Snow White
and the
VAMPIRE

MARINA MYLES

KENSINGTON BOOKS

Kensington Publishing Corp.

http://www.kensingtonbooks.com

KENSINGTON BOOKS are published by

Kensington Publishing Corp.
119 West 40th Street
New York, NY 10018

All Kensington titles, imprints, and distributed lines are available at special quantity discounts for bulk purchases for sales promotion, premiums, fund-raising, educational, or institutional use.

Special book excerpts or customized printings can also be created to fit specific needs. For details, write or phone the office of the Kensington Special Sales Manager: Attn. Special Sales Department. Kensington Publishing Corp., 119 West 40th Street, New York, NY 10018. Phone: 1-800-221-2647.

Kensington and the K logo Reg. U.S. Pat. & TM Off.

eISBN-13: 978-1-60183-100-2
eISBN-10: 1-60183-100-5
First Electronic Edition: December 2013

ISBN-13: 978-1-60183-139-2
ISBN-10: 1-60183-139-0
First Print Edition: December 2013

Printed in the United States of America

To my daughters, Alexa and Gianna.
Your hugs and your laughter mean everything to me.
I'll love you always.

Acknowledgments

Watching the second novel in my Cursed Princes series come to life has been a thrill. I'd like to offer heartfelt thanks to the extraordinary people who made *Snow White and the Vampire* possible:

Peter Senftleben, my tremendously talented editor who, thankfully, has a soft spot for Jack the Ripper stories.

Louise Fury, my wonderfully savvy agent who got my writing from the beginning.

Everyone at Kensington, from the seasoned copy editors to the visionary art department.

Fellow authors Terri Molina, Helen King, Cathy McDavid, Libby Banks, and Pamela Tracy. You've helped me so much with my writing. I hope I've returned the favor!

Lastly, I'd like to thank those of you who never tire of fairy tales. Your devotion keeps romance alive.

Hell is a city much like London.
A populous and a smoky city.

—P<small>ERCY</small> B<small>YSSHE</small> S<small>HELLEY</small>

When stars align at the hand of the Underworld God,
a chosen few are but puppets on strings.

—Ancient Egyptian proverb

Chapter One

London, 1888

Standing alone in the middle of a stranger's birthday party was hardly something Alba Spencer wanted to be doing. Struggling to inhale within the confines of her bustled *crepe lisse* gown—a dress she'd worn countless times before—she accepted a glass of champagne from a parlor maid. She took a healthy sip of the libation and squinted at a colorful banner suspended in the distance. Without the aid of her spectacles, which made her look more bookish than she preferred, the words gradually came into focus. *Happy 27th Birthday, Drake!*

Whoever you are, Drake, she thought, *you're late for your own dull party.*

Alba's gaze shifted to the party guests. Where was Edith, her best friend and chaperone for the night? No doubt the girl was getting into mischief, as usual.

Trying to disguise the fact that she would rather be tucked away in her dormitory reading law books, Alba focused on the banner again. She didn't know much about Drake Griffin. Her beau, Teddy Rollingsworth, met the gentleman at a haberdashery in Mayfair, after which the pair became fast friends. Other details of the situation hadn't interested her. After all, she was here as a favor to Teddy.

"Alba?" A well-bred voice drew her into the present. Tall and broad-shouldered, Teddy resumed his place by her side. With sparkling gray eyes, a strong jaw, and a finely cut evening suit that paid homage to his impeccable sense of fashion, he made for an impressive companion.

Alba smiled as he tucked his arm around her waist.

"Thank you for coming tonight," he said. "I thought it would take more than a party invitation to pry you away from your dormitory."

"You pleaded with me enough times to come, you goose." She swatted him softly on the shoulder.

He laughed and turned to the array of people dotting the drawing room. "I'm glad you did, because only a fraction of the guests I invited made an appearance."

"It's a fine turnout, nevertheless," Alba said. "You must have struck up quite a friendship with Dr. Griffin to be hosting a party in his honor."

"Drake is a good man—in addition to being a talented doctor."

"When did he take up the post at St. Bart's Hospital?" she asked, feigning curiosity.

"Three weeks ago." Teddy held her gaze before his stare wandered to the swell of her bosom.

Ah, Teddy. My patient suitor.

Only recently had Alba allowed their friendship to take a turn toward romance—and she was still trying to convince herself that Teddy was the man for her. He was astute, handsome, sensitive, and career-minded. Yet something was missing from their relationship. Could she ever get past his lack of luster?

"Drake is considered a top surgeon of his generation," Teddy continued. "Ah, he's just arrived."

"Where?" Alba craned her neck.

"In the foyer. There—he's the gentleman standing head and shoulders above the rest."

She set her champagne glass down on a side table. Straining to see without her spectacles, Alba took a step forward and caught sight of a dashing specimen of a man poised at the edge of the room. With an unusually pale face carved by high, angular cheekbones, the guest of honor stood his ground with a sense of resolution. His gleaming black hair, the front of which lay across his forehead in precise points, brushed the top of his stand-up collar and centered a pair of muscular shoulders.

Locking eyes with Alba, his lips spread into an entrancing smile. *What an attractive man*, she thought as he began to stride toward her. The nearer Drake Griffin came, the more she became the target of his fixated stare—and under captivating eyes more stunning than the deepest, richest topaz, her previous desire to be tucked away reading law books vanished like a rabbit from a magician's hat.

"Theodore." The princely gentleman quickly transferred his stare from Alba to his friend once he reached the couple.

"Please, Drake. I've urged you to call me Teddy—nearly everyone does."

"Very well." Drake shook Teddy's hand. "Thank you for planning this celebration. But I assure you, it was completely unnecessary."

The stranger's Romanian accent swirled around Alba like a melody. For an instant she was back in her native country. *But wait.* Had she heard that voice somewhere before?

"Of course the party was necessary!" Teddy's long nose twitched. "You're new to the city. As benefactors of the hospital, Father and I thought a party would give you the chance to meet some of London's upper crust."

"I'm sorry to hear your father isn't feeling well tonight," Drake said. His shimmering eyes darted back to Alba. She met their gold-flecked intensity by smiling.

"Allow me to introduce you to Miss Alba Spencer," Teddy offered. "She and I became acquainted in law school."

"Miss Spencer." The gentleman dipped his chin toward her politely.

She gave him her gloved hand, to which he pressed his lips. To her surprise, the warm contact penetrated the fabric and heated her limbs. Thoroughly uncomfortable, she was about to seek refuge in Teddy's bent elbow when a servant whispered something in his ear.

Teddy nodded. "Thank you, Reeves. If you'll excuse me, Drake, I must attend to a mishap with the caterer. Alba, do you mind keeping our guest company?"

Teddy disappeared into the crowd before Alba could answer. Now that she was alone with the mysterious doctor, nervousness seized her. She retrieved her champagne glass and pretended to study the tiny bubbles exploding within it. A brief silence passed between them while she searched the room for Edith again. Unable to locate her friend, she fumbled for something innocuous to say. "How are you enjoying London thus far?"

"Taking up a new residence can be rather daunting." Drake sighed. "Needless to say, I'm very grateful for Teddy's friendship—and for the opportunity to be introduced to the people he's acquainted with." He lowered his tone. "People like you, Miss Spencer."

The doctor's words encouraged the spattering of nervous blotches across her chest. "You're too kind," Alba murmured. "So you find this city a pleasant enough place to live?"

"Pleasant but for the brutal murderer who lurks in the Whitechapel District."

"Are you referring to the killer the newspapers are calling 'Leather Apron'?" she asked.

He evaluated her with interest yet said nothing.

"I understand this monster killed two unfortunates by ripping their abdomens wide open," she went on, making no attempt to sugarcoat her words since she was speaking with a surgeon.

"Where did you hear that, Miss Spencer?"

"It said so in the penny dreadfuls. Oh, not that I read them frequently . . ."

He raised an eyebrow.

What am I saying? She didn't normally babble on so, but this man had lit a fire beneath her. She felt odd in his presence, though she couldn't say why.

To her great relief, the doctor didn't seem to notice her jittering nerves. "Nasty business, preying on those unknowing women," he said. "I can't imagine a man treating any female that way. After all, women are beautiful creatures to be coddled. Admired. Cherished."

"That's a lovely thought." Alba repressed a girlish sigh. "It's a shame the killer does not share your school of thought."

Drake wrapped his hands behind his back. "I daresay the police believe this murderer will strike again."

"I fear that is why fewer guests came to your party this evening than Teddy anticipated. The city is gripped with fear." She paused to take a sip of champagne. "Perhaps we should talk about something more uplifting than murder."

"Yes." The surgeon took her glass and deposited it on a servant's tray. With his hand pressed to the small of her back, he guided her to a quiet corner of the drawing room. As she turned to face him, Alba could smell hot liquor fumes and the scent of his expensive aftershave. Surprisingly, she found that she liked the mixture of aromas.

"Teddy tells me you hail from Romania as well, Miss Spencer. What are the chances of that?"

"Slim, I daresay."

"You've lost a great deal of your accent, but if I had to guess, you are from Bucharest."

"I am." *How did he know?*

His features darkened. "It appears that we were destined to meet. And since we have, I'd be fascinated to know more about you."

Although Alba was taken aback by his boldness, nerves propelled her to continue their conversation in a blabbering rush. "I came to London when I was fourteen—to live with a family friend who runs the dormitory apartments of the Royal Opera's *corps de ballet*. Just this year, I graduated from law school. That's where Teddy and I met—at King's College. Recently, I've been assisting Teddy's father, Harold Rollingsworth, in the hopes that—"

"—you will become London's first female barrister," Drake completed her thought. Tilting his head to the side, he gazed at her with admiration. "Lovely, intelligent, and a pioneer. You are a rare gem, Miss Spencer."

The Romanian's hungry stare closed the small distance between them. Alba's cheeks burned. *We hardly know one another!*

Desperate to steer the conversation away from herself, she cleared her throat. "I have yet to wish you a happy birthday, Dr. Griffin."

"Thank you." The guest of honor did a cordial bow. "But 'Griffin' is merely my professional name."

Alba frowned. "What is your real name?"

"Dimitri Grigorescu."

Alba's limbs froze and the room started to take on a slow whirl. "That's curious," she murmured. "I knew someone by that name in Romania."

"And I once knew a girl named Alba Zăpăda," Dimitri said as a curtain of desire passed over his face. *"You."*

His lips thinned into a familiar smile and Alba's hand flew to her gaping mouth. *Curse my poor eyesight!* Now that she was this close to him she knew precisely who he was: Dimitri, the handsome Gypsy boy she'd fallen in love with at the tender age of fourteen.

Words escaped her while she gasped for air.

"Life is too short to be without the ones you love," Dimitri purred. "Don't you think?"

All at once, memories of the summer Alba spent in the Balkan countryside flashed through her mind:

The first kiss she and Dimitri shared amid a field of white poppies.

Simona, Dimitri's raven-haired friend.

And the terrifying night the three of them spent in a haunted graveyard.

Her blood raced and the room spun in faster circles.

"I've been waiting an eternity to return this to you," Dimitri whispered as he slipped a dried white poppy into her hand.

"But I thought you were dead," she said before everything went black.

Chapter Two

Dimitri caught Alba before she hit the ground. Taking no notice of the gawks and the curious whispers circulating around the room, he laid her limp body on the Persian carpet. A moment later, Teddy appeared by his side.

"What happened?" Teddy cried.

"She fainted," Dimitri answered, his heart hammering.

As Teddy took one of Alba's gloved hands, Dimitri longed to grasp the other one and press it to his cheek.

"Should you take her pulse?" Teddy asked in a panic.

Before Dimitri could answer, Edith Tuttlebaum, a garrulous girl with flaming red hair, rushed over. "Some chaperone I am!" she said. "I saw Alba's face from across the room and she looked as though she'd seen a ghost!"

Dimitri's gut clenched.

"Perhaps you should take her inside one of the bedrooms and examine her." Teddy snapped his eyes to Dimitri.

Dimitri shook his head. After all, he didn't want to draw further attention to his connection with Alba. "She drank her champagne too quickly," he replied. "She shall regain consciousness in a moment."

"Teddy, I think we should take Alba home," Edith argued. "I've never seen her look that way before. Perhaps she can't breathe inside this stuffy place."

"That's a good idea," Teddy said. "So sorry, my good man." He put a hand on Dimitri's shoulder. "It looks as though your party is over."

"Of course," Dimitri murmured.

Scooping Alba into his arms, Teddy plowed through the clusters of guests while Edith nipped at his heels. Dimitri rose and assured everyone that Alba would be fine. Meanwhile, he directed them to the front door. As the guests filtered out of the Rollingsworth home, they continued to gasp and whisper amongst themselves. Dimitri thanked each person for coming as cordially as he could, but inside he was screaming.

After the last guest climbed into an awaiting carriage, he rushed out of the house without looking back. Pulse speeding, he cut through the swirling fog that blanketed the affluent neighborhood of Belgravia and wondered if the evening could get any worse.

What was I thinking? That Alba would recognize me instantly? That she would throw her arms around me with abandon?

Well, she hadn't done either of those things. More than a decade had passed since their last encounter—and she'd been so shocked that she blacked out at the sight of him.

Glowering, Dimitri tapped his walking cane on the ground. Tonight he'd exuded the sophistication and confidence of a carefully bred gentleman. While that sophistication helped him orchestrate his first meeting with Teddy, Alba knew him better. Born an unsure Gypsy boy who lacked education, Dimitri made it his mission to become a man of society. Alba was his sole inspiration for the transformation. Had she liked it?

He released a sigh and watched it vaporize in the night air.

At least he'd reaped something positive from tonight's disaster: Alba felt like a warm, sweet angel when he'd caught her in his arms. With skin fairer than a dove's wing, eyes bluer than a delphinium, and black hair that shone like cut glass, she had stunned him anew. By far the loveliest woman in the room, she'd boasted more curves than a pirate's treasure map—and when she returned his curious stare from across the room, his heart threatened to leave his chest.

Although she hadn't recognized Dimitri until he spoke his name, he was every bit as in love with her as he'd been eleven years ago. And he could have sworn he sensed the allure of reciprocation when he kissed her hand.

But that was of no consequence now. *I'm in no position to reclaim Alba's love.* The irony chopped at Dimitri's emotions like a whirling blade. As he marched along the damp cobbles, he realized that there was no time for him to wallow in self-pity. He was here to protect Alba from a pair of terrifying curses.

The first was a prophecy cast upon both of them long ago—a curse that predicted they would become vampires. Now, blast the fact to hell, Dimitri was. His transformation had occurred two months ago when he was attacked by a bat in Wales. Because the deepest circle of hell was reserved for blood-lusting murderers, he was bent on preventing Alba from suffering the same fate. He knew there was truth to the hex, so he'd come to London to watch over her.

Unfortunately, the second curse Dimitri wanted to protect Alba from was just as horrendous. It involved an enchanted Egyptian amulet he'd given her in their youth—an amulet that, despite its dark prophecy, had been a token of his affection.

Both curses were evils Dimitri had brought to Alba's life, and the guilt that came with them wrenched his stomach. Of course, it hadn't been his intention to bring malice to Alba. The vampire's prophecy resulted from a foolish childhood dare and Dimitri gave Alba the enchanted amulet without believing in its curse.

Big Ben struck ten o'clock. Grimacing, Dimitri glanced down at the fog concealing his shining shoes and thought of his own immortality. His being in London might have set the hex of the Egyptian amulet into motion, but he was willing to protect Alba at the risk of dying again. And a broken neck or sharp stake through the heart could kill a vampire effectively.

Placing a hand over the organ in question, Dimitri passed a row of terraced houses. His determination to shield Alba increased with his stride. If he could persuade her to find solace in their rekindled friendship—*and* if he could resist biting her creamy neck—he might be able to save her from both curses.

His heels clicked along the empty street. A gust of cold air rippled his opera cloak, yet he felt no trace of the autumn chill. On the other hand, Dimitri could tell that his energy was decreasing at a dangerous rate. He'd fed off a homeless man earlier tonight—so that he wouldn't be tempted by the smell of Alba's blood—but the encounter had been interrupted and he hadn't drunk enough.

Fatigue pulling at his feet, he continued on toward Park Lane. A loud clanging noise rang out. Could it be the deranged killer from Whitechapel? Normally Dimitri would welcome the challenge, but not in his weakened state.

His eyes darted to a narrow alley. A calico cat had sprung off a rubbish bin, sending the lid clattering to the ground. Baring tiny, spiked teeth, the animal slinked into the shadows.

He struggled along until he reached the gate of the elegant mansion he'd purchased two weeks ago. It was a distance from St. Bart's Hospital where he worked as an emergency ward surgeon, but he'd fallen in love with the house at first sight. Anxious to get inside before sunrise, he raised his key to the lock. The house was void of servants, which meant no one knew his dark secret. And he intended to keep it that way.

He was about to turn the key when a flapping sound jerked his head skyward. A large bat dove at him, ruffling his hair and grazing his ear. Could it be the same creature that had attacked him in Wales? *If so, who is shape-shifting and following me?*

The animal dove in again, its red eyes glowing. Dimitri swatted it away in a panic. If he was bitten again, the bat would drain him of more precious energy. He craned his neck while the ugly creature streamed above a gas lamp. His vision blurred—and a wave of dizziness washed over him. Regretting that he'd drunk too much wine before he arrived at the party, Dimitri teetered sideways and struck his head against the iron palings of the gate. The scene before him became distorted—yet he could swear he saw a woman materialize from the fog.

Chapter Three

Alba regained consciousness inside a jostling hansom.

Lying on her back, she struggled to focus on the draped ceiling of the carriage. Her grogginess lingered and she half-expected to see Dimitri's handsome face leaning over her. At the memory of how dashing he looked at the party, Alba's heart pounded painfully against her ribs. She tried to blink away the image but it was no use. She found herself wishing Dimitri had been bold enough to move in for a kiss.

Gracious! What was she thinking? She needed Dimitri Grigorescu in her life like she needed a hole in the head.

The hansom rambled forward briskly. As she pulled herself to a sitting position, Teddy shifted beside her.

"Are you all right, darling?" he asked.

"Yes, but I'm dreadfully embarrassed," she said. "I hope I didn't put a damper on the party."

Teddy tsked. "Your health is more important."

"Do you feel ill?" Edith leaned forward on the opposite bench. She wore a monstrous plume in her hair that bobbed with the motion of the carriage. Her round face quivered with concern.

"I'm not sick," Alba said. "The champagne went to my head because of my empty stomach."

"But I saw you from across the room while you were speaking

with Dr. Griffin," Edith protested. "You looked as though you'd witnessed something extraordinary."

Shaking her head, Alba let out a nervous laugh. Teddy knew nothing of her past, including the fact that she'd changed her surname from Zăpăda to Spencer when she came to London.

"Teddy, isn't Drake Griffin the gentleman you brought backstage at the opera?" Edith asked.

Teddy nodded but remained silent. He seemed more interested in patting Alba's hand gently and drawing her near.

"Did Dr. Griffin say something inappropriate to you, Alba?" Edith's shrill voice disrupted the momentary silence.

"Not at all, Edith." Alba shot her an impatient look. "I told you, the champagne made me light-headed."

Teddy's muscles remained tense against her body until the carriage arrived at the ballet dormitories. Once Teddy and Edith helped Alba out of the hansom, Edith excused herself discreetly. Meanwhile Teddy hemmed and hawed.

"Shall I see you upstairs?" he asked, removing his hat.

It had been quite a night and Alba was desperate to be alone. "I'm sorry," she said. "But I'm rather tired . . ."

The hope in Teddy's down-turned eyes dimmed. "I understand." He paused. "Well, good night."

"Good night, Teddy." His hurt expression prompted her to force a smile. "I'm looking forward to having supper with you and your father tomorrow night."

"As am I." He tipped a bow as he climbed into the hansom.

Alba entered the dormitory's vestibule then ascended three flights of stairs. One level of the brownstone was a floor Alba occupied with Edith's six sisters. The girls were daughters of Widow Tuttlebaum—a woman who had been friends with Alba's deceased mother. Mrs. T., as Alba liked to call her, grew up with Alba's mother in London and the two had stayed close after Anastasia Zăpăda married and moved to Romania.

Now Mrs. T.'s daughters were Alba's dearest companions.

Exhausted, Alba swept into the cozy parlor.

"I'll make some tea while you rest," Edith said from the kitchen down the hall.

"Thank you." Alba crossed into the bedroom she shared with the seven girls and plopped into the vanity chair. Donning her spectacles, she stared into the mirror at her flushed cheeks and tousled hair. She was a mess. Worse yet, she had embarrassed herself by blacking out so theatrically at the party.

Pulling off her earrings, she rolled her eyes. At least she was alone and could think. Ella, Elaine, Evelyn, Eugenia, and the triplets, Ellen, Edwina, and Edith, were delightfully exuberant roommates, but Alba was glad that the majority of girls were performing *Don Quixote* tonight. It happened to be Edith's night off and Alba was grateful that her friend had accompanied her to the party. The Tuttlebaums were the only people in London who knew of Alba's harrowing history with her stepmother, yet they had no clue who Dimitri was.

Summoning the courage to look at the gift he'd given her long ago, she picked up her jewelry box and drew in a breath. Lifting its lid, she peeked at the ancient amulet—an object she hadn't touched for eleven years.

When she withdrew the smooth lapis stone by way of its silver chain, her chest tightened. Why had Dimitri given this to her in the first place? *Didn't he know it was cursed?*

Dimitri Grigorescu. The name shot emotion through Alba like a powerful pistol.

After the night they spent in the graveyard, she thought he was dead. That was why she hadn't recognized him in his resurrected form. Of course, Dimitri had changed considerably. He had materialized looking more handsome than ever in crisp white linens and an exquisitely cut evening suit. But what hadn't changed about Dimitri were his eyes. They spoke of the consuming love he and Alba shared back in Romania. His eyes also told her that he desired her the same way today.

It cannot be a coincidence that Dimitri has resurfaced in my life.

Alba was relieved that he'd survived that terrible night in the cemetery, but she was desperate to know more about his sudden appearance. After all, his presence could destroy the safety net she had so carefully constructed.

Edith entered the room, deposited a teacup on the desk, and studied Alba. "You look dreadful. Do you want to talk about what happened at the party?"

Alba nodded. She trusted Edith implicitly.

"You know, if I'd been standing that close to Dr. Griffin, I would have fainted too." The redheaded girl sat on one of the beds and smiled. "He's incredibly handsome."

"Yes, he is," Alba said dreamily.

Edith held a closed fist forward. "I didn't want to say anything in front of Teddy, but I saw Dimitri give you this before you fainted." She handed Alba the dried white poppy.

Alba's fingers shook as she accepted it. *It must have fallen out of my hand when I lost consciousness.*

"What does it mean?" Edith asked. "And why did Dr. Griffin give it to you?"

"That's not his real name," Alba said cryptically.

"Not his real name? What are you talking about?"

"Shush." Alba put a finger to her lips as she went about drawing the drapes. "We must whisper."

"Whisper? You *did* have too much champagne," Edith rattled on. "And the way the other guests gawked at you in the doctor's arms . . ."

"That's the least of my worries," Alba said, resuming her seat in the vanity chair. "Drake Griffin's real name is Dimitri Grigorescu. I knew him in Romania."

Edith leaned forward anxiously. "But you never speak of Romania."

"I must now." Alba paused. "I'm afraid."

"Afraid of what?" her friend asked gently.

"Of this." Alba unfurled her fist and revealed the Egyptian amulet.

"What is it?"

"A three-thousand-year-old curio from ancient Egypt."

"My word!" Edith's eyes widened.

"I should have gotten rid of it long ago, but I couldn't."

"Why not?"

"Dimitri gave it to me when I was fourteen. He was a sixteen-year-old Gypsy boy then—and we fell in love."

"He's a *Gypsy*? But he seems so refined."

"Believe me, he wasn't always."

Edith took the amulet from Alba and turned it over in her hand. "Why does this necklace scare you?"

"Because it comes with a curse—one Dimitri didn't inform me of when he presented it to me. I thought he was dead all this time, so I made myself forget about the amulet."

"You thought he was dead?" Edith looked excited. "Tell me everything."

"Where shall I start?" Alba exhaled. She ordered herself to relax, but the memory still shadowed her with distress. "Dimitri had a Gypsy friend named Simona. Simona dared Dimitri and me to sneak into an abandoned cemetery with her. The cemetery was located on the grounds of Vlad Dracul's castle."

"That sounds dangerous already," Edith said as her cheeks bloomed.

Alba suppressed a shiver. "We dug up a vampire's grave—a very special vampire's grave, in fact—but we got scared. We ran in different directions. Dimitri got hurt. His shoulder was torn open. He told me to leave him and get help. But no one would go with me to the cemetery to help him. When I went back alone, Dimitri was gone. I assumed he returned to his Gypsy camp, but when I paid the camp a visit, I was told that he'd never returned. Because he didn't contact me again, I thought he was dead."

"My God, Alba." Edith's fascinated expression melted into one of empathy. "That's a horrible story."

Tears stung Alba's eyes and she looked away. She had omitted the part about the vampire cursing all three of the trespassers as it'd roared out of its grave. "Dimitri gave me this necklace the morning we went to the castle," she said.

"What, exactly, does its curse foretell?"

"When I was at the British Museum," Alba said softly, "I was shocked when I spotted a story about this very amulet inside one of the display cases. It told of a princess named Tousret who invited a priest from her court to become her forbidden lover. The priest's name was Amenhotep—and as punishment for Amenhotep's deadly sin, the Underworld God saw to it that the princess was drawn to the priest by way of a fatal attraction. The god's dark forces willed Tousret to stab Amenhotep to death before she killed herself. Now any female who dons the amulet, even once, will commit suicide just as the princess did."

"That's another horrible story!" Edith exclaimed.

Alba's hands began to tremble around the amulet. "Inside the display case, the explanation of the curse rested beside a piece of jewelry called the bracelet of Amenhotep. Apparently, when this bracelet is placed on the wrist of the male lover involved, it has the power to neutralize the amulet's hex."

"That's good. Isn't it?" Edith asked.

"Yes. It's good that the prophecy can be severed, but the knowledge does me no good without the bracelet."

"I can see why you fainted when you saw Dimitri," Edith said.

Speaking aloud about her past sparked newfound fear in Alba. She worried that Dimitri's appearance would bring the amulet's curse one step closer to fruition. And if it did, there was no way she could get her hands on the magical bracelet. *What can I do to ensure my survival and his?*

Fortunately, she would only kill Dimitri if they became lovers. That was the last thing she planned to do . . .

"You said you loved Dimitri once," Edith said. "How do you feel about him now?"

"The night Dimitri and I stole into the graveyard was the night our relationship was ruined," Alba replied.

"If that's so, how do you know the amulet's curse isn't meant for Teddy?"

Her stomach roiled. "Teddy?"

"Maybe you're supposed to kill Teddy, not Dimitri." Edith's tone was impatient. "After all, Teddy is in love with you too."

The possibility left Alba breathless. Her pulse sped as her friend paced before her.

"All this talk of black magic is making me nervous," Edith said. "I thought it was something children imagine."

"No. It's very real." Thoughts of the Dark Arts closed the walls in on Alba. "Skeptics scoff at the power of the occult, but I've seen it firsthand. My stepmother, Ileana, delved into black magic, but she kept her spells and incantations private."

"You mean you spied on her?"

"Yes. I was curious, so I crept into Ileana's suites at the summer home we were leasing—to learn what she did in her chambers all day. What I witnessed terrified me."

"Perhaps it's best not to think about it. Or speak of this necklace." Edith handed the amulet back to Alba.

"No. I need to talk about it." Tears streamed down her face.

"All right," Edith said cautiously. "What did you see at this country manor?"

"I saw Ileana's pet rat—an evil, black rodent she fed spiders to—perched on a book of spells. Ileana was standing before a mirror that waved and shimmered on its own. The mirror spoke to Ileana and Ileana spoke back. She uttered a vow to kill me—her own stepdaughter." Alba buried her face in her hands.

Damn Dimitri! The last thing she needed was him coming here and conjuring up a collection of painful memories—memories that tugged at her like wind too forceful to resist.

"You poor thing." Edith sprang to her side and wrapped an arm around her.

While her friend tried to comfort her, images of Alba's past roared to life. Her assumption that Dimitri was dead. Her father dying from heart failure a week before they were to leave their country estate. And her suspicion that his passing was Ileana's murderous handiwork. Of course, she never got anyone to believe her.

"The days following my father's death were the worst in my life," she said through her tears. "The way Ileana resented me came out in the open. When I overheard her vowing to kill me in her mirror, I ran away and never looked back. That's when I came to London and sought refuge with you girls."

"There, there," Edith cooed. "We won't talk of it anymore tonight. That's that."

Trembling, Alba nodded in agreement. While she wiped away her tears, she glanced around the sparsely furnished flat. Eight brass beds covered with gingham counterpanes faced one another on opposing walls. An armoire, a dresser, and two desks bearing ink-blotters and glass oil lamps filled the corners of the large room. The lack of possessions reminded Alba that she didn't have much, but what she had, she'd earned. She had worked days at the library and nights as an office cleaner to put herself through the university. To become a barrister meant everything to her. It became imperative that she defend anyone who'd been mistreated or who faced injustice, just as she'd suffered at Ileana's hand.

Alba took a look at the ambrotype balanced on the edge of her night table. Her mother's wise, caring smile embraced her as it always did. *I miss you, Mama,* she whispered to herself. *What would you think if you could see me now?*

Alba hoped that, from her place in heaven, her mother would

understand why she had faked her own death. It was a plan she'd carried out with tremendous calculation. Unseen, she had scattered her best scarf, hat, and gloves around the forest that bordered Stelian Hall. The bloodstained, tattered articles had alarmed the household staff. When the servants were unable to find Alba, they came to the conclusion that she'd been consumed by a wild animal. All the while, she made the clandestine journey to London.

"Try and get some sleep," Edith urged. "I'll be in the parlor if you need me."

"Thank you." Alba smiled.

"Of course." Her friend stopped before she left the room. "I've thought of one more thing, Alba. If you staged your own death, do you suppose Dimitri thought you were dead all this time too?"

Edith's suggestion made Alba's blood run cold. Trying to chase away the idea, she thrust the amulet and the poppy inside the jewelry box and slipped into bed. Did she really care what Dimitri thought or felt after all these years? Determined to prevent him from alerting her stepmother about her whereabouts or revealing her new identity to everyone here in London, she finally slipped into a fitful dream—a dream that brought her back to her childhood.

Alba studied the needlepoint she held in her quivering hand. A moment ago, Ileana had strutted before her, criticizing her pattern. "Who on earth taught you needlepoint, child?" her stepmother had said. With her head held at a haughty angle, Ileana possessed a cruel beauty accentuated by cool, blond hair, sharply arched eyebrows, and commanding eyes the color of steel.

"My mother," Alba had replied in a small voice.

"Your mother, was it? Well, she did a pathetic job."

"Please don't talk about my mother that way," Alba had implored.

"Silence, you insolent girl!" Ileana had raised her hand to strike her.

Alba compressed her lips as she hurried to the front door. Letting out a shiver, she brushed a strand of dark hair from her eyes. At fourteen she was neither a child nor a woman, but many claimed that she had an unflappable confidence to be admired at any age. Well, she was confident enough to refuse to go back to her needlepoint lesson. No doubt the servants were looking for her after she fled the parlor, but she didn't care. She was a human being and she had every right to avoid a beating.

Her breathing slowed as she emerged from Stelian Hall. Sinking onto a carved marble bench, she gazed across the lawn. That was when she noticed a boy spying on her through the estate's palatial gates.

With black hair streaked with brown waves and a dirty, yet tremendously handsome face, the boy was crouched on his knees. His dazzling gold-brown eyes tugged at Alba, but she had been raised to avoid strangers. Especially Gypsies.

Alba folded her arms across her chest. "What are you doing here?" she called out.

Now that he'd been discovered, the boy squared his shoulders and stood. Embarrassment reddened his cheeks.

"I won't speak to you," she said. "My father, Ambassador Mihail Zăpăda, has instructed me not to consort with your kind. Gypsies are beggars and misfits and they mean nothing but trouble."

He made no reply. Was he ignoring her?

"My father, myself, and my stepmother will be here in this wretched countryside for five more weeks before we go back to Bucharest," she continued. "That is certainly not enough time to make friends."

"Who said I wanted to be your friend?" the boy asked as he wiped his smudged cheeks with a frayed shirtsleeve. "I only wanted to see who was living in Stelian Hall. And now that I see it's a snobbish, knock-kneed girl, I'll be on my way."

Alba sprang to her feet, her needlepoint ring tumbling from her lap. "Wait, boy! How dare you speak to me in that manner?" With impeccable posture that spoke of her up-bringing, she moved to the gate. The boy bravely stood his ground.

"You have a lot of nerve, Gypsy, but you are rather handsome. You may tell me your name." She clasped her hands behind her back the way she'd seen her father do when he talked to the servants.

"I'm Dimitri. Dimitri Grigorescu, and I am sixteen years old, so don't call me 'boy' again."

She nodded in compliance.

"And you, girl. What is your name?" he asked.

"I am Alba. Alba Zăpădă, and I'm fourteen, so don't call me 'girl' again."

The boy sputtered with laughter at the way she'd echoed his inflection. Alba joined in—reluctantly at first and then wholeheartedly.

Once their laughter subsided, the boy's tone became pensive. "Snow White. What a beautiful name."

"Thank you." She gave him a smile. "It was my mother's idea."

Over the next four weeks, admiration and infatuation came to pass between Alba and Dimitri. Seizing every opportunity to escape her stepmother's temper, Alba converged with her Gypsy boy beneath the bridge near the river and in the house's toolshed. They stole long looks in the high, swaying willows and relayed their deepest secrets in the tree-dotted forest . . . all the while falling completely and madly in love.

Those days were the happiest of Alba's life. She loved everything about Dimitri, from his intelligence to his quick wit. And when he'd kissed her for the first time at the end of that magical summer, he had fastened a white poppy in her hair . . .

Alba awoke for a moment, then fell back to sleep. Another dream took hold of her. In this one she was all grown up . . .

A mysterious stranger emerged from a wall of fog. Staring at Alba provocatively, he pressed a hand to the small of her back and led her into the inky shadows of Stelian Hall. He pinned her to the wall of the foyer while he lavished her with fiery kisses. Hot and hungry, his tongue twined with hers. Reaching beneath her white, flowing gown, he stroked her breast and the contact unleashed Alba's repressed desires. Heaving forward with a moan, she allowed the stranger to tease her nipple to a high peak while desire flushed through her with the force of a typhoon.

"You will be mine tonight." He hadn't spoken the words, but oddly, Alba could read his thoughts.

As she slithered her hands around his neck, she stared into his mesmerizing features. A strong brow topped his straight nose and his rich topaz eyes. Pulse accelerating, she watched his pupils transform to an unearthly red. He bent at the knees and whisked Alba to a plush divan—the only piece of furniture in the country manor. While he bore her down, a pair of gleaming fangs descended. She stared into his red eyes, knowing full well she was being hypnotized. She willingly opened to him as he feathered his fingertips along her exposed thigh—higher and higher until her folds were wet with arousal.

"I want to be yours," Alba said, her breath catching.

Nodding, the dark figure seared her lips with a kiss. Then he stroked her curls and edged his fingers inside her damp petals and smiled.

It was strange that the vampire seemed to be compelled not by evil but by genuine feeling. And because his eyes spoke of his admiration for her, she was eager to succumb to him.

Bunching up the material of her nightgown, the elegant vampire held the garment against her hips with one hand. Lowering his trousers with the other, his stone-hard erection brushed against her leg, and when he guided it inside her wet channel, Alba's eyes fluttered open.

"I've loved you since we were children," he said suddenly.

She let out a gasp. Now that he'd spoken, she realized the vampire was Dimitri.

Chapter Four

While London slept, a dark figure stepped from a wall of shadows like a ghostly apparition. Wearing a silk top hat and a swirling cloak, the elegant phantom seemed out of place in the filth and stench of Whitechapel. A cesspool plaguing London's East End, the district was home to an assortment of drunkards, gamblers, criminals, and garishly painted prossers, or prostitutes. It was a place few sophisticated gentlemen frequented.

Ducking in and out of the inky shadows, the killer strode toward the end of the main thoroughfare and then turned onto Berner Street. With cold, unfeeling eyes, he spied a likely victim in a tart who was parading at a gate that led to Dutfield's Yard. He watched as the middle-aged whore shouted out suggestions to several gentlemen as they exited the International Workingmen's Educational Club.

"Lookin' for a bit o' sport, are ya, guv'na?" The prosser's voice sounded dry and weathered as she spoke to a man who rushed by her. "Do ya like what ya see, eh, Cock?"

Once she'd been passed over by several men, the woman finally noticed the stranger. Her face broadened into a seductive smile and she peeled up her bottom petticoat. After the man in the top hat emerged from his shadowy hiding spot, he laced a hand through the crook of her arm.

They walked silently through the wooden gate while the public din off Whitechapel's main thoroughfare faded behind them. The gentleman directed the prosser to an edge of the large yard, where she laughed merrily.

"What is your name?" he asked.

"Elizabeth. But you can call me Liz," she teased.

He nodded.

"I see yer carryin' a doctor's bag," she said. "Are ya gonna *examine* me?" The smell of liquor rolled off her tongue.

The man said nothing.

Up one side of the illuminated yard sat a row of small, dirty-looking houses. By the glow filtering through their windows, the houses appeared to be fully tenanted. The International Working-men's Educational Club, founded by immigrant Jewish socialists, flanked the yard's other side. The killer boldly stepped in and nuzzled Liz's neck beneath the amber lights.

"Yer an elegant one, aren't ya, guv'na?" the prostitute said with a glint in her eye. "From the looks of your clothin' maybe I should be chargin' ya double!"

Her hearty laughter rang out into the night while the killer remained solemn. In a low voice, he suggested she lift up her skirt. Stinking of other men, Liz took a step back and did as her client asked. The killer pulled a red scarf from his waistcoat pocket and stroked it with his hands.

"Wrap this pretty scarf around your neck," he commanded.

Liz shrugged. She took the scarf from him and did as she'd been told. "Are ya dressin' me up?"

The killer dipped his chin. "Now unbutton your jacket and show me your corset."

As one hand worked at further exposing her breasts and the other clasped a bag of breath sweets, the prosser's hands were occupied. The madman pulled a knife from his bag and rushed to grab her from behind. Grasping the ends of the scarf, he yanked her head back until the length of her neck was exposed.

With tears of fear pooling in her gray eyes, the forty-four-year-old woman was in no position to cry out. The man remained silent as he sliced her throat from her carotid artery across her windpipe. Proud of his deed, he watched his victim slip to the ground, stripped of all her dignity.

The murderer knelt down and whispered into her ear, "Now there's one less woman in the world."

* * *

Dimitri awoke inside the narrow shipping crate that doubled as his coffin. He rubbed his aching temple, then touched the warm trickle of blood at his mouth. A familiar, musty smell permeated his nostrils. *How the hell did I get to my basement after I struck my head on the gate paling?*

And the blood at my mouth. Did I feed?

Someone must have helped him inside the house and into the crate. He wanted to think it was Alba, but her fainting spell proved otherwise. Perhaps he should have sent her a letter instead of stunning her like that. Or called upon her alone. He would have done things differently in retrospect, but it was too late now.

Dimitri exhaled as he pushed himself out of the crate. Alba knew he was here—and he needed to start protecting her.

While he climbed upstairs to shave and dress, his thoughts flashed to the chilling events that led him to London.

"Alba and I are in love," Dimitri informed his friend, Simona Popovici. They were headed to the small village of Braşov nestled below the snow-tipped Carpathian Mountains. Both of them had turned sixteen last month, but they'd known one another since they were five years old.

"Alba caught you spying on her four weeks ago and you're already in love?" feisty Simona asked with disdain. The raven-haired girl was prone to trouble, but she was the only member of the Szgamy tribe close to Dimitri's age.

"I do love her," he replied, his breath vaporizing in the crisp, mountain air. "And someday I plan to marry her. For now, I'm going to give her this." He withdrew a ring made from alderwood from his pocket. "I carved it myself."

"How sweet!" Simona taunted him with a laugh.

He glowered at her.

"Your handiwork is horribly rustic," she went on. "Do you really think it will impress a sophisticated girl like Alba Zăpăda?"

Dimitri stuffed the ring back in his pocket. "It's all I have to give her."

"Maybe not."

"What are you talking about?" he asked.

From beneath her vest, Simona produced a stunning lapis amulet attached to a silver chain. The markings on the stone were Egyptian and bore intricate inlays of gleaming coral and onyx.

Dimitri gasped and took a step back. "You stole that necklace from Rosa Spera! If you're found out, Rosa will use her dark powers to punish you."

"Calm down," *Simona said.* "She won't find out. Rosa Spera may be the leader of our tribe, but she's dim-witted."

"Why did you steal it?" *Dimitri prodded.*

"To give it to you, silly. And I didn't hear a thank-you."

"The amulet is cursed."

"It is?" *Simona feigned ignorance.*

"Stop it, Simona. I'm sure you remember the story the elders told us when we were children."

"The story about the Egyptian princess who killed her lover before she stabbed herself to death?"

"Yes," *Dimitri growled.* "That one."

Simona's eyes narrowed. "The story is rubbish."

Dimitri shook his head. "Rosa's grandmother, Marga Yavidovich, found the amulet when our people were in England. She stored it away—to protect the world from its dark powers. Now it's Rosa's job to guard it."

"I don't see why she has to guard it. How can something so old still fuel a curse?"

Simona had a point, Dimitri considered.

Smiling slyly, she handed the necklace over. He took a moment to study it. He had to admit it was an impressive piece of jewelry that must be very valuable.

"You're a Gypsy, Dimitri." *Simona tossed her long hair in the wind. She was a striking girl, but one who was too full of fire and brimstone for his taste.* "That means your beginnings are far from respectable. Give Alba the necklace. You'd be smart to use anything you can get your hands on."

He looked ashamed. "Do you really think I should give it to her?"

"Yes." *Simona smiled.* "You do want Alba to like you, right?"

"I want her to do more than that. I want her to marry me."

Simona put her hands on her hips. "Marry you? Have you thought this out, Dimitri?"

He thought he had.

"Giving Alba the amulet will bring you one step closer to winning her over. But can you convince her—or her family—that you're worthy of marriage?"

Dimitri frowned. "I don't have to convince her family of anything. She plans to run away with me."

Simona's laughter floated around them. "Are you sure?"

"Alba's stepmother is cruel and vain," he said. "All she does is stand in front of a huge mirror her husband built for her, staring at her reflection all day. She pays no attention to Alba—except when she rants at her in a jealous rage. She envies Alba's youth and beauty so much that she's considering sending her to boarding school in England."

"Poor little Alba," Simona said with manufactured sympathy. "And you want to save her from all that? If she agrees to run away with you, where will you take her, Dimitri? What money will you use? It's hopeless, you foolish Gypsy boy."

"Hold your tongue, Simona!"

Her eyes darkened with anger before they twinkled with mischief. "We both agree that you're not wealthy or sophisticated, but maybe you can win Alba's father over with your bravery."

"What are you babbling on about?" He slid a glance her way.

"Suppose you and I do something daring, something . . . unbelievable. Perhaps little Miss Pure As the Fallen Snow will come along as a witness. Afterward she'll brag to her father that you are the bravest boy she's ever met and you'll be accepted into the family."

Simona had managed to capture his attention. "What kind of dare are you talking about?"

"I say we steal up to Castle Bran and hunt for vampires!"

A sense of unease skittered across Dimitri's skin. From high upon a cliff, Castle Bran loomed over the Transylvanian countryside like a terrifying gateway to hell. Once the resi-

dence of a sadistic fifteenth-century prince named Vlad Dracul, the infamous castle had been the site of countless atrocities. Known as the first lord of vampires, Dracul ruled as the Prince of Wallachia. During his reign, he commanded upward of a hundred thousand people to be murdered by means of impalement on a sharpened stake. The prince also condemned his citizens to be burned, boiled, or skinned. As his reward, Dracul enjoyed drinking the blood of his victims . . . all at Castle Bran.

The very suggestion that he go anywhere near the castle gripped Dimitri like a vise. Men of the Szgamy Gypsy tribe were prone to curses, and if he awoke a vampire who used to be a member of his tribe, that was precisely what he would become.

"Alba will never agree to come with us," he told Simona, although he suspected that the girl he loved was braver than he was.

The following night, the trio made their way to Castle Bran. Beneath a full moon, its ominous white bricks and red turrets glowed like beacons on a lonely sea. Entering the graveyard, Dimitri noticed that the ebony shadows and bright margins cast by the moonlight lent it the look of a black-and-white checkerboard. It appeared to be a place still vibrant with the dancing spirits of violence and death . . . a perfect place for a dare.

The three youths hid behind an enormous tomb.

"Is everyone ready to dig up a vampire?" Simona asked.

Dimitri gripped his shovel. "What if we dig up a Szgamy?"

"No Szgamys are buried here," Simona replied in a sharp whisper. "Only Vlad Dracul's soldiers—the ones he impaled."

Alba gulped.

Dimitri looked at her. "I can't believe you talked us into this, Simona."

Simona snorted. "You can go back to camp right now, Dimitri. No one is holding a gun to your head."

"A dare is a dare," he countered.

"I don't like this any more than you do." Alba fingered the

amulet Dimitri had given her that morning. "But I wasn't about to let your friend call me a spooked cat behind my back." She cast Simona a look that shot daggers.

"It's not my intention to frighten you, little princess. By coming here, Dimitri and I are returning to our heritage. Our ancestors served Vlad Dracul by carrying his caskets on these very grounds. He wanted our loyalty forever, so he enchanted a stream beneath his castle. The Szgamys drank from it and that's how they attained their magical powers."

Alba dug her fingertips into Dimitri's arm.

"Never mind the history lesson. Just tell us what we need to do to find a bloodsucker's grave," he ordered sharply.

Simona flung her waist-length black hair over her shoulder. "To find a true vampire we must look for finger-sized holes in the dirt. Because vampires can change into a mist, people say they can escape from their graves at night by way of these holes."

"How are we going to spot the holes through this damned fog?" Dimitri asked.

"Well," snapped Simona, "if we'd brought a black horse with us, the horse would circle the grave instead of walking across it. Since we don't have a horse, do you have a better suggestion?"

Dimitri rolled his eyes.

"If we dig up a grave," Simona hissed, "and if the corpse makes a groaning sound at being disturbed, then we've found our vampire. We'll place these wild rosebud stems around its sleeping body to prevent the vampire from moving." She handed Dimitri and Alba two stems each. "Finally, we must all touch the corpse with our bare hands. Agreed?"

They nodded.

Dimitri took Alba's hand in his while Simona went in the other direction. They moved hesitantly about the graveyard, their necks craned downward in search of finger-sized holes. After a few minutes, Simona stopped before an unmarked grave and called her companions over. "I've found one!" she proclaimed proudly. "Start digging."

With the shovels they'd brought with them, they began to catch the moist earth and fling it aside. It seemed forever be-

fore Dimitri's shovel tip came into contact with something solid. "I think I hit the top of a casket!" he cried.

He lay facedown on the ground, his heart pounding. With the tip of the shovel, he pried open the four-hundred-year-old lid. Inside the casket sat a hideous corpse. The female figure, dressed in a royal gown, rested in eerie slumber while maggots bored holes in her cheekbones. Her slender hands lay folded across her chest and glowed an unearthly purple beneath the waning moonlight.

Simona wiped a layer of mud from the surface of the headstone and read the name on it. "Oh my God. We've found Petra Laskov!"

Dimitri's face went pale. "I didn't mean to . . ."

"Who is Petra Laskov?" Alba asked. "Was she a Szgamy Gypsy?"

"Yes," answered Simona in a panicked voice. "She was also Dracul's mistress. Dracul lured her away from her Gypsy camp and seduced her. When she grew tired of his advances, she tried to leave him. Legend has it that the prince turned her into a vampire himself, so that she would serve him for all eternity."

The corpse emitted at low, guttural moan and the trio exchanged terrified glances. Before Simona could lower the wild rosebuds into the desecrated grave, Petra Laskov's eyelids flashed open to reveal a pair of red pupils aflame with madness.

The vampire streamed out of the casket, baring its gleaming fangs. The friends scattered about the graveyard in two different directions, Simona toward the rear gate of the cemetery and Alba and Dimitri toward the tunnel they dug under the fence.

"How dare you disturb my slumber!" The vampire's fangs caught the moonlight.

Dimitri drew back against the fence's wrought-iron palings.

"I hereby damn all of you to the same fate I suffer: an eternity spent as the undead!" the vampire seethed.

Alba screamed.

"Quick," Dimitri yelled. "Slide under the fence!"

She did as Dimitri urged. Before he could follow her, the vampire seized him in a choke hold and held him against the square palings. Dimitri clutched the shovel to his throat as protection against the creature's razor-sharp fangs. The vampire raised him off the ground, then flung him like a rag doll onto the sharp points of a stone cross that topped a headstone in the distance.

"Dimitri!" Alba cried.

The outburst caused the vampire to turn in her direction. "You're next!"

While the vampire moved toward Alba, Dimitri worked his shoulder free of the headstone's sharp point. Grimacing, he dislodged the stone crucifix and raised it to eye level. "Go back to hell!" He stepped toward the creature.

The vampire cowered at the sight of the religious symbol.

Still holding the cross at arm's length, Dimitri made his way to the fence. He managed to shimmy beneath it and join Alba on the other side. Assuming that Simona must have reached safety too, the frightened pair ran to a clearing. Dimitri stopped and pitched to his knees, his shoulder bleeding profusely.

Alba fought back tears as she tried to press her hand against the wound. But nothing would stop the gush of blood.

Dimitri looked up at her with sorrowful eyes. "You must get help."

"I don't want to leave you."

"You must! I'll bleed to death."

Alba nodded. "I'll fetch Dr. Rhessa. He's the physician who tends to my stepmother's hemophilic condition when we travel. He'll know what to do."

"Go. And hurry!"

Alba touched the amulet around her neck in a silent caress. Then with a tortured look, she disappeared into the forest.

Dimitri groaned. He tried to concentrate on the hope that Alba would return quickly. Was she running the entire two miles—through town and up the mountainside—until she reached Stelian Hall?

The rattle of a horse-drawn wagon seized his attention.

Dimitri jerked his head to the right. A kindly-faced man with thick spectacles pulled his cart to a halt and jumped down to the ground.

He studied Dimitri's bloody jacket. "What the devil happened to you, young man?"

"It's my shoulder. If you don't want to help me, you can take me to my camp."

"I don't care that you're a Gypsy. I'm a doctor—and from what I can tell, you've lost too much blood to be moved at the moment." *He paused.* "Let's get you out of the road and into the wagon."

"What is your name?" *Dimitri asked as the tall physician helped him to his feet.*

"Ionel Rhessa."

"You're the doctor Alba went to fetch at Stelian Hall. She cut through the woods, so she must not have seen you."

"If that's the case, you must be Dimitri. Alba speaks of you often."

Dimitri groaned in pain. Perspiration soaked his dark hair and dripped in streams along his temples as the physician peeled off his ripped jacket.

The physician, a man approaching middle age, began to treat Dimitri's jagged tear in the moonlight. An awkward silence hung in the back of the wagon.

Where is Alba?

Dr. Rhessa cleared his throat. "What were you doing when you got this nasty slice on your shoulder, young man?"

"Fighting a vampire," *Dimitri answered him without hesitation. Petra Laskov, of all creatures.*

Dr. Rhessa simply nodded. "So you're as brave as Alba claims."

Dimitri grimaced as Rhessa stitched his skin with a sturdy needle and wire thread.

"Drink this, my boy. It will help." *The doctor, whose eyes seemed comically large behind his thick glasses, produced a flask of whiskey.* "Mind you, I brought Alba into this world. Unfortunately, she will acquiesce to her parents' demands that she have nothing to do with you out of respect. But nothing will ever change what she feels inside unless she wills it *so. She is that headstrong." He paused. "As for you, my boy, it's obvious that you will never be allowed anywhere near her again."*

"You think her parents will forbid me to see her?" The thought mortified Dimitri.

"Yes. Especially if Alba returns home tonight scared out of her mind, splattered with blood." Rhessa clipped the wire off the needle. "The Zăpădas are planning to return to Bucharest sooner than expected—all in an attempt to sever your relationship with Alba."

"But I love her more than anything." Tears stung Dimitri's eyes. He took another swig of the fiery alcohol.

Rhessa applied a layer of soothing liniment, and bandaged the wound before he sighed at the dejection in Dimitri's eyes. "I too know what it is like to love someone so deeply they become a consummation of your soul. My wife, she . . ."

"Yes?"

"My wife was a very beautiful woman," Rhessa continued slowly. "But she left my son and me when Jochen was just a baby. It is something that still troubles him."

"I'm sorry," Dimitri said. "Where is your wife now?"

"I have no idea."

Growing paler by the minute, Dimitri withdrew the promise ring from his pocket. "I made this so that I would never lose Alba. Silly, isn't it?"

"Nothing that symbolizes love is ever silly." The doctor set his instruments down and took the ring. He held it up in the moonlight and studied the phrase of love Dimitri had carved into its interior curve. "Impressive. It shows a very steady hand."

"Thank you."

He handed the ring back to Dimitri. "You've exhibited fortitude and courage this evening."

Dimitri said nothing.

"Young man, have you ever considered becoming a surgeon? Fortitude, courage, and a steady hand are precisely what the profession requires."

Dimitri laughed. "Me? A surgeon? I wasn't able to join

the village children in primary school because of my lack of education."

The doctor stuffed his instruments into his bag. "No formal education, granted, but you're obviously intelligent and determined. Do you happen to read and write?"

Dimitri wiped the perspiration from his brow with his shirtsleeve. "I taught myself with books I found here and there."

"Excellent! Assuming you have no money saved, I can arrange for you to enter a secondary school in Bucharest where you will live in my apartment with my son, Jochen, and his governess. My son desperately needs companionship. He also needs someone he can learn a sense of character and discipline from. I have no doubt you will be a good influence."

Dimitri took another swig of the liquor.

The doctor continued. "It is my hope that you will later gain access to my alma mater, the University of Bucharest, on scholarship."

"Why are you being so nice to me?"

"You have impressed me, my boy. But please understand, you must have the proper grades to get in the university. Upon graduation, perhaps you will go on to attend my other alma mater, the Royal College of Physicians in Edinburgh, Scotland—also on scholarship. These are Jochen's plans as well." Rhessa paused.

"What is the catch?"

"No catch, young Dimitri. But there is one obstacle."

"What is that?"

"You must learn to speak English," Rhessa said.

"You would arrange for me to attend medical school—on scholarship?"

"Let me make this clear," the doctor replied. "I can recommend you as a student, but you must have excellent grades, my boy, in order to qualify for the scholarship."

"No one has ever been this kind to me," Dimitri said excitedly. "Still, I don't know—"

"For heaven's sake, boy! Offers of help come few and far

between. Besides, this may be the way to win over your princess. Transform yourself into a proper gentleman so that you may seek her out when you're older."

Dimitri hesitated. *"I don't want to leave Alba now."*

"I've told you, she will be leaving this countryside very soon. Besides, you won't be alone," Rhessa reminded him. *"As I said, my son, Jochen, is planning to go the very same route. Although I'm not sure he has the discipline to become a surgeon, I must be supportive, eh?"*

"I'll show Alba that I can make something of myself." Dimitri drew confidence into his voice. *"And I'll convince her parents that I'm not worthless at the same time."*

"That's it!" Rhessa cried. *"I'll send correspondence to the secondary school in Bucharest immediately. If all goes well, you will start in a matter of weeks since the new school year is nearly upon us."*

"Thank you, Dr. Rhessa. I shall never forget your kindness. I hope to repay you for it someday."

"Repay me by succeeding, Dimitri. My instincts tell me you have the makings of a fine surgeon. And God knows the world needs more of those."

"I'll do my best." Dimitri paused. *"Are you going back to Stelian Hall now?"*

Looking embarrassed, the physician shook his head. *"Ileana Zăpăda terminated my post. She claims I have not tended to her well enough."*

"I'm sorry," Dimitri said. *"But since you aren't going back, could you to send a message to Alba—telling her what I plan to do?"*

"I'd be happy to."

Dimitri pulled in a breath. *"Do you really think I could become a doctor?"*

"In such things I am never wrong. Now let's get you to my apartment in Bucharest so you can heal."

Chapter Five

Shaking away the memory, Dimitri entered the bathroom and peeled his shirt off. Although he'd had all the mirrors removed from the house, he'd grown accustomed to shaving without one—and he certainly didn't need to see his reflection to know what the scar on his shoulder looked like.

Scowling, he ran his fingertips over the puckered skin. He'd never forgotten the pain from that night—and he didn't think he ever would.

He ran the sink water while the image of Alba's long, white neck seared his mind like a mad temptation. *If she knew I was a vampire, what would she think of me?*

Since their time together in Romania, he'd gone from rough Gypsy boy to refined gentleman—yet Alba had no inkling of his worst identity. If Dimitri could continue to disguise the heinous monster he'd become, he might gain back her friendship and trust.

As he wiped the mysterious blood from his mouth, the wall sconce blew out. Alarmed, he whirled around and peered into the darkness.

A tiny blaze ignited in the center of the bathroom. His nerves jumped as the candle illuminated the face of a woman. She looked at him from beneath a riot of black wavy hair, her lips an other-worldly hue of purple.

"Simona?"

"Greetings, Dimitri." She sauntered toward him, the nipples of her small breasts leading the way beneath a plunging gown.

Years ago, he'd turned to Simona in his anguish over losing Alba. She had followed him from Transylvania to Bucharest with the intention of lending him her support. But once Simona's seductive wiles became too demanding, everything had changed between them. He'd chosen to leave Romania to attend the Royal College in Scotland. When he abandoned Simona, she became a woman scorned. Rail thin and deathly white, she lacked the vibrancy she'd emanated in her youth.

"You're alive!" he cried.

The eerie figure tightened her fingers around the candle. Her lips changed from a frosted purple to a deep blood red. "You look as good as ever without a shirt, Dimitri."

"What are you doing here? I thought you vanished off the face of the earth."

She shook her head slowly.

"You look so . . . different," Dimitri said.

She made no reply.

"Word reached me that you disappeared in Romania," he went on. "Are you all right?"

"I am now," she whispered.

His eyes narrowed. "What became of you after I left Bucharest?"

"The same thing that happened to you, Dimitri."

He took a step back. "You became a vampire?" He remembered Simona as strong-willed. Demanding. Possessive. The kind of woman who would make a terrifying vampire.

"Yes. In fact, I'm the one who carried you over."

"It *was* you. You were the bat that drained me of my blood in Wales. But why?"

She put a hand to his bare chest. Her icy breath gusted across his face. "It's in our destiny to become vampires."

His hands curled into fists and he shot her a glare. "Did you bite me again last night?"

"I did. You were so weak that you would have perished. I bit you to incapacitate you—while I pierced my wrist and allowed you to drink my blood. Now you feel good, extraordinarily potent, do you not?"

Fury flushed through him. "I would hardly have perished, Simona."

She frowned. "It seems you underestimate your need to feed," she said. "You must accept your fate as a vampire, Dimitri."

"Stop saying that." He fought the urge to strangle her. "If anything, I think our fates were sealed the moment you stole that amulet from Rosa Spera."

"I beg to differ."

"I'll ask you again." He grasped her fragile arm. "Why have you done this to me?"

"I brought you over because I knew you are still in love with Alba. It's also why I urged you to pass the amulet on to her."

"Giving the amulet to Alba was a mistake."

"It was a brilliant idea, but I didn't come up with it on my own," Simona scoffed.

"What do you mean?"

"Alba's stepmother persuaded me to steal the necklace from our camp."

Alarm feathered up Dimitri's spine. "Her *stepmother*?"

"Ileana Zăpăda is a witch. She dabbles in black magic. She knew about the Egyptian amulet and its curse. That's why she came to me. She gave me money to take the stone and give it to you. *To curse Alba.*"

"And you agreed?"

"Yes," she said flatly. "You loved Alba when you should have loved me. Now I've turned you into a vampire so that you and I may be together. The strength I've given you will lead to a clearer mind—with which to choose either me or Alba."

His eyes flashed. "I'll show you that you cannot play with people's lives this way, Simona!"

"If you think I'm evil," she purred, "you should meet Ileana Zăpăda. She will stop at nothing until Alba is dead." She lowered her voice even more. "The woman knows where Alba is."

Dimitri's stomach dropped. "How?"

"In looking for you, I inadvertently found Alba and informed Ileana."

A scalding fury heated Dimitri's blood. He hurled his razor against the wall.

"Don't you miss what we had in Bucharest?" Simona pressed herself against him, but he flung her away. "Tell me you didn't like the warmth of my body beside you."

It was true that Simona had shown Dimitri carnal pleasures in bed, overcoming his inexperience, aiding the pain he felt over losing Alba. But their physical relationship had been short-lived. Once he'd come to his senses, he knew their brief intimacy was a mistake. He also knew he would never stop loving Alba.

"After you left me in Bucharest, I returned to the countryside with my tail between my legs," Simona explained. "I couldn't stomach the fact that you should have loved me but didn't, so I drowned myself in the Olt River. According to Romanian folklore, you know what happens to someone who commits suicide, don't you?"

"They become a vampire," Dimitri murmured.

She nodded. "Now we have more in common than ever. Perhaps it is our destiny to live the same existence."

"I may not live at all if the amulet drives Alba to kill me."

"You are immortal," Simona reminded him with a frown.

"We'll see about that," he replied. "A stake through the heart can stop both of us in our tracks."

Simona gave a shudder. "Time will tell if you and Alba will meet the fate of the amulet. In the meantime, think of the story surrounding its prophecy, Dimitri. You'd have to become lovers to set the curse into motion."

"That's why I will avoid making love to Alba at all costs."

"Can you?" Simona teased, stroking the tip of her breast with her fingertip. "You always were a tiger in bed . . ."

"You disgust me," Dimitri bellowed.

"And you always know the right things to say." She laughed. "Well, I have another surprise for you."

"To hell with your surprises!"

She pulled the bulk of her hair seductively over one shoulder. "Oh, you'll want to hear the details of this one. If you dare become Alba's lover, *you will destroy her yourself.*"

"What are you talking about?" He ground his back teeth together.

She stepped forward and clutched his arm. Then her touch grazed lower, to his shaft. She began to rub it slowly, entrancingly, causing an involuntary arousal.

Snapping to his senses, Dimitri shoved her hand away.

"You are a Szgamy Gypsy, remember?" Her eyes blazed. "Our band is tied to Vlad the Impaler. That means we, as Szgamys, have the capability of becoming *mulo* vampires when we cross over," she said.

"What the hell are you talking about?"

"*Mulos* crave blood, but we can also drain the energy from our victims in a special way. I'm a *mulo*, and because you drank from me last night, your sexual appetite will increase substantially. With that comes the danger of exhausting your human partner to the point of illness—or even death—through your lovemaking. Don't you see, Dimitri? You and I can make love with no problem. But Alba . . . She is still human. She will become the victim of your sexual hunger in bed."

"You are as just as wicked as Ileana Zăpădă!"

"Sticks and stones, Dimitri." She sneered.

He turned to go but she blocked his way.

"You'll destroy Alba if you make love to her, Dimitri, so you really should avoid it. I suggest you wait for her to drive a stake through your heart just before she kills herself." She threw her head back in eerie laughter.

"Don't go near her!" he thundered.

"I hate the idea of you bedding Alba, but the thought of you destroying her makes up for it. Of course, if none of this happens as quickly as I prefer, I will turn Alba into a vampire myself."

"You viper. I have the mind to drive a stake through *your* heart!" He glanced around for something sharp enough to do the job.

She dropped her smile and took a step back. "I'll go. But first, a word of advice, since you are so tenderly new at being a vampire."

"Don't ever pair the words 'tender' and 'vampire.'" Dimitri growled.

"Right now you can't help but take your victims quickly, hungrily. Eventually you will learn to hypnotize your victims so that they will remember nothing of the encounter."

Guilt seized him every time he took someone's life, so he forced himself to listen to her.

"Try out your powers of persuasion tonight, Dimitri," she said. "After you hypnotize your victim, feed where you won't be seen. But heed this warning: you *will* come back to me."

Simona crumbled the candle into a cloud of dust. Then, morphing into a small bat, she disappeared through the open bathroom window.

Simona was the vilest creature ever to plague Dimitri's life and he vowed to have his revenge on her. But at the moment, all he could think of was his hunger for blood. He quickly changed his clothes, then twirled in circles while holding his opera cloak away from his body. In no time, he evaporated into an ominous, bluish mist—a mist insubstantial enough to seep up the chimney chute.

Dimitri soared through the sky like a nimble bird. It was extraordinary how every sight and sound was magnified at this altitude. But soon his senses became painfully exaggerated. His ears pounded and his heartbeat boomed. He felt crazed. Heady. Omnipotent.

His heart ached for Alba, and all he wanted was to change the past—to go back to the time before the curses snared them in their nets. Before he allowed them to be separated.

He transported himself over Mayfair and Chelsea Harbour, to the less prestigious neighborhood of Bloomsbury. Hidden away, Dimitri changed back to human form. As he began to search the gaslit streets for any vagrant who'd been cast aside by society, he spotted an outcast slumped in a deserted back alley. Catatonic, the drunken hobo lay next to a rubbish bin.

Steam from McGroder's Pub wafted into the narrow dead end. Dimitri shook the vagrant.

The degenerate's eyes opened only to slide closed again. Deciding that it was no use trying to hypnotize him, Dimitri went about feeding.

As Simona described, he took his victim by storm, consuming the man's blood in an uncontrolled frenzy. Once he was finished drinking and the hobo was lifeless, guilt seized him. He morphed back into a ball of mist as his thoughts turned to Alba. She would be terrified if she learned of the encounter. She would be even more frightened to know that Simona had told Ileana where she was. Therefore, he should tell her nothing. That way she might allow him to be close by if either of the venomous witches paid her a visit.

Still, getting close to Alba meant that the sweet scent of her blood and the warmth of her flesh would madden him—and drive him insane. Dimitri had known about *mulo* vampires, but he'd blocked their existence out of his mind. Now he remembered that their unstoppable powers were the stuff that frightened Gypsy children around the campfire.

As he left the alley in search of Alba's dormitory, he wondered, *Can I protect Alba and prevent myself from consuming her at the same time?*

Chapter Six

The conversation Teddy and his father shared circled around the Rollingsworth dining room in a dull drone. Tuning it out, Alba looked up at the crystal chandelier that canopied the dining table. She became mesmerized by the way the gaslights caught the facets of the cut glass. Her thoughts wandered to Dimitri.

How did he find me after all these years?

Where does he live?

Should I ask Teddy if he's been in contact with Dimitri?

No, she decided. She shouldn't let Teddy know that she was curious about her former love. After all, her pulse hadn't yet slowed under the memory of Dimitri's black-fringed stare—and Teddy might notice.

The sound of the kitchen door burst her daydream bubble. A servant appeared with a tray of unappealing beef Wellington, and the evening seemed a total loss. That is, until Harold Rollingsworth raised a topic that caught Alba's attention.

"Two more unfortunates were murdered in Whitechapel last night," the middle-aged barrister said. "The first woman was a prostitute by the name of Elizabeth Stride. A hawker discovered her body at Dutfield's Yard a few hours after midnight." He sat back in his chair, folding his hands over his protruding belly. "The second was another prosser by the name of Catherine Eddowes."

Alba gripped her napkin and glanced at Teddy. Aside from the substantial belly, Teddy resembled his father in every way. Both men sported reddish blond hair and the same solemn gray eyes. And each possessed a gentle demeanor. In fact, the two men were so alike that it seemed natural for Teddy to follow in his father's footsteps at Crown Court.

"Poor sods." Teddy shook his head. "Robbed of all dignity."

Alba frowned thoughtfully. "Were the prostitutes mutilated like the first two women?"

"No. And that's the curious part," Mr. Rollingsworth said. "Elizabeth Stride's throat was cut—but there were no other marks on her body. Police seem to think the killer was interrupted."

"How long after the murder did the hawker find the body?" Alba asked.

"Minutes, apparently. In fact, the blood was so fresh that authorities believe the killer may have been lurking in the shadows while the hawker ran for help."

"The madman barely got away this time," Alba murmured.

"He walked a mere twelve minutes to find another victim in Mitre Square," Harold Rollingsworth went on. "The blood on the knife hadn't even dried when the Ripper butchered Catherine Eddowes."

Enthralled, Alba leaned over her plate. "So Scotland Yard believes this is all the work of the same killer?"

"That's their assumption." Harold nodded.

"I'd bet money this is the work of a copycat," Teddy chimed in.

"I don't think so," Alba protested. She turned back toward the elder Rollingsworth. "Do the police have a suspect?"

Harold frowned. "They have several, but no arrests have been made. I presume their barrier is lack of evidence."

"No one saw or heard anything?" she asked.

"Apparently not. The only thing the police have to go on is the assumption that the killer possesses anatomical—even medical—knowledge."

"Who are these suspects?" she asked.

Teddy put a gentle hand over hers. "Alba, the dinner table is hardly the place to discuss such matters."

"But this case is precisely what we've spent years preparing for," she said. "This is how my mind works. I piece clues together to form a perfect puzzle. Only then can the real answer stare me in the face."

"She's right, my boy," Harold said to Teddy. "Now that you're both part of the firm, I suggest you get accustomed to discussions of lurid details among barristers."

"Part of the firm? Pardon me, sir?" Teddy's eyes widened.

Harold laughed as he shoved his thumbs into the tiny pockets of his vest. "I intended to save my announcement for dessert, but I suppose now is as good a time as any. I've decided that both of you are ready to bring your pupilage to the next level. You've passed the Bar Vocational Exam and have shadowed me for six months. Now it's time you undertook some real courtroom work. The youthful energy and passion for the truth you possess is just what's needed in the Crowe trial."

"You mean we will be acting as barristers, along with you?" Alba asked, squeezing Teddy's arm.

"You'll be acting as *pupil* barristers, yes," Harold replied. "You've been sitting in on the trial all along, so you know that all the witnesses have been called—except our number-one suspect, Tabitha Crowe."

Teddy and Alba nodded enthusiastically.

"Alba, since you are a woman, I want you to question Mrs. Crowe. I have a feeling you will give the procedure just the right touch. Teddy, you will present closing arguments."

"Thank you, Father," Teddy cried.

"Yes, thank you, Mr. Rollingsworth," Alba said. "You won't regret your decision!"

Teddy turned toward Alba and beamed. "Congratulations to you."

"Likewise." She grinned as they embraced.

"You know, Alba"—Harold's voice developed a more serious tone—"if you step into the role of London's first female barrister, you will have many eyes upon you. Are you certain you can withstand the pressure?"

Alba smiled. "I can think of no challenge I'd relish more."

"That's what I like to hear," he said. "Now, if you both do well, you may go on to share chambers with me."

Teddy reached for Alba's hand. She looked into his gray eyes where she recognized the adoration he'd always held for her. Her heart warmed.

"Teddy, my boy. Having your own career means you'll be in fine position to take a wife and carry on the Rollingsworth bloodline." Harold Rollingsworth's eyes twinkled as they flitted to Alba. She blushed in return. Oddly, Teddy didn't smile or respond.

Dessert wasn't served a moment too soon. A butler poured steaming coffee from an ornate silver carafe while a maid sliced a delectable apple tart dusted with confectioner's sugar. Alba, suddenly famished, consumed two of them with zest.

The evening proved enjoyable after all. As it came to a close, she bid good night to her generous host and climbed into a hansom with Teddy. They journeyed back to Bloomsbury, chattering on excitedly.

"I've never seen my father more proud than he was tonight," Teddy informed her amid the glow of the gaslights. "Proud of you, that is."

Alba flung him a dubious glance. "Your father is proud of both of us."

Teddy shook his head. She had to admit that he was extremely handsome in a straight-backed, honorable kind of way. With his fashionable sideburns and square jaw, he could make any number of girls pay attention. And his easygoing temperament made him a prized suitor. At the moment, however, his eyes took on a strange, haunted aura.

"I suppose I shouldn't hang on Father's every word," he said.

"If it's not too bold to say, you seemed unusually quiet when your father suggested you marry soon."

"It wasn't his mention of marriage that bothered me."

"What was it?"

"It was his suggestion that I carry on the Rollingsworth bloodline."

"Don't you want children, Teddy?"

He sucked in a breath. "I do, but I'm not Harold Rollingsworth's real son."

Alba put a hand to her mouth. "You're . . . adopted? You never told me."

Nodding, he reached for her hand. "My adoption is something I don't like to speak of. Nor does my father."

"Go on," she said compassionately.

He hesitated. "My parents decided to offer a home to an unnatural child when my mother was declared barren."

"I would never have guessed you were adopted since you and your father look so much alike."

"I suppose that was the whole idea." Teddy smiled and the haunted look disappeared. "Presumably, my red hair helped me out of the 'baby factory,' as it's known in the East End."

Alba knew of this "factory"—a place one would never frequent unless one was forced to go there. It was a means to an end for prostitutes or for young mothers who found themselves precariously with child.

"I'm so sorry." She squeezed his hand. "But from what I can see, Mr. Rollingsworth loves you just as much as he would any child of his own."

Teddy nodded.

"Did you know your adoptive mother?"

"No," Teddy said. "Madeline Rollingsworth died shortly after she brought me home. But my father raised me lovingly. He's a wonderful man."

They traveled the rest of the way in silence. The hansom stopped in front of Alba's building and Teddy hurried to help her out. She opened her handbag and fished for her key. Meanwhile, he cleared his throat.

She looked up. "What is it, Teddy?"

"I meant to ask you something the last time I took you home, but I lost my nerve. Even when Edith went inside."

"You can ask me anything," Alba said gently.

"Well, I'm curious . . . as to how you *actually* feel about me."

She cupped his cheek with the palm of her hand. "I consider you the dearest man in the world."

His expression darkened. "I'd hoped you'd say something more passionate." He took a step toward her. "Alba, it's my wish that someday you will be my wife."

She looked up at him, trying to digest what he had just said.

"It would be a smart match, the two of us," he went on.

Her brow puckered and she didn't reply.

"Alba, would it be acceptable if I kissed you?"

She swallowed and smiled tremulously. "Of course."

Teddy shifted toward her. In a stiff motion, his arms encircled her waist and he gathered her close. Tall enough to give the illusion that his head was scraping the night clouds, he bent in and clamped his mouth over hers. During the lengthy kiss, he neither moved, moaned, nor twitched. Alba stood rigidly as well. The embrace made her feel as if someone had erased a beautiful love sonnet from a piece of paper. She felt blank.

He drew back and stared into her eyes. "That was very pleasant, wasn't it?"

"Oh, yes." She smoothed a strand of flyaway hair. "Most pleasant."

"I hope one day you will look at me as you did Drake Griffin. I saw your expression when you spotted him at the party."

Guilt and frustration churned her stomach. Could she ever view another man with the same desire she'd felt for Dimitri? And was it fair to withhold the truth from Teddy? "I haven't been completely honest with you, Teddy. Drake's real name is Dimitri Grigorescu. He is someone I knew in Romania. In fact, we were very much in love in our adolescence. I was shocked to see him again."

"What a coincidence." Dejection shadowed his face. "But why didn't Drake—I mean Dimitri—tell me he knew you?"

"It was very long ago." She paused. "I don't know why Dimitri changed his name, but promise me you won't reveal it to anyone."

"I promise," he said as concern surfaced in his voice. "But I want to know how you feel about him now."

"I'm not sure," she said.

Teddy forced a smile. "I suppose I'll settle for your confusion." She turned to leave.

"I hope my curiosity hasn't strained our relationship," he called out.

Alba looked at him over her shoulder. "Not at all."

"Get some sleep, my fair princess."

With a heavy heart, she climbed the staircase to the third floor. She knew she shouldn't string Teddy along, but he always provided her with a much-needed sense of comfort. If she married him, they could share a life full of common interests and easy companionship. He would never intrude on her independence—nor would he ever consider her his weaker half. Although she might not have passionate feelings for him at the moment, they could possibly form a deep love someday.

Still, as wonderful as those things sounded, something was stopping her.

Alba entered the bedroom and hung her wrap inside the armoire. Grateful that all of the girls were performing tonight, she put a match to an oil lamp and stepped behind a dressing screen to remove her other garments. The sound of someone breathing filled the silence. Pulse stuttering, she peeked around the screen. The silhouette of a man materialized on her windowsill and she screamed.

Chapter Seven

"You should lock your window, Alba." Dimitri's sultry whisper drifted through the darkness. "There's a demonic killer on the loose."

"How dare you barge in here!" Clutching her dress to her chest, she brought the flickering oil lamp closer to him.

As he sat on the window ledge, his back resting against the frame, Dimitri watched her from under a veil of black lashes. His white teeth flashed in the light and his piercing eyes made her knees wobble.

Alba sucked in a breath.

"Correction," Dimitri said with a wry smile. "I haven't actually 'barged in.' I'm still waiting for an invitation."

"You seem to enjoy surprising me," she said crisply. "And you know I loathe surprises."

"Some things never change." His topaz eyes burned a deep desire for her even now. "How about that invitation?"

She hesitated.

"Well?"

Struggling to hold her garment across her chest and balance the heavy lamp in her other hand, Alba looked out the window. She saw no trace of a ladder. "How did you get up here?"

"I climbed the trellis."

"But the trellis doesn't seem strong enough to hold you."

"That's my Alba. A brilliant barrister someday you'll make."

"I'm no longer 'your' Alba." Her tone was bitter.

He sighed as he drew one leg up and rested his arm on it. The position, which showcased the snug fit of his trousers and his ample bulge, gave Alba an enticing view.

"If we must talk from here, I want you to know that I didn't believe the rumors swirling around Bucharest. Not for a moment," he said.

Her gaze softened. "Which rumors?"

"The ones about you being dead." He drew in a breath through his straight nose. "I knew you were a survivor—and that you had probably orchestrated a plan to disappear."

"I did have a plan. To get as far away from my stepmother as possible," she said. "But none of that matters now."

"The past does matter. It makes us who we are," Dimitri insisted in a subdued tone.

She looked away from him. Her body stiffened—yet curiosity made her lock eyes with him again. "How did you survive? The tear in your shoulder . . . you lost so much blood."

"Dr. Rhessa happened upon me on the road. He sewed up my shoulder and bandaged it. I told him to send word to you at Stelian Hall—to let you know that I was about to leave Romania in order to get the education he convinced me I should get."

"If Dr. Rhessa sent correspondence, my stepmother must have intercepted it." Alba's voice quaked.

"Regardless," he said with a smile, "we've been reunited. Though I admit our reunion didn't go according to plan with you fainting on the spot."

She studied his face. He hadn't shaved and she found the look incredibly appealing. But wasn't she supposed to be angry with him? "All these years, I pined for you, Dimitri. I went to your camp to inquire about you, but a Gypsy woman told me you never returned. That's why I assumed you were dead."

"I'm sorry, Alba. I left the countryside without saying good-bye to anyone."

"Why?"

"Because you were all that mattered to me. Your family did not approve of me, so I slipped away—determined to make myself worthy of you."

"When you came to London, how did you know that I wasn't betrothed or married?" Alba asked.

"It's hard to explain, but I have—visions," he replied.

"Visions?"

"More like feelings."

"Did you see Teddy in this vision?" She cast him a rueful smile.

"Yes, but I sensed you don't return his affections."

"Well, now that you're here, I want to return the Egyptian amulet to you." She snapped out of the sentimental moment. "I cannot believe you had the nerve to give it to me when it was cursed in the first place."

Remorse surfaced in his eyes. She ignored it. Setting the lamp on a side table, she retreated to her nightstand to get the amulet. "Here." She held the necklace toward him with an outstretched hand. "I want you to take it away."

Dimitri cast his eyes from the light. The action told her that he refused to take it. "Alba, I hate to be the bearer of bad news, but if a woman dons the amulet even once, she will be affected by its curse. Or so the story goes."

"I already know that." Sarcasm ran rampant in her voice.

"Then there is no reason for me to take it."

Her anger grew. *I just want everything to go away.* She twined the amulet's chain around her hand with a scowl. "Why didn't you tell me who you were when we were introduced at your birthday party?"

"I should have," he replied. "Both of us have resorted to fabricated names, but I should have told you who I was straightaway."

She stood rigidly in the middle of the room. "I changed my name so that my stepmother couldn't find me. Why did you change yours?"

"For a simpler reason." Dimitri shifted his position. "The people of Great Britain are friendly, but they are even friendlier to somebody who has an English name. Besides, 'Griffin' is much easier to spell than 'Grigorescu.'"

Refusing to join in on the joke, Alba gave a little snort. The dress slipped from her grasp and gave Dimitri a glimpse at her cleavage above her corset. He raised a winged eyebrow as she tried to compose herself.

"I'm getting tired of sitting on this narrow ledge," he said. "Won't you invite me in for a drink?"

She hesitated.

"Come along, Alba. It's the least you could do for an old friend."

"Very well. You may come in." She disappeared behind the screen in order to put her dress back on. Meanwhile, Dimitri made his way to the tiny kitchen at the back of the apartment.

"Do you have any wine?" she heard him ask.

"In the cabinet above the stove."

A minute later, he joined her holding a bottle of Cabernet and two glasses. She watched him pour the wine with steady hands— strong hands that seemed capable of anything. After he passed her one of the glasses, he raised his own in a salute. "To us. Friends reunited after an eternity apart."

Alba forced a dry lump down her throat. She met Dimitri's stare with wide eyes. "We were more than friends . . . although our love was innocent enough."

"We were very young," he admitted.

"I try not to dwell on the past."

His warm smile melted her icy demeanor. "Come now. Don't you wonder what would have happened if we ran away together that night?"

Instead of answering him, she took another sip of wine. The fiery golden hue of Dimitri's irises dazzled her. Her heart fluttered.

"I don't dwell on what-ifs either."

"You've gotten crusty on me, my dear Alba." He smiled dashingly.

"Bad memories will do that to a person," she countered. A tingle of guilt seized her and she paused. "Our separation is something I never forgave my stepmother for. My father was away on business, so I went to Ileana for help the night you got hurt in the graveyard. She had just terminated Dr. Rhessa's post and she refused to summon another doctor for you." Alba looked away. "As you can see by my modest existence, I cut myself off from her when my father died."

Dimitri's gaze was sincere. "That's very commendable. But then I always knew you were extraordinary."

Her cheeks flushed at the compliment. She moved into the kitchen, to the tiny stove, and leaned against it. "And you have always been persistent. Now that you are a successful doctor, have you had no interest in finding a Mrs. Grigorescu?"

His tawny eyes turned darker and she fought the urge to swoon.

"No," he said. "I've never loved another woman."

"Please don't say things like that."

Dimitri set his glass on the kitchen table. He came nearer and took her by the shoulders. Her skin felt as though it would burst open under his touch. She nearly caved forward against his chest as his breath feathered over her face, but she forced herself to stiffen.

"What things shouldn't I say?" he asked.

"That you've never had feelings for anyone but me. Too much time has passed—"

"I only want to be your friend, Alba," he said.

Friends? That's all he wants to be? Embarrassment and disappointment coursed through her with fervency—disappointment being the more powerful of the two emotions. Dimitri had always had the ability to convince her that she was the only woman in the world by just one stare. As Alba watched his black hair glisten in the light and his jaw harden, she wanted him to gather her into a crushing kiss, yet she told herself to remain on the defensive.

"It may sound crazy, but when I found out you were in London, I accepted the position at St. Bart's to be near you," Dimitri said.

Alba's heart missed a beat. So this *had* been planned. His admission warned her to brace herself for something dangerous—something that might have to do with the amulet.

"I want to know more about the necklace you gave me in Romania, Dimitri."

He pivoted away. "Must we talk of it?"

She placed a trembling hand on his arm. "Please."

"I want to talk about something else." He paused. "Where were you tonight?"

"I was at the Rollingsworth home. Harold Rollingsworth offered me time in court."

"Congratulations," Dimitri said, striding to the other side of the room.

She wanted to say so many things to him. She wanted to tell him that she'd cried herself to sleep for weeks after he disappeared from her life. She wanted to tell him that she had enjoyed kisses from several men, but no one had ever kissed her the way he had. And she was desperate for him to know that, at twenty-five years of age, she was still a respectable virgin.

She'd thrown herself into a career to forget the pain of being without him. Yet, assuming that the words wouldn't come out right, she said none of it.

She moved to him. "You have some wine on the corner of your mouth." Dimitri nodded and withdrew a handkerchief from his pocket. Then he glided to a hanging mirror. Alba followed him but once they reached the mirror, he whirled around to face her and grabbed her by the shoulders. "Do you mind if we continue our conversation in the park?"

She was surprised by his strange actions but conceded anyway. "I'll get my coat."

Chapter Eight

Dimitri felt like an imbecile. Alba had nearly seen his lack of reflection. How would he have explained that?

As they strolled beneath a canopy of low-lying trees, he managed to compose himself. The moon bathed the park in a romantic glow and he slid a glance her way. He could hardly believe the woman he would sacrifice his life for was walking beside him. Alba still possessed a charmingly round forehead and a delicate nose, but her facial shape was defined by a woman's beauty now—a beauty that was immeasurable. Under the bright moonlight, her skin appeared as luminescent as a dew-drenched flower, and the gloss of her cherry-red lips lured him closer.

They meandered farther along the pathway, and it took all of Dimitri's willpower to resist reaching for her hand and biting down on the curve of her neck. He clasped her elbow firmly as they strolled. And when he inched closer to her, the scent of her blood made his loins burn and his cock harden.

Thank God for my billowing cloak.

Under a blanket of twinkling stars and amid a cool, intoxicating breeze the park's ambience was magical, but Dimitri reminded himself why he was here. He must gain Alba's trust. Once he did, he would inform her of Simona's visit—and the fact that her stepmother knew she was in London. But the timing must be right. At that point, he could persuade Alba to leave this place and hide away with him. But he didn't dare tell her that he would have to leave her once she was safe from Ileana and from the vampire's curse. After all, he couldn't afford to make love to her, because it would destroy her.

"Those in the field of law may question my abilities as a woman," Alba was saying. "But I'm up for the challenge."

"You should be very proud of yourself." Dimitri forced his attention back to their conversation. "I hope to see more women in the medical field as well. I believe they bring a new level of compassion to the science."

She met his gaze. When he focused on her blue eyes, what he saw in them was hard to read. Did she feel anything for him at all?

The pounding of Alba's pulse beneath her creamy neck was a maddening sound. Then again, Dimitri was an inexperienced vampire—and the slightest hint of hunger drove him to seek blood. At the moment, he had the impulse to tug Alba closer and penetrate her throbbing vein.

His fangs descended against his will—and as he ran the tip of his tongue beneath their sharp points, his mouth watered. It took every ounce of restraint he could muster to make them recede.

Christ, man! Remember why you are here.

Instead of seducing Alba, he must become her friend all over again. He cleared his throat. "How did Teddy react to his father's announcement of your time in court?"

She lit up. "That's the best part! Mr. Rollingsworth offered Teddy the same opportunity too. We intend to work side by side on the case."

"Ah." Dimitri smiled. "I must congratulate Teddy. He is a good man." The longer Dimitri gazed upon Alba's spectacular beauty, the more his body heated.

A brief silence passed. She blushed when she spotted a couple walking toward them hand in hand.

"I know you are not officially engaged to Teddy," Dimitri said. "He told me as much. However, it's Teddy's wish that you two will head toward marriage."

She frowned as they stopped walking. "How do you know that?"

"He mentioned it the day before my birthday party."

She looked down at her hands.

"How do you feel about the possibility?" he asked.

"This must be my night for interrogation," she replied as her forehead creased.

Dimitri squared his shoulders. "I apologize. It is none of my business."

They sat on a stone bench and fell into silence. Alba watched the couple pass by. Dimitri followed her stare and decided it was a perfect opportunity to reach for her hand. He slid closer—until their thighs touched—and gathered it, but she moved it away.

"I'm sorry, Dimitri." She turned to look into his eyes. "Your appearance has taken me by surprise."

"And you hate surprises." He smiled wryly.

She nodded.

"And you've worked hard to come this far in your life."

She nodded again.

"And I am interrupting the plans you've laid out." He paused as she laughed. "You see?" he said. "Despite the years that separated us, I still know you."

"I suppose you do." She matched his rueful smile, but dropped the expression an instant later. "I didn't think I'd ever see you again, Dimitri."

Another wave of hunger pinged inside him. He longed to bundle her in his arms, taste her lips, consume her delectable blood . . .

"I know you didn't," he said.

"But now that you're here, look how far you have come in your life," she said, changing the subject. "Surgeon at St. Bart's. That's quite an accomplishment."

I did it all for you.

He leaned forward. Her water-lily scent filled his nostrils, and her breasts rose and fell alluringly with every breath she took. He was tempted to kiss her, yet she seemed uncomfortable with his close proximity. What's more, he'd told her he merely wanted to be friends—

She shifted away from him. "Tell me about the hospital. It must be an awfully busy place."

"It is. We have 676 beds that cater to 6,000 inpatient and 100,000 outpatient visitors. It's a place that smells like death, hope, and strong carbolic soap."

She chuckled at the description. "And I suppose you love it."

"I do."

"It seems you've found what it is you're meant to do," she re-marked softly.

"I have." *If only I can continue to resist all the blood.*

Cupping her delicate chin in his hand, he urged her face back in his direction. "Did you recognize me at all last night, Alba?"

"You've changed so much," she stammered. "You've certainly become a handsome man—if it isn't too bold for me to say."

"And you've blossomed into an incredible woman. In fact, you're more beautiful than I could have imagined." He reached for her hand again and brought it to his lips.

When she smiled, Dimitri could see the familiar attraction in her eyes. For the briefest of moments they were back in the flower-laden hills of Romania, lying in the tall, waving grass. Nostalgia nearly persuaded him to spill the truth: that the curse cast upon them in the graveyard had come true for him and Simona. But he didn't want to scare her away.

Alba's show of affection vanished as quickly as it had appeared. "You're confusing me, Dimitri. You say you want to be friends, but I see more in your eyes."

He made no reply as his internal debate continued.

"Is there something you'd like to tell me?" she asked.

"Not at the moment."

"It's no matter." Alba frowned. "Unfortunately, we can't turn back the hands of time. Now we're very different people with very different lives. I'm shocked to learn you've made London your home."

Stabbed with rejection, he thought of Simona's words. *Use your powers to hypnotize Alba.* But he quickly chased the thought away since she was too precious to him.

She withdrew her hand and stood. "It's been lovely catching up with you, Dimitri, but I think it's best if we distanced ourselves. You must understand that I have a new existence now."

He surged to his feet. "I don't want to complicate your life, Alba. I want to enhance it."

"I left Romania for a reason," she said firmly. "You're part of a past I want to forget."

His heart was breaking on the inside. "Please, Alba. I'm here to try and reverse the curse of the amulet."

"The amulet." She glowered. "You showed bravery in coming to London. After all, I might kill you at any given time."

He looked away as his face flamed.

"I . . . I'm sorry I said that."

"Please, Alba. I'll take you back to your dormitory if you promise me one thing."

She didn't reply.

"Promise me you will have dinner with me Friday night."

"Dimitri," she said, "I just told you that I don't want to see you again."

"Please. In honor of our friendship. After our dinner, I promise to leave you alone."

She hesitated.

"Please?" he repeated.

After a moment, she raised an eyebrow. "Agreed."

"You make me a very happy man. I'll send a hansom round for you at eight o'clock."

Chapter Nine

Dimitri awoke the next night in the dim haze of the basement.

Removing the lid of the shipping crate, he climbed over its edge and pulled himself to his feet. Although he felt a mild sense of lethargy, gone was his insane urge to feed. He hadn't meant to satiate himself with the vagabond behind McGroder's Pub, but that was what happened. Devastated that he'd killed the unlucky fellow, Dimitri was determined to hypnotize his next victim into submission. That way he could take what he wanted and leave his subject alive—as Simona had suggested.

He bathed and dressed in a suit of gray twill accompanied by a silver silk tie. Completing the ensemble was his cloak filled with native soil. Of course, once he reached St. Bart's he would change into less formal clothes and don his leather apron.

He was fortunate that his schedule allowed him to work at night. Even before he became a vampire, he'd grown accustomed to staying up late during medical school, and it was a good thing he had, for the worst of the hospital's patients seemed to arrive in the middle of the night.

Alcoholics with ruptured livers.

Children with appendicitis.

Women delivering babies in the Cesarean manner.

Yet Dimitri loved his work. He liked the aspect of helping people—and his reward was curing their ailments. However, it was becoming more and more difficult to ignore all the blood. At the hospital, his temples pulsated at its smell, and that growing thirst pounded his brain.

Being a surgeon and a vampire is a paradox—a polar-opposite kind of existence.

Dimitri locked the front door of his mansion and walked to the awaiting hansom.

Thank God I lack the need to feed at the present time.

Just as Dimitri climbed into the hansom St. Bart's had sent round for him, a dark figure emerged from the shadows across the street. A foreigner of medium height and build, the man gathered the collar of his frayed jacket around his throat.

Shivering against the cutting October breeze that would have blown his short hair about if it weren't for his deerstalker cap, the man crossed to Dimitri's mansion. He would wait for the doctor to return, and if he was lucky, he'd be able to remain by the gate undisturbed in this affluent neighborhood of London.

Sitting on the cobbled sidewalk, the homeless man folded his arms over the bump of his knees and lowered his head for a long nap.

Dimitri panicked during his shift. An appendix removal took much longer than he had anticipated. He sewed up his patient as hastily but as expertly as he could. It was five o'clock in the morning, and the sun would rise in just one hour. Dawn's cresting meant that he would lose all his strength, and worse, he'd be burned by the bright rays of the sun as he made his way home.

When the hansom deposited him in front of his home, he swung out of the carriage and spotted a ragged-looking man slumped by the gate. The man was barring the way to his home.

"Excuse me, sir," Dimitri called out in a hurry.

The figure didn't move.

He reached over and shook the thinly clad man by the shoulder. The degenerate roused in a bleary state. The stranger looked up and Dimitri raised an eyebrow. It was Jochen, the son of Dr. Rhessa—the physician who'd given him his start! He hadn't seen Jochen since the young man unexpectedly dropped out of the Royal College of Physicians in Edinburgh after their first year of study. Dimitri had lost contact with him after that.

"Jochen! What the devil are you doing here?" he said, offering a hand to help him stand.

"My old friend." Jochen spoke in his native Romanian. "It's so good to see you."

Dimitri pulled away from the man's embrace. His friend smelled worse than a pile of rubbish left out in the sun. "I say, you look downtrodden."

"I've come upon hard times, Dimitri."

"Indeed." A brief paused passed. "Where are my manners? Please. Come in. I'll pour us some brandy and we can sit by a warm fire."

Jochen looked surprised. "You are inviting me in?"

"Of course." Dimitri smiled. "It is the least I can do for an old friend." He stole a look at the gray haze of dawn. In his estimation, he had thirty minutes or so before the sun rose. "After you."

Jochen grasped Dimitri's arm in a sign of gratitude and they escaped out of the autumn chill and into the parlor. An eerie wind began to screech against the windows. Jochen took a seat in front of the hearth while Dimitri set fire to the coal scuttle. After Jochen extended his hands toward the rising flames, he eagerly accepted a snifter of brandy and downed the entire glass before Dimitri could sit in the matching armchair.

"I'm embarrassed to say I have no food in the house," Dimitri said. "I've only been in London for a few weeks and haven't had a chance to hire any servants."

Jochen shook his head. "I'm grateful for the drink." His eyes darted about the place and seemed to take in every detail.

"I'd like nothing more than to catch up." Dimitri tried to disguise a yawn. "But I just completed a long shift at the hospital. I need some sleep."

"I'll go, then." Jochen started to push himself out of the chair.

Dimitri put up a hand in protest. "You may rest here by the fire. I'm so tired that I might sleep until evening, but when I awaken we will chat some more."

Jochen nodded. Dimitri left the room and stole down to the basement. As he climbed inside his makeshift coffin, yesterday's newspaper headline came to mind:

MAN IN DEERSTALKER CAP PLACED AT SCENE OF RIPPER KILLINGS

Dimitri pitied his old friend, but at the same time, he wondered if Jochen could be the stocky man the article had gone on to describe. The possibility that Jochen Rhessa had a hand in the gruesome "Leather Apron" mutilations seized him with alarm. Yet all he could do was hope he'd be safe during his deep sleep.

Dimitri rose when dusk materialized. After he bathed, shaved, and dressed, he found Jochen in the parlor where he'd left him. His friend had prepared tea and laid out a small tray of food.

"What a nice surprise," Dimitri said warmly. "But where did you get—"

"I went out in the late afternoon and spent my last shilling on some pastries."

"You didn't have to do that, Jochen," Dimitri said.

"I wanted to."

"Unfortunately I never eat before I go to the hospital, but I'll have some tea." Dimitri smiled and pretended to drink the steaming liquid. Then he studied his friend in the rekindled firelight.

Jochen glanced nervously about the room, as he'd done when he arrived.

"Now, tell me," Dimitri urged, "how on earth did you find me?"

Jochen rubbed his bloodshot eyes. His lips seemed painfully dry. "I was in a brawl a few weeks past. Got pretty roughed up. My friends took me to St. Bart's. While I was there, you were being shown around by a staff member. You were dressed in a fine suit and when I inquired about you, a pretty nurse told me that your name was Drake Griffin." He paused. "But the name and your clothing could not fool me. I knew it was you."

"What a coincidence—for our paths to cross in London, I mean."

Jochen nestled his head between the wings of the chair and closed his eyes. "It's a small world, is it not?"

As his friend spoke, Dimitri eyed the dirt caked beneath his fingernails and the soot that soiled his clothes. A nasty gash marred Jochen's left cheek and it was obvious that he'd either lost the bandage the hospital had supplied him with or he'd simply yanked it away.

"I understand why you were at St. Bart's," Dimitri said. "But why are you here in London?"

"A girl," Jochen answered in a state of delusion. "A lousy girl coaxed me here and now she's up and left me."

From the sight of the full glass Jochen held in his hands, he'd helped himself to more brandy during the day. Dimitri's friend raised it now to accentuate his point and the amber liquid sloshed over the brim and onto the carpet. "Never do that. Never allow a female to dictate your life, Dimitri. Females . . . lousy lot."

"I beg to differ." Dimitri frowned. "Being with an intelligent, beautiful female is the joy of life. In fact, I came to London for the same reason you did: to pursue the woman of my dreams. Do you remember Miss Alba Zăpăda?"

"How could I forget that name?" Jochen gave a crooked, yellow smile. "She's all you talked about in medical school."

"Now I see!" Dimitri let out a hearty laugh. "Is that why you dropped out and found another roommate?"

Jochen's eyes darkened and Dimitri assumed his joke hadn't been appreciated. He rubbed his chin. "I'm sorry. After all these years it's none of my business."

"I found another roommate because I could hardly measure up to you." Jochen's voice was solemn. "You got better grades than I and you were far more focused and handsome."

Sitting in a mesmerized state before the hearth, the down-and-out man fell silent.

Dimitri's brow shot up. Jochen was as odd as he remembered, but he was to be dealt with compassionately nonetheless. The kindness Jochen's father had showed Dimitri flooded his mind. So far he'd been unable to repay the good doctor for setting him on his career path, but this could be his opportunity to set things straight.

He set his teacup down. "What's passed is past, Jochen. But now that you have shown up here, I want to repay your father for all that he did for me."

Jochen stared at him with a blank expression.

Dimitri's heart sank. "How is your father, by the way?"

"He's dead."

"Dead?"

"Yes."

"I'm very sorry." Dimitri cleared his throat in order to keep his composure. "Still, I feel that he would like you to stay with me. As

I told you, I've yet to hire any servants. Would you like to work here as my butler?"

Jochen hesitated while his bushy mustache twitched.

"You make outstanding tea, after all." Dimitri grinned.

This made Jochen smile, and the look, however fleeting, reminded Dimitri of their jovial schooldays ... before Jochen had sunk into a depression over his failing grades. It wouldn't be easy for Dimitri to have someone in the house, but if he explained nothing and made Jochen promise not to ask any questions, it might work.

The stocky man stood and pressed his palm into Dimitri's. "I will gladly work for you, my friend. And I shall never forget your kindness."

Dimitri nodded. "Splendid. But first I must warn you that I keep very odd hours. And very odd habits. You'll find I have no mirrors in the house. It is a personal quirk of mine. Furthermore, I've been sleeping in the basement since I haven't had time to install curtains over the windows. You see, I'm very sensitive to light." He paused. "The basement is a place you needn't clean."

Jochen nodded his head. "Understood. You will never know I am here, except when I am needed."

"I shall pay you bimonthly," Dimitri said, looking into his friend's rough-hewn face. Jochen's eyes were beady and his jowls sagged over the corners of his thin lips, but he saw determination there. Determination, Dimitri hoped, that would lead to Jochen turning his life around.

Jochen set his brandy snifter down and tugged on the edge of his jacket. He followed Dimitri into the foyer.

"I'll show you to your room," Dimitri said. "It has an adjoining washroom. Clean up and I will lay out a nightshirt and a change of clothes. You may buy a new wardrobe and get a shave and haircut tomorrow with the advance I'll give you."

"Thank you again for your generosity," he heard Jochen say as they ascended the main staircase.

Dimitri turned around with a smile. "It's the least I can do in your father's honor."

Chapter Ten

Damn Dimitri.

As Alba sat at her desk at Gray's Inn, she doodled his name on a piece of paper like a schoolgirl. Glancing dreamily out the window, her gaze reached the archways of the Royal Courts of Justice. Harold Rollingsworth had been due there ten minutes ago, but he was too busy bellowing about a late-paying client in the other room.

Of course, Alba wasn't one to judge. Productivity had escaped her today as well—thanks to thoughts of Sunday night. When Dimitri had caressed her with his eyes in the park, she'd felt adored and completely prized. Teddy showered her with attention, but she was starting to realize that his affections couldn't compare.

Her brows drew together. *What exactly does Dimitri want with me?* She sensed there were things he wanted to tell her. What were they?

While Dimitri claimed he only wanted to be her friend, his body language said otherwise. To complicate things further, the way he made Alba feel left her to wonder if she could keep her own feelings at bay.

Letting out a sigh, she squared her shoulders and forced her thoughts back to the Crowe murder case. Mr. Rollingsworth was defending Greta Crowe, a woman accused of slowly poisoning her husband. Hefty and red-faced, Greta was prone to long bouts of crying, and during their witness rehearsals, Alba found it difficult to interject her questions between displays of the woman's highly strung demeanor. Needless to say, Alba needed to be detailed in her research in Greta's case. The evidence against the middle-aged wife of Seymour Crowe was daunting. The prosecuting barrister possessed proof that Mrs. Crowe had purchased strychnine at a nearby apothecary. Allegedly, Greta brought it home in a brown-wrapped package and kept it under the washstand where several friends had seen it.

The drawn-out poisoning took place over the course of the next few months. Nervous Greta insisted her mother-in-law, the charmingly fragile Tabitha Crowe, had killed Seymour. The elderly woman's motive? Greta claimed that Tabitha had been treated cruelly in her old age by Seymour, her down-and-out son.

Alba faced a challenge by putting Tabitha Crowe on the witness stand. Who wouldn't believe the ninety-year-old lady with the sparkling periwinkle eyes and softly powdered face over her brambly daughter-in-law?

Exhausted, Alba was still mulling over the case when she returned to the Bloomsbury dormitory. Her glance shifted to the clock on the kitchen wall.

Seven-thirty. *Time to change for my dinner with Dimitri.*

After donning a shrimp-pink dress with a basque front, she secured its cravat bow and gazed at her reflection in the mirror. She looked as breathless as a young girl about to get her first kiss. Should she apply blush and lip stain? Would it seem that she was trying too hard?

Pinching her cheeks instead of applying rouge, she proceeded to pile her long mane on top of her head in the latest style. Satisfied with her appearance, Alba sat on her bed and waited.

At precisely eight sharp, a hansom rumbled to a stop below her window. Her heart bounced inside her rib cage.

It was a short ride to Dimitri's Park Lane home. In the rich darkness of night, the hansom pulled to the curb of the impressive house and Alba heard the driver jump down from his box. While she waited for him to open the door, she studied the house before her. The three-story, square-set structure boasted a beautiful Georgian façade and rows of Ionic columns. Designed in a C shape, the mansion was centered by a lush courtyard framed with ornate gates.

Alba placed a hand over her stomach to subdue its fluttering. It wouldn't do for Dimitri to see her lose control. Grabbing hold of her nerves, she exited the coach and made her way to the front door. As she raised her fist to knock, Dimitri opened the door wearing a smile as warm as a summer's day.

"You must be psychic!" she said.

He put a finger to his temple and laughed. "I told you. I have visions." After studying her in her best dress he said, "You look lovely."

"Thank you." She blushed.

"Where are my manners? Please come in." He swept his arm gallantly across the threshold.

Alba stepped inside the opulent house and her jaw dropped. It wasn't as though she was unaccustomed to luxury. After all, her father had been a wealthy Romanian ambassador for many years. Rather, she was in awe of Dimitri's accomplishment. Considering his humble beginnings, he gave new meaning to the phrase "pulling oneself up by one's bootstraps."

"May I take your coat?" Dimitri offered with a hint of the boyish awkwardness he'd shown in Romania.

"Yes. Thank you."

As he peeled the garment from Alba's shoulders, his touch on her dress made her wish her shoulders were bare. Clearing her throat, she watched Dimitri drape her coat over his arm in a confident flourish. And when he pivoted to hang it inside the hall closet, Alba admired the width of his shoulders beneath his crisp white shirt and expensively cut waistcoat. Her eyes traveled from the corded muscles of his thighs to his firm backside, and her cheeks heated.

It would be so pleasurable to rekindle the attraction they'd once shared, but she forced away her giddy reaction to him.

Dimitri turned with a smile and steered her into the drawing room. "I've taken the liberty of arranging an indoor picnic for us—to celebrate times long past."

Alba sucked in a breath at the grand display. In the center of the room was a white tablecloth spread over a plush Oriental rug. Mounds of chicken, red grapes, decadent pastries, and shimmering wineglasses covered the tablecloth, and in its center stood a single candle.

Dimitri placed his hands on Alba's shoulders. She could feel his breath on her neck—and a jolt of lust shot through her. Her eyes fluttered shut in the heat of the moment until she snapped them open in alarm. If she let her defenses melt like the candle dwindling before them, she might throw herself at him.

"The food looks wonderful," she commented as steadily as she could.

"There's a Romanian delicatessen off Parker Street. I bought all the *placinte*, *mamaliga*, and *tuica* Mr. Livadaria had in stock. Please." Dimitri directed Alba to sit with a wave of his hand.

She gathered her skirts and settled at the edge of the cloth. Dimitri planted himself at her side. When their shoulders touched, an ember of attraction kindled. She turned her head and met Dimitri's stunning topaz stare. Alba's eyes remained locked on his—until the intenseness between them prompted him to smile. He inclined his head to the side, as if he were about to kiss her, but then somebody entered the room.

"Good evening, Miss Zăpăda."

Alba turned to look at the man poised at the edge of the parlor. She recognized the thick-set figure after a moment. "Jochen?" Wide-eyed, she made a move to get up. *Jochen Rhessa.* She remembered playing with him when they were children. In fact, he had been her only playmate more often than not.

"It's good to see you, Miss Zăpăda." He smiled, showing badly cared-for teeth.

"It's good to see you too, Jochen. I had no idea you were in London."

"It's odd that we are all here, isn't it?"

"How do you know Dimitri?" she asked in confusion.

Dimitri stood as well. "After Jochen's father tended to my shoulder wound, he arranged for me and Jochen to room together during medical school."

"Now Dimitri has been generous enough to offer me a post."

"I've employed Jochen as my butler," Dimitri explained.

"I can tell by your fine livery." She smiled. "And how is your father?"

The pleasant expression on Jochen's face vanished. "I'm afraid he's dead."

Alba's heart stuttered. "I'm sorry. He was such a kind man."

"Yes, he was." He turned his attention to Dimitri. "Is there anything you need before I leave for a few hours, Doctor?"

Dimitri shook his head. "No, thank you."

"Then I will take my leave. Please enjoy your evening."

Alba's face flushed as she watched Jochen depart. "I'm sorry I mentioned his father."

"It's sad that Dr. Rhessa has passed on," Dimitri said softly. "He was the first person to give me an encouraging word."

Dimitri remained solemn. They sat again and Alba tried to lighten the mood. "How did you and Jochen meet up here in London?"

"I came home the other night and he was sitting on my doorstep. Apparently, he had nowhere else to go. So I gave him a job."

She suppressed the urge to place her hand over his. "That was very generous of you. I suppose you need a lot of help in this place."

"I do need help, but I much prefer to be alone. *With you.*" His eyes darkened as he reached for her hand.

Flustered, Alba removed it from his grasp. She picked up a glass filled with *tuica* and smelled its rich, plum scent. "I thought we were having dinner as old friends."

"That is what I said." Frowning, he poured himself some of the potent liquid and took a long sip.

"I'm sorry," she said. "I'm afraid that living on my own has given me a bold sense of self." Alba dared look at him again. Her heartbeat surged as he licked the gloss of the drink from his lips.

"Your straightforwardness is something I admire about you," he said. "In fact, it's what struck me most when we first met."

"I remember that day," she replied as sentiment enveloped her. "I was sitting on a bench outside Stelian Hall. And you were spying on me."

Dimitri laughed. "You were beautiful enough to force my eyes away from that half-baked groundskeeper of yours."

Alba clamped a hand over her mouth to suppress a hearty giggle. "You mean Cruvinksy?"

"If he's the fellow who never wore a belt and always lost his trousers, then yes."

They shared a laugh at the old man's expense. When their

chuckling subsided, Dimitri sighed. "Do you remember what we carved in the oak tree by the pond?"

She blushed furiously and looked down at her plate. "Yes. 'Dimitri loves Alba. And she loves him back.'" She could almost feel the deep indentations in the rough tree bark. After all, she had traced the letters a thousand times when Dimitri disappeared from her life.

"That summer was magical, wasn't it?" he asked.

She raised her stare to meet his. "Yes."

The twinkle in his topaz eyes enchanted Alba as it had in her youth. Suddenly she missed the way he had wrapped her in his arms when she was fourteen—and the way he had whispered his undying devotion. Dispelling the notion, she bit into a drumstick.

Dimitri drank more *tuica*. "We got into a great deal of trouble the last time we were together in Romania."

"I hate to think of it," Alba said darkly.

"We shouldn't have gone to Bran Castle in the first place. I regret dragging you into that horror."

"As much as I try to put the dare out of my mind, I still dream of it."

In the dancing candlelight, his golden brown eyes shimmered and his hair glistened with every shade of brown and black imaginable. She put a hand to her heart to slow its hasty thrumming.

"I dream of that night too," he whispered.

A spine-tingling silence filled the air. Dimitri reached up and traced the line of her jaw.

Buzzing with inner excitement, Alba watched him lean in for a kiss. His mouth claimed hers gently at first, but when eagerness prompted her to whisper his name, every lustful emotion they'd shared came surging forward. Inflamed, Dimitri gathered her to him. The feel of his body crumbled her every defense and awakened her every desire. Head reeling, Alba let him squeeze her in his arms.

Dimitri's tongue plundered its way past her lips. He dropped his hand from her face to her waist, and her heartbeat accelerated again. *Can he hear its beating?* Alba wondered. *Can he feel the heat rippling through me?*

A thrill danced along her spine. Her muscles tightened and a warm quiver vibrated between her legs.

With his mouth still clamped to hers, Dimitri bore her back. He inched his knee between her thighs, cradling her head with the kind of gentleness one uses with a baby. Then, as his fingers got lost in her hair, he spread his weight on top of her. He murmured ear-blushing compliments along the column of her neck, and happiness overcame her—a feeling she hadn't experienced in a very long time.

Dimitri used his confident hands to find her breast through the fabric of her dress. And as he fondled it with abandon, Alba felt dizzy, as if she were caught in a whirlpool. Her pulse spiked as he unbuttoned the front of her dress and exposed her breast. In a sensual motion, he licked his fingertips and then stroked her darkened nub erotically. A surge of moisture flooded the space between her legs.

Dimitri seared her lips with another hot kiss. Tears sprang to Alba's eyes because she had finally released the sense of loneliness that had gripped her ever since she came to London.

My God. It had only been six days since he'd appeared with his beguiling smile and dark allure and he was already bringing out her vulnerabilities. Suddenly their intimacy felt wrong.

I must be careful. For all I know, Ileana sent Dimitri.

"I can't," Alba cried. Breaking free, she sat upright. "I'm sorry—"

Dimitri bolted to a sitting position as well. Face flushed, he raked a hand through his precisely layered hair. "No, no. It's my fault. I shouldn't have kissed you."

She felt the color drain from her face. As her tears threatened to spill, she spun her head away.

Dimitri covered her quaking fingers with his steady ones. "I'm still so attracted to you. But I will settle for being your friend."

Alba allowed him to see her tears. He reached up and swept them off her face. His touch was as hot as a fully charged fire.

"I cannot be your friend because I must protect my emotions," she said. "To be honest with you, I'm frightened to see what you might bring back to my life. Your being here reminds me of all the terrible things I left behind. My stepmother—"

"—knows you're here in London," he interrupted.

Alba jerked back. Her hand flew to her mouth. "How does Ileana know where I am?"

Dimitri's expression dimmed, taking with it the desire she had seen in his eyes a moment ago. "I wasn't going to tell you, but I think you deserve to know. Simona paid me a visit."

"Simona? I heard she'd drowned herself in the Olt River."

"She did."

"Then I don't understand. If she's dead, how could she have told you about my stepmother?"

Dimitri shifted in an uncomfortable manner. "Simona committed suicide. And according to Romanian folklore, you know what happens to someone who takes their own life, don't you?"

The words sent a blow to Alba's abdomen. "They become a vampire." *The prediction from the graveyard . . .*

"Simona has remained connected to the Dark Arts," Dimitri said. "It was she who stole the amulet and convinced me to give it to you. She claims that your stepmother contacted her with the idea."

"What?"

"Once you wore it, you became cursed. That was her intention."

Panic seized Alba as it always did when she thought of Ileana. She bit her lip until it throbbed with pain.

Dimitri went on. "Simona told me that your stepmother knows you are in London. If that's the case, I haven't arrived here a moment too soon."

"Why didn't you tell me this before?"

"I didn't want to worry you."

She made no attempt to hide her anger. "What else are you keeping from me?"

His face went red.

"Tell me this," she said. "How did Simona know where to find me?"

"During her search for me, she found you too," Dimitri replied. "Then she sent word to Ileana."

A gust of hot fury filled Alba's lungs. *That snake of a girl.* From the moment they met, Simona's attraction to Dimitri was apparent— as was Simona's disapproval of her. Even in death, the Gypsy girl continued to manipulate things. Together she and Ileana were a very dangerous team.

Will I become a vampire? Or will I fall victim to my destructive stepmother? Or maybe I'll go down the morbid path laid down by the Egyptian amulet . . .

Alba's fate seemed doomed any way she looked at it, and it was all Dimitri's fault. He had introduced her to all these curses, and if he hadn't come to London, Simona would never have found her. *Damn him.*

Dimitri reached for her hand while a sympathetic expression spread across his face. "I'm sorry I exposed you to any of this, Alba. I was young—"

"No!" She snatched her hand away. "We can't blame bad judgment on our youth anymore. We are adults now and Simona has succumbed to the vampire's prophecy. Who will be next, Dimitri? You or me?"

Dimitri scowled. "You don't understand. I'm here to prevent anything from happening to you."

"I can't be around you. I can't trust the man who drove me toward this evil in the first place."

He clutched a hand to his heart, as if she had pierced it with an unrelenting blade. "I never meant to hurt you."

Her lip trembled. "But you did."

"Why won't you let me protect you?" he asked. "You speak of evil but you have no idea the depth of that wickedness."

"I don't want to know. I just want to forget all of it happened."

"Do you think these curses will just go away?" Dimitri growled. "Do you think they'll disappear if you simply ignore them?"

Her voice shook with emotion. "All I know is that you brought these hexes into my life."

She stared straight ahead, clasping her hands together in her lap.

Prompted by the sight of Alba closing herself off, Dimitri's lips formed a hard, straight line. "Well, I see no reason to take up any more of your night."

He rose, helped her to her feet, and gathered her wrap. A moment later, they stood outside in wait of a hansom—the tension between them so thick the sharpest axe could not have severed it.

Chapter Eleven

As they waited for a hansom, Alba's harsh words rolled over Dimitri like a crushing boulder. He broke the heavy silence by offering to accompany her home. She refused. When he argued that he needed her to be open to his guidance, she ignored the plea and continued to retreat into her blasted, defensive shell.

I shouldn't have kissed you, he thought as he watched her cross her arms. He'd known it would lead to arousal—and eventually danger.

Once Alba disappeared into the hansom, Dimitri glanced up and down the street. The hair on the back of his neck stood up. He knew in his heart that Simona had been watching them.

I shouldn't have brought Alba here. Will Simona follow her home?

Cursing his bad judgment, he marched back into the house and slammed the door. During the indoor picnic, he'd eaten nothing. In fact, he hadn't consumed food since he became a vampire. The smell and texture nauseated him. Liquor and blood were the only things he put to his lips, and at the moment, he could think of nothing else but the latter. When Dimitri had leaned into Alba's sweet scent and firm curves, his fangs had descended. It meant that every minute she spent with him she was in peril of being consumed. If he was smart, he'd leave this city and never return. But he couldn't.

Not only did he feel responsible for Alba's fate, he needed her like a drug.

She was his soul . . . his everything.

After settling for the last drop of *tuica*, Dimitri retrieved his cloak and tall hat and rushed into the night. Although it was late, he managed to hail a carriage. Settling on its back bench, he yanked the velvet drapes together for privacy. His thoughts were wild now, jump-started by his lust for Alba. As her image filled his mind, his cock hardened.

He'd blurted out the truth about Simona being in London because he wanted Alba to be prepared for a visit from her. But the reaction Alba gave him struck his heart like a speeding arrow. She wanted nothing to do with him, but he had to get her the hell out of this mess.

Will she ever trust me again?

Dimitri arched a brow as the carriage rambled toward Bloomsbury Street. *I've made mistakes in the past, but I will not leave Alba as bait for the hounds.*

It was Saturday morning and Alba was still reeling over Dimitri withholding information from her. Ileana knew where she was—which meant that this was the calm before the storm. She would have to sleep with one eye open from now on and trust no one.

To steady herself, Alba grabbed the newspaper Edith left on the bedside table. As she held up the paper with quivering hands, her eye was drawn to the front headline.

Is There Another Murderer in Town?

The article went on to report that a vagabond had been killed several nights ago. The police were linking this murder to an attack on a homeless man several nights previous. While the first vagrant had survived thanks to an interruption in his assault, both victims had been drained of their blood by two puncture holes to the neck.

A vampire at work.

The suggestion that a creature of the night was on the loose cut off the air in Alba's lungs. Some would say the idea was nonsense—

insisting that a delusional person was simulating the way a vampire sucks a victim's blood. But Alba didn't think so.

Had Simona killed this vagabond?

She flung the newspaper down. A knock at the door gave her another start. The girls had just gone off to their morning ballet class.

"Who's there?" she called.

"It's me. Teddy."

"Come in."

The door swung open. "Good morning." Teddy smiled. "I passed the girls on the stairwell, and Miss Edith told me to come up."

Alba drew her dressing robe together. "This is highly unusual, Teddy—"

"I know. But I have breakfast and a newspaper."

She laughed as she held hers up for him to see.

He shook his head as he stepped into the bedroom. "That's my girl. Always one step ahead."

Teddy took a large book from a shelf and set a paper bag on top of it. When he brought the makeshift tray to Alba, she extracted a scone and took a bite.

"Good?" he asked as he sat on the bed with her.

She nodded since her mouth was full.

Teddy looked rather dashing this morning. His clean-shaven face showcased his strong jaw, and the silver suit he wore highlighted his steely eyes. He smelled of citrus cologne and expensive soap, and when he smiled his eyes crinkled handsomely at the corners.

"Did you get the scones from the Captain?"

The Captain was a colorful street vendor who always positioned his cart outside the dormitory. Word had it that he was an ex-captain in Britain's Royal Navy who had gladly hung up his military hat for a life of freedom as a vendor.

"Yes," Teddy replied. "His apple ones are your favorite, right?"

"They are." She took another bite.

"So what do you make of this 'vampire killer'?" he queried. "Do you think he's some crackpot trying to steal Jack the Ripper's thunder? Or do you think our sadistic serial killer has changed his *modus operandi*?"

"Jack the Ripper a merciless vampire? I don't think so." Alba scrunched her nose in refusal. "The Ripper is a monster who will stop at nothing to satisfy his lust for blood—but I think he prefers to draw blood another way."

It frightened her to think this killer's anger stretched beyond the furthest realm of violence the authorities had ever seen. He seemed capable of anything.

"I suppose you're right." Teddy pointed to the newspaper that lay on top of the coverlet. "This is probably the work of an imitator. I just hope London doesn't become infiltrated with crazies trying to snatch up the criminal spotlight."

She nodded. Realizing that she'd lost her sleep cap in the middle of the night, she became self-conscious of her rumpled hair. She tried to fix it with her fingers, but her mane had tumbled impossibly loose from its braid.

Silence fell between them. Teddy reached over and slipped a finger into one of her large, lazy curls.

"You look beautiful, Alba," he whispered. "I know it isn't proper to call on you alone—or this early in the morning. But I wanted to see you."

She said nothing as he cupped her chin in his hand and leaned in for a kiss. His lips were soft and cool, contrasting Dimitri's fiery ones. His tongue flickered gently across her mouth, as if it were knocking on the door for entry. Parting her lips mechanically, she allowed Teddy's tongue to intertwine with hers. How she wanted to love him—to desire him the way she had swooned under Dimitri's hot kiss. But to her enormous disappointment, nothing about Teddy excited her.

He took her in his arms and cradled her against him. With the hand that rested on her shoulder, he slipped her dressing gown to the side and exposed a patch of bare skin. Ever so lightly, he caressed it with his fingertips, then circled his touch downward toward her breast. She froze. As mad as she was at Dimitri, she felt like a betrayer of the worst kind being here with Teddy. Of course, Teddy knew nothing of her encounter with Dimitri—and she wasn't about to tell him—but Alba wanted to feel clean before she allowed any intimacy between them. The last thing she wanted to do was hurt Teddy.

She was about to break free of his contact when Justina, her Persian cat, leapt across the newspaper. Nerves jittering, Alba cried out. Teddy managed to grab Justina before the creature pounced to the ground.

"Are you all right?" he asked, studying Alba's pale face.

She gulped and nodded.

Teddy turned his attention to the cat. "I know, pretty girl." He stroked its silky fur and smiled. "You were protecting Alba, weren't you? But you must know that I would never hurt her."

Justina, as if she understood what Teddy was saying, purred excitedly before she shot off his lap.

Alba blushed furiously. "I should get dressed."

Teddy looked embarrassed as well. "Forgive my forwardness."

"I'm sorry, I'm just not ready," she murmured softly.

"Then we shall take things as slowly as we need to." His eyes sparkled with kindness.

She slipped out of bed and walked him to the front door.

"I would like to take you for a ride in the park today," he said. "Are you free?"

"I would love to, but it's my turn to clean the dormitory."

"Have you no maid?" he asked in mock horror.

"Not all of us are as rich as you, Teddy." She laughed.

"If and when you become Mrs. Theodore Rollingsworth, you shall have five maids attending to you. No more cleaning for you."

She studied her slippers.

"Would you like me to help you?"

"Thank you, but I can manage it."

"Then I shall see you bright and early at the office Monday morning?"

"Yes. We still have a lot of work to do to prepare for the Crowe trial."

"We do, indeed." He turned to go.

"Teddy?"

"Hmm?" He spun around.

"Thank you for the scones. They were delicious."

"You're welcome." He gave her a peck on the cheek before he left.

Alba knew she should get started on the washing up, but she sank on the sofa instead. Since the moment Dimitri told her Ileana knew where she was, she'd become a bundle of nerves. Few people knew what her stepmother was capable of, but Alba did. It frightened her. It also incensed her—as did the fact that Dimitri hadn't been loyal enough to tell her about Ileana right away. But this wasn't about loyalty. She refused to let someone who underestimated Ileana protect her.

Sighing, she rose and began her housework.

Dimitri had instructed the hansom driver to deposit him at Alba's dormitory, where he'd stolen across the street. Swathed in the cold shadows, he had watched the building until the sun began to rise . . . until he knew Simona would have to sleep too.

Under the purplish glow of dawn, Dimitri morphed into a bat and streamed home. As all the signs of night disappeared, he entered his house like a quiet thief. He began to tiptoe toward the basement door when he felt a hand on his shoulder. He sucked in a startled breath.

"Are you all right?" Jochen asked.

Dimitri pivoted around. His shoulders sagged when he spotted his friend. "Yes, I'm fine."

Jochen, with his puffy face and uneasy eyes, looked as though he'd been awake all night too. Dimitri had given his new butler the evening off, but the whiskey fumes on Jochen's breath told him that his friend had already squandered his first round of wages.

"Jochen, don't you think you ought to stay away from the pub? It's where you seem to get into trouble."

"I did my best to stay away." The butler clenched his fists. "In the future I will, I promise."

Dimitri gave him a casual smile. "I'm not chastising you. I'm just offering some sound advice as a friend."

"I appreciate your concern," Jochen said as anger flashed in his shifty eyes. "But what I do on my off hours needn't worry you. I will always abide by my work schedule."

"Good," Dimitri said as he felt the weariness of dawn drape over him. He made a move to open the door. "Now I must get some sleep."

"I left this morning's newspaper on the entry table," Jochen called out before he disappeared into the kitchen.

Dimitri retrieved it and stopped when he read the headline. *Bloody hell.* The police had already been on high alert for the Ripper, but now they were hunting for vampires. Then he looked at the report a different way as he descended the stairs to the basement: maybe the police would capture Simona during their new search.

Chapter Twelve

Two weeks had passed since Alba's tense parting with Dimitri. She'd spent the better part of them tormenting herself with the presumption that he'd left town, and with nothing left to do but prepare for Greta Crowe's trial, she had purposefully thrown herself into work.

On this chilly October morning, the Old Bailey, London's foremost courtroom for press-worthy crimes, smelled of tradition, honor, and real-life drama. Sunlight slanted into the room through high, rectangular windows—and when it settled on the tiered seats designated for those lucky enough to gain entry as audience members, the entire place came to life.

This is the culmination of all my years of schooling, Alba considered.

Donning her spectacles, she pushed herself to her feet and met a sea of riveted eyes. Trying not to brim with pride, her gaze shifted to Harold Rollingsworth. He nodded as if to say, "Have the courage to proceed."

Alba called Tabitha Crowe to the witness box. Rosy-cheeked and freshly powdered, the old woman stood on unsure feet. As she walked past the members of the jury, she gave them a gentle smile. Then, with a sense of frailness, she grasped an officer's arm and teetered to her place inside the box.

Alba plastered a smile on her face. "Please state your name for the court."

"My name is Tabitha Loretta Crowe."

"How are you today, Mrs. Crowe?"

"With the shock of my Seymour passing, I'm feeling very weak, Miss Spencer. After all, I am ninety years old—and an old woman's heart is a very delicate thing."

"I'm sorry for your failing health. Do you think you can answer my questions?"

Tabitha clutched her handbag to her chest and nodded. "I'll try."

"On August tenth of this year, your son, Seymour Darby Crowe, died from strychnine poisoning in the Chelmsford home you shared with him and his family. Is that correct?"

"I think we've established that over these long, arduous weeks, haven't we?" Tabitha flung her eyes wide.

The response brought out a few chuckles, as well as stains of humility on Alba's cheeks. She laced her hands together tensely. "Mrs. Crowe—"

"Please call me Tabitha."

"Very well, Tabitha. Did you ever see your daughter-in-law administer poison to your son?"

"No," the elderly woman replied carefully. "But my rooms were on the top floor of the flat. And I take frequent naps."

"I see. So you are saying that you didn't see much of Greta and Seymour Crowe?"

"That's right." The elderly woman sat back in her seat, her lips pressed together.

Alba moved to the defense counsel's table to retrieve a piece of paper. "I beg to differ, Mrs. Crowe. Your daughter-in-law has stated that you ate every meal with her, Seymour, and their three children. She says you took tea together as well. Furthermore, Greta Crowe helped you with your knitting projects, hosted your bridge games, took you to your doctor's appointments, and accompanied you to church."

Tabitha's expression darkened. "What are you getting at?"

"Did you witness any rows between Greta and Seymour?"

"They were always fighting. I daresay Greta nagged Seymour incessantly about his being out of work."

"I believe with six mouths to feed, I would have insisted my husband look for work too," Alba said as diplomatically as she could.

Tabitha made a disgruntled noise.

"Mrs. Crowe, isn't it true that you were the one who fought with Seymour most frequently?"

"Not at all!" Tabitha put a hand to her heart.

Alba straightened her horsehair wig and looked at the paper again. "Mildred and Harry Willows. Frank Tatino. Sisters Erin and Heather O'Rourke. These neighbors have provided sworn testimony that you argued with your son night and day."

The elderly woman's lips quirked and quivered as if they were playing a harmonica. Tears sprang to her eyes as she glared at Alba.

"Mrs. Crowe," Alba continued firmly, "during your police interview, you asserted that you think Greta Crowe took your son's life via a slow and methodical exposure to poison. Is that still your belief?"

"Yes. She was depressed and she was very frustrated with Seymour," Tabitha said, dabbing her tears with a lace handkerchief. Her soft sobbing drew empathetic stares from several reporters.

"May I remind you that our expert witness, Dr. Clive Hughes, has testified that one cannot tolerate the taste of strychnine by itself," Alba said. "Rather it is best administered in something like tea. Such as the tea you always insisted on preparing for Seymour Crowe *yourself*."

Tabitha merely shook her head and blew her nose loudly into her handkerchief.

Alba took a breath. It was just as she and Harold Rollingsworth had planned. She would ask Tabitha the easy questions first, leading the jury to suspect the elderly woman before she went in for the kill, but a sense of hesitation was beginning to seize her.

She moved to the witness box. Tabitha continued to dab her nose, unable to hide the fact that she was twittering uncontrollably. Alba placed her hands on the wooden frame and leaned forward.

"Now, Mrs. Crowe," she began, "we can't have these lovely people believing anything that contradicts the evidence we have against you. Bill Plumpton, shop owner of Plumpton's Apothecary, says it was you who sent your daughter-in-law, Greta, in to purchase large doses of strychnine. You told her that you needed the poison for your own medicinal purposes. But you never provided a physician's order, did you?"

"No," Tabitha said after a long hesitation.

"You knew Mr. Plumpton would fill the order because he was familiar with Greta, a diabetic."

The elderly woman's cheeks went pale.

"Mrs. Crowe, it is common knowledge that strychnine, even if it's given in small grains over a long period of time, is toxic."

"I didn't kill my son!" she cried. Her face drained completely of color and she started to unravel like a ball of yarn.

Alba glanced at Greta, who sat between Teddy and his father. Greta's face had turned crimson and she looked as if she were about to bolt out of her seat. Teddy grasped one of one the defendant's arms to steady her.

"I know everything about your murderous plan, Mrs. Crowe," Alba said. "There is no denying that you kept the poison in a brown paper package beneath your washstand. You wouldn't allow Greta to open it, but you urged her to purchase the poison in the first place. You claimed you were too ill to go out, but that was a lie."

"You're wrong." Tabitha sobbed.

Alba's heart surged. It was a pitiful to watch a ninety-year-old woman fight for her life.

"The truth is"—she softened her tone—"your son was a brute. A bad lot who drank too much. He was a man who refused to work. A man who abused you with his words and his lack of respect. He was a man who deserved to die, wasn't he?"

Tabitha raised her watery, forlorn eyes. "Yes!"

Everyone in the courtroom gasped. Even the Honorable Judge Oliver Wentwood sank back in his seat with disbelief.

Tabitha sputtered, "Seymour was rotten, even as a child. He was all the things you've mentioned, but the worst thing about him was his lack of respect. He would deny me food and beat his children!"

"Still, you were going to let me hang for his death!" Greta sprang up.

"I'm truly sorry, my dear, but I do hate the idea of a noose around my neck. I tried my best to convince them that you had a good reason to kill Seymour. Can you ever forgive me?"

Judge Wentwood hammered his gavel to subdue the chaos in the courtroom. "In light of your admission, Mrs. Crowe, I hereby release your daughter-in-law, Greta Crowe, from the crime she's been accused of."

There was a final slam of the gavel and Greta dropped back into her chair with relief.

Alba joined Harold Rollingsworth and Teddy at counsel's semi-circular table as the bailiff escorted Tabitha Crowe out of the courtroom.

"Good show, Alba!" Teddy said.

Harold untied his cravat. "Your steady questioning made for a more dramatic reveal."

Teddy looked at Alba admiringly. "You were brilliant."

"Thank you."

"It will be your turn to shine next, my boy," Rollingsworth promised. "After all, the old woman's confession dispelled any need for closing arguments."

Teddy cast his eyes down. "Oh. Of course."

Alba's gut wrenched. She glanced at the spot where Tabitha Crowe had stood. She'd won her first case. Why did she feel so bad?

Harold noticed her queer expression. "What's wrong, Alba?"

"I know justice has been served, but I can't help feeling sorry for Tabitha," she said. "Her son was a lousy degenerate and she refused to put up with him any longer. Perhaps one can admire a woman like that."

"She killed her own son and didn't care if her daughter-in-law hanged for it," Teddy reminded her.

Alba knew what it was like to detest a relative, but he wouldn't understand.

"I admit this was a very unusual case, Alba," Rollingsworth said. "But you'll harden in the courtroom eventually. Besides, if we had the chance to bring someone like Jack the Ripper to justice, you would have no problem condemning him to the gallows."

Alba supposed he had a point there.

With the eyes of a hawk, Jack the Ripper watched Alba Spencer move about the courtroom. She was a smart, sophisticated, and savvy woman—unlike the tarts he had killed.

The ruthless killer reached down and patted the leather bag secured against his chair. Last night, he had cleaned his set of sharp, gleaming instruments to a high shine. Now he longed to run his fingertips over them and kill again.

He had cleaned off every last trace of Polly Nichols's, Annie Chapman's, Elizabeth Stride's, and Catherine Eddowes's blood because the ritual of cleaning meant a new start and an erased past.

So far I have killed four women. And those incompetent men who call themselves police officers have no idea who I am. The authorities from Scotland Yard, the Metropolitan Police, and the City of London's own police team have joined forces to catch me. But they can't.

No one will ever catch me. I will go on to kill any woman who is unlucky enough to encounter me alone on a dark night.

Chapter Thirteen

Alba entered the empty dormitory rooms with a sigh of relief. She had begged off a celebration with Mr. Rollingsworth and Teddy by telling them she had a headache.

It felt strange to be alone after winning her first case, but there was only one person she could think of who would be truly happy for her accomplishment: Dimitri. He was the one who had listened patiently to her dreams of becoming a barrister when she was a young girl. In fact, it was Dimitri who had encouraged her—even when her dear father had guffawed at the possibility.

Alba hadn't heard anything from him since she'd refused him at his house. She'd tried to convince herself that was best, but in the past it had never been easy to forget him.

If he hadn't left town yet, perhaps Dimitri would grow tired of London and return to Romania. That too was probably the best scenario, but the thought of him leaving stabbed at her heart. Her anger had dissipated in their days apart because the guilt she had seen in his eyes tugged at her. And when he spilled the truth—that Ileana was aware of Alba's location—his guilt had probably worsened.

Alba knew Dimitri. She knew that he prided himself on telling the truth. That could mean only one thing: he was actually trying to protect her.

Justina emerged and slinked around her feet. As dusk settled outside, the room filled with an eerie, lavender haze. Alba's spine prickled. Something didn't feel right.

Apprehension drew her lips together. She searched the bedrooms, the bathroom, and the kitchen, but turned up nothing.

Unable to shake away the feeling that something terrible was about to happen, Alba sat rigidly on a three-cushioned settee. Justina jumped onto her lap. "Do you feel it too, pretty girl?"

Staring into space, Justina arched up dramatically and bared her spiked teeth.

"What is it, Justina?" Alba glanced about again. There was no one there.

Goose bumps sprang on her arm and her lungs hitched. Animals could sense things—preternatural things.

A soft scratching came from the front door. Nerves racing, Alba cracked the portal open and saw a stunning Persian cat sitting at its threshold. The cat looked up at her with sorrowful eyes.

"Why, hullo!" she said. "However did you get up here?"

The cat took a diminutive step back and purred.

"It's fine, you little darling. I won't hurt you."

The intelligence in the cat's eyes was obvious. It bowed its head and put a paw out.

"Very well," said Alba. "You may come in. Maybe I can return you to your proper owner."

The cat purred again and crossed into the dormitory.

"See, Justina?" Alba smiled. "It's just another cat. Perhaps you two can be friends."

The door shut and the cat's eyes darkened to an inky, malevolent black. In a whirl of mist, the animal evaporated and Simona's lithe body replaced it. She stood before Alba, a slip of her former self, as pale and thin as a ghost. Simona's dull black hair swung against her waist while her mouth twisted into a cruel smile.

"What are you doing here?" Alba cried.

Simona strode closer. "Thank you for inviting me in."

Alba's heart slammed against her ribs.

"It seems I've finally found you alone," Simona said.

"What is it you want?" Alba managed to stammer.

"I want you to be frightened. Frightened the way you were in the graveyard all those years ago. Nothing has given me as much pleasure since. Nothing, that is, except Dimitri's hard, naked body next to mine."

Dimitri and Simona were lovers? Bile rose in Alba's throat. "You're lying!"

"Dimitri was mine after you left Romania," Simona raged. "Running away from Stelian Hall was a big mistake, Alba. You lost everything—and in the end your well-planned scheme to avoid your stepmother has backfired. Ileana Zăpăda is a very powerful witch. Now it's her turn to plan something carefully."

"What is she going to do?" Alba barked.

"Arrange your death."

"Get out of here!" Alba blinked against a curtain of tears.

"You think Dimitri is a hero who's come to protect you against Ileana? Well, you're wrong. While Dimitri watches over you, he is keeping a very dark secret hidden. If he doesn't reveal it to you soon, I shall."

"What are you talking about?"

Simona's voice dropped to a whisper. "It is a secret that might put you in more danger than Ileana's scheme."

"Tell me," Alba said desperately.

Instead of replying, Simona bared her fangs. Alba inched backward and grabbed a poker and a broom from the mantel stand. When she raised the makeshift crucifix in front of Simona, the female vampire hissed. Simona shielded her eyes as she untied the sash laced around her black frock. "I leave you with a gift from your stepmother!" she thundered as she threw the sash on the floor.

As Simona vanished into a ball of blue light, the long ribbon transformed into a coiled cobra. The venomous serpent reared up and fanned out its head. Alba froze. She opened her mouth to scream, but her dry throat clogged the sound. While the snake waved its upper half in the air, Alba forced herself to creep forward with the sharp poker drawn. Her heart pumped wildly as she met the cobra's evil stare. Its crimson eyes and jutting tongue signaled its plan to strike.

Can it bite me from this distance?

Before she could decide what to do next, the door burst open. Mrs. T. entered the dormitory followed by her seven daughters. The door's thrust batted the snake against the rear wall with tremendous force. The girls were chattering excitedly—until they heard the snake hit the wall and saw Alba's drawn face.

"What's the matter, dear?" Lorna Tuttlebaum asked.

"Stay where you are!" Alba quickly shut the door and smashed the disoriented cobra with the poker. The snake writhed on the ground for a moment before it stopped moving. Alba sank down on the floor beside it, shaking like a child in the cold.

"My stars!" Mrs. T. screeched. She extended her hand and drew Alba to her feet. "What is that thing doing in here?"

"It seems my stepmother has found me," Alba said. "This is her warped idea of a reunion gift."

All eight Tuttlebaums gasped.

"Ileana Zăpăda knows where you are?" Mrs. T. asked.

"Yes." Alba could hardly get the word out.

"This is bad, my dear. This is very bad," the large woman said with concern. "Ella and Edith, check all the rooms for anything out of the ordinary."

"Right, Mum," the girls said in unison.

Alba was very grateful that the brood had arrived when they did. With shoulder-length red hair that waved in shimmering curls and skin that gleamed like porcelain, the seven sisters were beautiful, yet they possessed very different personalities. Ella was the eldest and the leader. Elaine, the second eldest, was overly energetic, while Evelyn was a bit lazy. Being a hypochondriac kept Eugenia under the weather most of the time, while the triplets had their distinct personalities as well. The spark that surfaced in Edith's blue eyes whenever she saw food kept her pleasantly plump, and Ellen was a girl who constantly quoted Shakespeare, her favorite author. Lastly, there was Edwina. She was the smallest and most fragile of the girls, and while she didn't possess the sharpest mind, she did have the biggest heart.

"There's no one here," Ella reported as she and her sister came back.

"Good," Mrs. T. said. "Now, Evelyn, I want you to dispose of this vile serpent."

"Do I have to, Mum?"

"Yes. Now, go on."

As Evelyn retrieved a dust bin, Mrs. T. turned to Alba. "You could have been killed, my dear."

"I know," Alba replied softly. She looked into the woman's hazel eyes, unable to hide her fear. Mrs. T. knew that Ileana was the one person Alba was deathly afraid of.

"Come now." Mrs. T. patted her hand and directed her to sit with her on the sofa. "We won't let any harm come to you on Ileana's account. There is one of her—and eight of us. We shall protect you."

"Thank you," Alba said earnestly. "But I've told you what she's capable of."

To that, Mrs. T. made no reply. She plastered on a congenial face, but inside Alba knew what she was thinking: *Satan's favorite hound has just been released from hell.*

The girls crowded around, cooing reassuring words and offering comforting hugs.

"Did your ballet class get canceled?" Alba asked.

Ella nodded. "Madame Salinsky fell and broke her hip. I've always said she was too old and clumsy to be the head ballet mistress."

"Poor woman," Mrs. T. added. "Reginald will simply have to step in for her when he returns from Bath." She sighed. "Now, Alba. I was at the café this morning having my morning tea—oh, I was also enjoying some of those scrumptious raspberry scones; the ones with the cream cheese topping? Of course, they weren't as good as the pastries Chef Frederick made. Poor man got fired last week—"

"Mother!" Edith cried. "For God's sakes!"

"Sorry, dear. Now, where was I?"

"In the café," Edith reminded her. "But please get to the point."

"Oh, yes. Anyway, the gossipmongers were out in full force. I overheard someone claim they saw you faint at a birthday party—a party for some fellow named Drake Griffin."

"His real name is Dimitri Grigorescu," Alba said shakily. "He's someone I knew back in Romania." *And considering Simona's information, he is still here in London.*

"We've met him!" Elaine's eyes fluttered. "Oh, Alba, he is perfectly dashing."

That he is.

Evelyn pushed her shoulders back with an air of importance.

"He was in Teddy's box at Covent Garden. You know, on opening night for *Don Quixote*. Teddy brought him backstage and introduced him to all the dancers. He's a surgeon at St. Bart's. We had no idea you knew him!"

"Once . . . long ago." Alba's eyes glazed over. "Edith met Dimitri at the party—before I fainted."

Edith corroborated the story.

"Well, this Dr. Grigorescu may be handsome," Evelyn continued, "but there are some torrid rumors floating around town about him."

"What rumors?" Alba asked.

"That he's mysterious and keeps strange, nocturnal hours."

"Good gracious," cried Edith. "He's a doctor! And don't people have anything better to do than gossip?"

Mrs. T. frowned at Alba. "Yes. I'm sure this Mr. Grit-gross-goo is perfectly normal. But we can't have you fainting on the spot when you see him, my dear. You're stronger than that."

Clucking with dissatisfaction, Mrs. T. reached for Alba and thrust her head against her ample bosom. Lorna Tuttlebaum smelled of toffee creams and dusting powder.

As the kindly woman stroked her hair, Alba's mind sped. She was embarrassed that her fainting spell was the talk of the town. And no doubt Teddy was suffering through a string of harsh gossip too, thanks to her. But what bothered Alba most was the attempt Simona had made on her life.

Will Simona come back soon to see if I'm dead?

"Now," Mrs. T. said as she prompted Alba to an upright position, "have you considered that the appearance of this handsome surgeon may coincide with Ileana discovering where you are?" She talked rapidly now, apparently impressed with her own powers of deduction.

"Yes. I've thought of that," replied Alba.

"I beg you not to jeopardize your relationship with Teddy. Look at my girls. I'm trying to marry all seven of them off to respectable gentlemen. And Teddy Rollingsworth defines 'respectable.'"

"You mean he defines 'horribly dull,'" Evelyn chimed in with a wrinkle of her pert nose.

"He is not dull," said Edwina, who held a girlish infatuation for Teddy. "He's tall, and intelligent, and incredibly serious."

And he'll be faithful to me, Alba thought. *He won't leap into someone else's bed—as Dimitri did with Simona.* "I didn't say I'm tempted to jeopardize anything for Dimitri."

"Oh, you don't have to say it, dear," Mrs. T. said. "I see the love you hold for him in your eyes."

Alba's heart missed a beat. She tore a string from the sofa's fringe and wound it nervously around her finger. The tip of her finger went white. She wanted to know the truth: had Dimitri and Simona been lovers? It shouldn't matter, of course. That was many years ago, and she had denied Dimitri's current efforts to reunite with her. But it *did* matter. It mattered to her so desperately that her stomach wrenched with emotion. *With me out of the way, Simona and Dimitri can resume their affair.*

Jealousy built inside her. She wanted to seek Dimitri out—to inquire about his "dark secret" and to tell him that he'd been right about Simona. *There is no doubt I'm in dire danger. If only I'd listened to him.*

After this final encounter with Dimitri, Alba planned to be done with him.

But she didn't believe that any more than she believed Mrs. T. would stop eating raspberry scones and toffee creams.

Chapter Fourteen

Alba lay awake listening to Edith's soft, wheezy snore. Desperate to talk to Dimitri, she had waited until everyone was asleep so that she could slip out of the dormitory unnoticed. After all, Mrs. T. and the girls would never have let her steal out alone.

Craning her head toward her night table clock, Alba saw that it was three-thirty A.M. She climbed out of bed and treaded carefully over a field of coats, gloves, scarves, and high-button boots. She managed to pull on a dress without disturbing anyone, but when she made her way to the washroom to fix her hair, a floorboard creaked beneath her feet.

Edith sprang up in bed and Alba winced.

"Gracious!" Edith whispered sharply. "Why are you dressed at this hour?"

Alba hastened to the girl's bed and grasped her hand. "I need to go somewhere. But you mustn't tell anyone."

"Why?" Edith rubbed her eyes through a yawn. Then, as if struck by a revelation, the girl's eyes flew open. "You are going to meet that doctor. *That handsome surgeon.*"

"Yes—but it isn't what you think."

Edith laughed loudly before she clamped a hand over her mouth. "Sorry. But meeting a man you used to know, a good-looking one at that, can only mean one thing."

Alba's patience went raw. "Edith, I'm in danger and Dimitri is the only person who can help me."

The redhead's expression changed. "Is that true?"

"Yes." She patted her friend's hand. "Promise me you won't tell anyone I've gone to meet him. He'll be getting off his shift at the hospital soon."

"How do you know?"

"I checked his schedule earlier today."

"Aren't you terrified to be on the streets of London alone? Your stepmother is after you and there's a madman on the loose—in case you've forgotten."

Alba sat on the edge of the bed. "I'd be lying if I said I wasn't scared. But asking one of you girls to accompany me would be selfish. You needn't place yourselves in danger because of me."

"I'll go with you," Edith offered.

"No," Alba replied.

"If you don't let me come, I'll wake up this entire dormitory right now."

Alba's shoulders rolled forward in defeat. "Very well. Hurry and get dressed."

Once Edith was ready, she and Alba maneuvered their way out of the dormitory without being heard. They hailed a hansom and instructed its driver to take them to St. Bart's Hospital in Smithfield. The driver nodded from his box.

As Alba bumped along inside the carriage, she found herself searching the streets for Simona. Through the window, her eyes scrutinized every cloud of fog, every alley cat, and every person. There was no sign of the baneful girl.

Once the hansom neared St. Bart's, Alba's anger toward Dimitri evaporated completely.

He had put her in this predicament, but he'd also traveled endless miles and relocated his residence to find and protect her. The moment she saw him peering at her through the gates of Stelian Hall all those years ago, she'd known he was trouble. But she also realized that the second she opened her mouth to talk to him, her fate had been sealed.

The carriage jerked to a stop. Alba emerged and paid the driver. "Would you mind waiting for me?" she asked him. "I won't be long."

The driver nodded in agreement. After exchanging emotional looks with Edith, Alba crossed the street and gathered her collar against the biting October wind. She peered up at the hospital's gates, remembering the day Teddy had driven her past this spot. It was the one time he had persuaded her to skip classes at the university in order to accompany him on a city tour.

Alba gave a nod to the enormous statue of Henry VIII located in an alcove above the gates as she ducked into St. Bart's front courtyard. Maneuvering through a beautiful garden, she reached the main vestibule, where she climbed a staircase leading to the Great Hall. Cheeks flushed, she hurried past a wall of plaques bearing names of the hospital's benefactors until she reached an information desk.

A pretty, golden-haired nurse looked up. The nurse set her pencil down and folded her hands in front of her. "May I help you, miss?"

"Good evening. I'm looking for the emergency ward."

"The emergency ward? Are you hurt?"

"No. I—"

"Is someone in your party hurt?"

Alba arched an eyebrow and looked behind her. "I am with no party."

"So you are here alone? And you want to go to the emergency ward?"

"Yes. I need to see Dr. Griffin." Alba studied the difficult girl. With her shiny blond hair swept off her face and her glowing skin, the nurse was attractive. However, she didn't appear to be very intelligent. Worse, she seemed to have taken an instant dislike to Alba.

The girl raised an eyebrow. "I'm afraid Dr. Griffin is . . ."

Alba felt a hand on her shoulder. She spun around and looked into the face of an elderly nurse. "Are you Miss Alba Spencer?"

"Yes," she said, confused.

"I'll take care of this, Mona." The older nurse gave a nod to the flustered girl before she wrapped an arm around Alba's shoulder. The nurse guided her to the back of the Great Hall and down a flight of stairs.

"How do you know my name?" Alba asked.

"Dr. Griffin told me you were coming."

Alba's heart thumped. It seemed Dimitri did have visions. *My world is becoming stranger by the minute.*

The two women treaded through a starkly lit corridor that smelled of carbolic acid and blood. Screams of agony filled the air while crying infants could be heard in the distance. Alba cringed and wondered how Dimitri tolerated such atrocities.

"Dr. Griffin isn't finished with his shift until four A.M. But you may wait here for him." The nurse indicated a bench.

Alba glanced at the kindly nurse's name plate. *Emily Donovan.* "Thank you, Nurse Donovan."

"You're welcome. My, you are a right pretty thing. Just how Dr. Griffin described you," she said, smiling.

Alba blushed. She took a seat on the bench and laced her fingers together nervously. She spotted Dimitri through a glass partition. He had his sleeves rolled up, revealing muscular forearms and corded veins. And as he sewed up a patient's sliced arm, blood gushed from the wound in all directions. Alba felt her stomach roil. However, the more she watched Dimitri work, the more her queasiness subsided. In fact, she began to study him with awe. By barking orders and tending to patient after patient, he took complete control of the room. He was a hero here, dedicating himself to the practice of medicine and to helping people—and the thought flushed desire through her.

A few minutes later, he looked over and met her stare. His welcoming expression sent relief rushing through her. She had been an ice queen when they parted last, but all she wanted to do now was tell him he'd been right about the danger she was in. She wished she could race into his arms, bloody sleeves and all, and tell him she was sorry for distrusting him.

He came around the glass partition and gave her a rueful smile. "Alba."

She stirred under the low timbre of his voice. A strand of black hair hung over his left eye and she resisted the urge to brush it away. Heart racing, she stood and clutched her handbag with both hands. "I . . . I had to see you. Simona—"

"Did she hurt you?"

"She tried to."

"Wait for me in the Great Hall," Dimitri said. "I'll wash up and meet you there shortly."

She forced a dry lump down her throat. At least he was speaking with her. She stood and retraced her steps back to the Great Hall. The blond nurse was still at the information desk. Catching sight of Alba, the nurse quickly stuffed a copy of the penny dreadfuls into a drawer. Of course, Alba couldn't blame the girl for reading the scandal sheets. She too got a great deal of fascinating information from them.

Dimitri appeared a few minutes later and took her by the arm. As he began to usher her down the staircase, they heard the young nurse call out, "Good night, Dr. Griffin."

"Good night, Mona."

Alba shot him a sideways glance. "She seems rather protective of you."

"She's just a child," was his response.

Since she hadn't detected any attraction in Dimitri's voice, Alba forced her jealousy away.

He looked at her with concern and when he squeezed her arm gently, her breath caught.

"You informed Nurse Donovan that I might be coming here tonight," she said. "How did you know?"

He looked away. "I just did."

They reached the ground floor and Dimitri pushed his way through a back door. "We can talk in my hansom while I return you to the dormitory."

"You have a private coach?"

"It's provided to me by the hospital." He released Alba's arm as he swung his greatcoat over his shoulders. "The driver has my schedule committed to memory."

As they moved to the carriage, which sat in a dark alley behind St. Bart's, Alba and Dimitri's breath frosted in the air. Alba swept her skirts off the ground, and with Dimitri's assistance, she climbed into the hansom. After she settled against its squabs, she heard him give the driver her street address. Then he joined her inside.

"Can we pull around to the front of the hospital? Edith is waiting for me there."

Dimitri nodded and shouted the instruction to his driver. The carriage jerked to life while he peered at Alba through the shadows. With his topaz eyes flashing and his eyebrow cocked in a curious manner, he looked devastatingly handsome. But more than that, he looked intrigued, as if he wanted to know precisely why she'd sought him out.

Alba said nothing until she sent Edith home. When Dimitri shifted toward her, she tried to reorder her thoughts.

"Now what's this about Simona?" he asked.

Once she verified that the curtains were drawn for privacy, she delved into her explanation. "She came to see me in the dormitory."

Dimitri reached for her hand and clenched it firmly.

"She told me that Ileana is planning my demise. Using Ileana's black magic, she transformed her dress sash into a poisonous snake meant to kill me."

"My God." His eyes flashed with anger. "Are you all right?"

She nodded. "The girls and Mrs. T. helped me kill it."

"Damn the fact that I didn't protect you from her!"

She squeezed his hand.

"I won't let her come near you again," he vowed. "Now tell me exactly what she said."

She recounted the episode, ending with Simona's claim that she and Dimitri had been lovers.

Dimitri didn't reply.

"You don't have to tell me if it's true because it doesn't matter." Alba was lying, but she was in no position to demand the truth. She and Dimitri had never been intimate. What's more, she was no angel herself. She had joined Simona and Dimitri willingly in the graveyard that night. No one had forced her to desecrate the vampire's grave—the very sin that had led to their troubles.

As Dimitri shifted his face away, she studied his profile. Half of it was darkened by the shadows, the other half illuminated by lights of the neighboring carriages. She admired the flare of his nose and the way his hair brushed the top of his collar, and when she stole a look at his broad shoulders and able hands—hands that saved people's lives—her heart skipped a beat. In that moment, it seemed he could do anything. Set fire to water. Even move a mountain with one push of his powerful shoulder. It sent a pulsing heat to her core, suggesting that maybe she was the type of woman who was attracted to trouble.

"Go on," Dimitri said in a rich voice.

Alba swallowed hard. "What alarmed me almost as much as the

cobra was Simona's assertion that you have a dark secret. She said this secret could present more danger to me than Ileana."

Dimitri let go of her hand and raked his thick hair. The layers ruffled and fell precisely back into place. "Do you believe that?"

Tears surfaced in Alba's eyes. She shook her head and stared down at her gloved hands. "I did at first. But now it's her I don't trust. Seeing Simona convinced me that you are trying to protect me. It's obvious that evil girl means to hurt me with every move she makes."

He nodded gently. "She's the enemy, not me." Slipping his arm around her shoulder, he drew her close.

Alba buried her face against his chest. He smelled purely masculine, a mixture of musk-based cologne and his own, warm chemistry. Comforted by the steady beat of his heart, she tried to hold back her tears. "I'm so scared."

Unable to stop herself, she began to cry. Dimitri hushed her sobs with low words.

Reaching into her hair, he loosened the pins and stroked the curls that tumbled free. "I told you, Alba, that's why I'm here. To protect you."

"I thought you might hate me after I stormed out of your house," she said.

"I could never hate you. I wanted your anger to cool, so I didn't contact you for a while, but I've been guarding you the entire time. Nothing in the world could ever deter me from you."

He held her so tightly that she thought she'd been captured by chains. She was a fiercely independent woman who'd sworn she'd never let anyone clasp her so possessively, but strangely, she reveled in it.

Turning her face up, she looked into Dimitri's golden brown eyes. Heat spiraled to every inch of her body. "That's just it," she said. "You know everything about my past, Dimitri. You're the only one who *can* protect me."

"Letting you go was the biggest mistake I ever made." He looked as if he was about to kiss her, but then he seemed to change his mind.

Alba's heart began to thump so fast it nearly flew out of her chest. She hadn't been very responsive to his last kiss, so he might be hesitant now.

Perhaps, she thought with morbidity, *he will never try and kiss me again.*

In a moment of insanity, she dove forward and pressed her lips to his. She sensed Dimitri's surprise, but he didn't draw back. Instead, he groaned against her mouth and clutched her urgently. His lips were velvety soft and warm, but best of all, they were familiar. Clinging to him as if her life depended on it, Alba began to cry all over again—for the kiss transported her back to a time when he was everything she wanted. And the deeper he kissed her back, the more she realized he was all she wanted again.

Dimitri's breath came in rasps. Pulling her hard against him, he uttered words that assured her she'd done the right thing. As their tongues entangled, electricity sparked within Alba, escalating the fervor she'd restrained ever since Dimitri had sauntered toward her at his birthday party. Her muscles quivered as his hand strayed from her waist to her back. When he caressed the length of it, she grabbed his wrist and moved his hand to her bosom. Dimitri didn't need additional prompting. He fondled her breast through her coat, and Alba's body lurched. She matched him kiss for kiss while he arched her back across the carriage bench. Tearing her coat and gloves away, Dimitri traced his tongue along the outline of her mouth. It felt fiery hot, like coal set aflame.

His hand glided along the trail of buttons that barred him from touching the rise of her breasts, and he grunted with impatience. Loud snaps and rips filled the cabin—and Alba saw the buttons of her dress flying through the air.

The noise seemed to excite Dimitri even more. He yanked her dress aside so that he could tug at the material of her chemise. After slipping the thin strap from her shoulder, a breast spilled out. He studied it with dark desire and wet his lips.

"You are so beautiful, Alba," he whispered. "I've thought of nothing but you these eleven years."

His words couldn't have provoked more excitement in Alba. Inflamed, she welcomed Dimitri's hand as it furled erotically around her breast. He laid his body over hers and she could feel his erection against her thigh. Letting out a little cry, she instinctively pressed her leg against it—making his long penis as hard as steel. Dimitri's mouth skimmed her throat while he stroked the oval of her breast.

And when the tip of his tongue dipped into her hollowed spot, she wiggled uncontrollably against the sensation.

Dimitri brushed his head along her chest until his mouth reached her nipple. With his lips and teeth moving simultaneously, he sucked urgently at the nub until it grew to a new height inside his mouth. Moaning, Alba cupped the back of his head as he worked his magic on her hardened point. And as he thumbed her other pink nipple to a hard charge, she drew in a sharp breath.

To Alba, being here with Dimitri was an unearthly pleasure; it was what she'd been missing all these years. Tonight he had been a savior to those poor hospital patients and now, in this carriage, he was *her* hero—and she lusted for every inch of him.

Dimitri banged on the roof of the hansom.

"Yes, sir?" the driver called out.

"Take us to my house, Drummond."

A tremor of desire convulsed through Alba. *Will we make love tonight?* She wanted to. She wanted to feel Dimitri holding her, rocking into her. Regardless of her reputation . . . in spite of her loyalty to Teddy.

While the carriage reversed directions, Dimitri reached beneath the hem of Alba's dress. She closed her eyes as the pads of his fingers traced her ankle. As difficult as it was, she held her breath while his fingers slid up her thigh. When his touch reached the thatch of hair at the top of her legs, moisture pooled at Alba's center, hot and wild. She whimpered pleading sounds as he pulled away. Holding her gaze, he gave her a look as if to ask, "Are you ready?" Her answer took the form of a wild gaze. Dimitri pulled her nipple deep into his mouth and sank two fingers into her folds at the same time. It hurt at first but then a cataclysm of pleasure imploded within her. Alba pulsated around his fingers and she let her head drop back against the seat. Pressing her eyes shut, she raised her chin skyward and arched her back as Dimitri continued to plunge his fingers in and out of her. The friction brought her to the edge of madness—and to a tremendous climax.

Her limbs stiffened and she remained still to enjoy the throbbing sensation.

"My God." She choked the words out. "That feels so good."

She yanked off her gloves and reached for him now. She wanted to feel him, touch him, and become part of him. Her hand traveled down his trousers until she found his arousal through the heavy material. She grasped it and fondled it, hoping her inexperience wouldn't matter. Emitting a groan, Dimitri rose up to catch her lips with an openmouthed kiss. He crushed her against his chest, mashing her breasts while she rubbed his shaft.

Just then the hansom rolled to a stop and the driver announced their arrival at Dimitri's mansion.

Dimitri pushed himself up and stared down at Alba. She was a vision, an angel with flowing black hair fanned across the bench like the exotic plumes of a peacock. The way her steaming, cobalt eyes gleamed at him rocked him to the core—and the sight of her breasts standing at attention made him ache for her even more.

The fact that Alba had initiated a kiss was like a dream come true. Regardless of her independent streak, it proved that she longed for approval and love above all else. The realization filled Dimitri's blank life with the color he'd been yearning for, so much so that he knew he had to have her at all costs. If he used self-restraint against the temptation of blood, maybe he could make love to her without harming her. Of course, if they made love, he'd have to pay a visit to the British Museum to get his hands on the bracelet of Amenhotep.

He kicked the carriage door open. "I'm taking you inside." His voice was gruff with desire.

Since he'd ripped Alba's dress clean open, he pinched it together, then wrapped her coat around her shoulders for coverage. With her head nestled against his shoulder, he burst out of the hansom and hastened inside the house. He didn't bother to light an oil lamp, but moved to the darkened drawing room where he laid her on the divan.

As he hovered over her, he kissed her deeply. And after he peeled the coat off her shoulders, he knelt before her and parted her frayed dress like a pair of curtains. Alba let out a gasp while he sucked the mounds into his mouth again.

Dimitri urged himself to slow down. He intended to make love to Alba slowly, with an intense focus and an unhurried purpose. She was precious to him, the only woman he'd ever loved. And he had never forgotten the magic of her smile—or the earnestness of her character.

Now she was his to claim completely.

After he flicked his eyes to Alba's face, he continued to feast on her tawny nipples, and his cock became painfully rigid. When he saw that a fire lit her eyes too, his shaft started to pump.

"My God," she moaned, unable to catch her breath.

Control, Dimitri told himself. He must maintain control and not spill his seed too early. It had been years since he'd made love to a woman, and having Alba writhe beneath his touch was maddening. But he wanted to show her how much he cared for her, how much he treasured her. And once he was inside her, he wanted her to peak first.

Releasing his mouth from her nipple, Dimitri swept his hands inside her torn dress, feeling Alba's sculpted body. Her skin was warm and soft and supple, just as God intended the perfect woman to be. His shaft remained hard between his legs, but he tried to concentrate on lavishing Alba with kisses. All the emotion he'd felt after their violent separation sprang up inside him, escaping his body by way of those kisses. Alba, as if she sensed just that, opened her mouth to him and received his tongue with anxiousness.

He grasped the back of her neck while her mane tumbled loose and free over her shoulders. She skated her hands along his shirt and fumbled with the buttons. Once she had his shirt open, she trailed down his hairless chest until her caress reached his belt.

A shudder ran through Dimitri. As Alba started to unclasp his trousers, his fangs descended. Heart racing, his body shook as he tried to restrain himself from biting her. She had her hands around his cock, and it was hell trying to resist piercing her creamy neck.

Christ. What was he thinking? If he made love to her, he might kill her. He must stop.

Before he could make another move, there was an insistent knock at the door.

"What the devil?" he said, jerking his head up. Luckily the interruption made his fangs recede.

He and Alba froze for a moment as the knocking continued.

"Could it be Jochen?" Alba pulled her dress closed.

"Maybe he lost his key," Dimitri said, scowling.

The knocking became more insistent.

"Damn it!" he hissed.

She sat up. "You should see who it is."

Signs of a misty sunrise streamed through the drawing room windows. Dimitri stood, but the heavy lethargy that always accompanied daylight began to overcome him. *I'm a bloody fool. I didn't make note of the time when I took Alba home.*

His feet felt like thick pieces of cement as he trudged to the door. Alba followed. He swung the door open as she placed a quivering hand on his shoulder. Standing before him wasn't Jochen or the hansom driver. It was Teddy.

Chapter Fifteen

"Teddy!" Alba gasped.

Glowering, Dimitri reached back and shoved her behind him. "Bloody hell, Rollingsworth. What are you doing here?"

Teddy eyed Dimitri's bare chest then raised an urgent eyebrow at the sight of Alba's frayed dress and mussed hair. "Are you all right, my darling? What did you do to her, Grigorescu?"

"It's none of your business." Dimitri gritted his teeth. *How does Teddy know my real name?*

"It sure as hell is," Teddy said. "Alba is my betrothed."

Dimitri glanced beyond the door—to the sunlight that bathed the open courtyard. Fatigue pulled at him and he could hardly stand, let alone fight Teddy. "She isn't engaged to you, Rollingsworth. I see no ring."

"Stop arguing!" Alba stepped forward.

Reaching toward her, Teddy yanked her out of the house.

"Alba—" Dimitri cried. He made a move to go after her, but the sunlight seared his outstretched hand. Alba looked back to see smoke rising from his charred skin. Her hand flew to her mouth. She gave him a staggering stare while Teddy forced her into his awaiting carriage.

Dimitri is a vampire. Alba wormed her way to the far side of the hansom against the morbid thought.

Seeing the sun's rays burn his skin convinced her that he was a bloodsucking monster—and the realization gripped her with terror. *He would have disintegrated into a pile of ashes if he'd gone after me.*

Her gut wrenched. When was Dimitri going to tell her what he had become? What Simona was and what, eventually, she might become? *Was he going to tell me after he bit my neck in the throes of passion?*

Shuddering, Alba buried her face against the window.

"Rotten bastard!" Teddy slammed the carriage door. The sound set the hansom into motion. "No gallantry. He didn't make an attempt to come after you."

Alba tried to hide her tears. "How did you know I was here?"

"Edith came to me, concerned out of her mind. She knew you'd gone with Dimitri and she begged me to find you."

Alba scowled. She would have to have a few words with Edith about her secret-keeping skills.

Teddy analyzed her disheveled state and shock replaced the anger in his eyes. "Apparently Dimitri attacked you. That's the story we shall stick with when it comes to the gossipmongers."

"You said you wouldn't speak his real name. What's more, why do you care about the rumor mill?" she asked sourly, gathering the collar of her torn dress together.

"We must leave your reputation intact, Alba. To protect you." His body stiffened. "I am willing to forget this incident ever happened."

Goose bumps sprang along Alba's arm. Never before had she heard Teddy speak with such frigidity. It made her think she didn't know him at all.

"You drive me to madness, Alba." He met her stare. "I don't know what I would do if anything happened to you."

I wish I felt the same way about you.

"Don't I get a thank-you for being your rescuer?" he asked as his expression softened. He slid closer to her.

She said nothing.

When she stiffened, he turned away. "That heinous Grigorescu. I didn't believe what people are saying about him, until now."

"What are people saying?"

She watched Teddy's brows dip together as he continued. "That Dimitri has a dark side," he said. "Apparently, he turns down every social invitation presented to him and keeps completely to himself. People are jabbering on about his nighttime hours. They say he may be a vampire."

Alba's blood chilled. *He is.*

"I think he may be responsible for killing that vagabond last month," Teddy said.

"There are no such things as vampires," Alba shot back.

"Of course not. But maybe he did the Ripper killings."

Her blood chilled at the suggestion. Still, she managed to keep her horror hidden. "You and I both know Dimitri isn't capable of such butchery."

Teddy reached for her hand but instead of accepting it, she clutched her torn dress. Tilting her head, she rested it against the seat and closed her eyes. She was humiliated and exhausted and she would have told Teddy to go to hell—if she wasn't so confused.

What am I to do now that I know Dimitri's secret? His thirst for blood was extremely dangerous and she wondered if it led to the killing spree in Whitechapel.

Would Dimitri harm her?

As a beam of sunlight streamed through the carriage window and landed over her face, she wondered one more thing. Would the amulet's curse apply to either of them since Dimitri was immortal?

The sadistic Jack the Ripper slowly tugged on his black pigskin gloves. As he jammed each finger against the cold material, a sly smile formed on his lips. He was close to Alba now, almost close enough to touch her. He had watched her as she came to Dimitri Grigorescu's home and he saw her leave it. The woman intrigued him. He'd known her for years, and her transformation into a beautiful, confident woman fascinated him. She was one of the few women he respected. He didn't want to kill her yet.

Looming in the shadows, listening to the clip-clop of horses' hooves—that was what suited him. It was where he did his best thinking.

All of London remains in an uproar over the murders I've committed. It caused pride to shoot through him because he knew the city was terrified under his influence.

It had taken notice of his unique calling card: leaving his victims' mutilated bodies in plain sight. What murderer did that? What murderer welcomed the police's attention so soon after committing a crime worthy of the gallows? He did. He was clever enough to challenge the authorities. But now he had a new strategy.

I will take a respite. It will lead people to think I'm finished. But I will strike again.

As he sat in the gray shadows, the Ripper closed his eyes and concentrated on the sound of the hansom rolling down Harley Street.

Cradling his burnt hand, Dimitri made his way inside the house. He managed to bandage the burn before he stumbled to the basement. He didn't want to ask for Jochen's help because he was too tired and too angry to think straight. It was a bizarre combination indeed.

Blasted Teddy! What had the man been thinking?

Obviously Teddy didn't trust Alba—and the thought made Dimitri smile a little despite the throbbing pain in his hand. *Teddy must have suspected that Alba still had feelings for me, and tonight she proved just that.*

Wincing, Dimitri dragged himself inside the shipping crate. After he settled over the rough straw, he pulled the lid closed with an unprecedented weariness.

Did Alba put two and two together when she saw my smoking hand? How could she have not?

His mortifying identity had been revealed, and it made Dimitri sick with shame. Before Teddy shoved Alba into the carriage, she'd looked back at him with eyes flooded with terror. *Christ. I let Teddy steal Alba away as easily as someone yanks a sucker out of a child's hand.*

Have I lost her forever?

Dimitri knew he must gain back Alba's trust, but how?

Then he knew. He would find Ileana and kill her.

Folding his arms, Dimitri closed his eyes to the sleep of death. A hand sliding up his leg awakened him. A lithe woman lay close. Groggy, Dimitri moaned with pleasure as the woman's hand reached his shaft. With just the right touch, she rubbed, teased, and stroked his cock through his trousers.

Alba. Had she escaped Teddy's grasp—explaining nothing but wanting everything Dimitri could offer her?

It was dark inside the crate. He was half-awake and he couldn't make out the woman's face. Pressing her cool lips to his, the woman shifted on top of him, her long, silky hair spilling across his chest. The tips of her breasts compressed against him as she inspired his sex to a full arousal with her handiwork.

Could this be a dream?

Dimitri flattened his palm and located the tight juncture between his companion's thighs. The woman moaned softly. Then, with playful, unhurried strokes, he caressed her nether hair through the material of her dress, and when she started to unclasp the buttons of his shirt, he pulled up her skirt.

She feathered a hand along his leg and he was struck by how strangely cold her skin felt. What's more, the woman's thigh was incredibly thin, unlike Alba's rounded limb.

Dimitri's eyes sprang open with alarm and he burst out of the crate. When he looked down at Simona's smug face, his erection deflated.

"What the hell?" he thundered.

"It's me, my love."

"What are you doing here, Simona?"

She ignored the question. "I could tell that you wanted me just now."

"I thought you were Alba."

"Did you?" Her eyes formed serpent-like slits. "Fooling you is so much fun!"

"I'm warning you, I'll kill you myself if you try and harm Alba again," said Dimitri.

Simona watched him stuff his shirttails back inside his trousers. "Alba is fine."

"This time," he raged.

"I've been watching you, Dimitri, from the shadows and from the air. You almost got Alba to trust you, but now she knows you are a vampire, doesn't she?"

"It's likely." He scowled.

Simona tsked. She floated out of the crate and made her way to his side. "Poor Dimitri. Whatever will you do now?"

"I probably chased Alba away forever." Anger flared in his throat. "But why am I discussing this with you? Get out of here, you snake!"

She pouted dramatically.

"Don't act wounded, Simona. Despite what happens between me and Alba, you and I have no future together."

She raised her chin. "I just wanted you to know that Ileana is here in London and she plans to destroy Alba very soon."

"Why are you warning me?"

Simona shrugged her shoulders. "Because I am impartial."

"What the hell does that mean?"

"It means that even if you and Alba evade Ileana's wrath, you will eventually destroy her because you are a *mulo*. Don't you see? I win either way."

"Get out!" Dimitri roared.

He lunged for her but Simona was quicker than he. She morphed into a bat and escaped through the basement window with a loud flapping sound.

Temper quickened, Dimitri paced the floor of the basement. As much as he loathed Simona, maybe it was time he took her advice. Perhaps he should mesmerize Alba in order to gain control of her. Now that she knew he was a vampire, she might shrink from him and refuse his help. If that was the case, he must use his preternatural powers to persuade her back into his arms. That's where he secretly wanted her.

Up to this point, he'd been foolish—completely consumed by his need to impress her. But he was the one who'd doomed her to end his life before she took hers. Ending his bloodlust would be a godsend—there was no doubt about that—but this wasn't about him. Knowing that Alba would suffer after he was dead was something Dimitri would not stand for.

As he made his way upstairs to shave and dress, he vowed to find Ileana and hypnotize Alba before her stepmother got to her . . . before the dark prophecy began to see the light of day.

Chapter Sixteen

Ileana Zăpăda strolled through the foyer of Atwood Hall with the drama of a queen on parade. She had arrived in London by train during the night and was staying in the house her late husband owned. Years ago, the neglected Kensington home had belonged to Mihail's first wife, Anastasia Zăpăda, a pathetically feeble invalid. Although Mihail never mentioned the house to Ileana, she became aware of its existence when she overheard a conversation between him and Alba.

Now, Ileana thought slyly, *it belongs to me.*

The Georgian-style house with its stunning painted-glass windows and its elegant brickwork was nestled inside a respectable district of London. Yet it had stood unoccupied for more than a decade and had fallen into disrepair. Considering that Ileana demanded the best of everything, the run-down interior of Atwood Hall simply wouldn't do.

She moved toward the vast drawing room while Otterbourne, her pet rat, sat perched on her left shoulder. Amid the dark shadows, Ileana nearly tripped over a pile of steamer trunks.

"Giselle!" She screamed for her mute housemaid, the only servant who had accompanied her to London. Ileana had told the elderly woman that she would have to tend to the laundry, the cooking, and all of the cleaning herself for the time being.

Giselle emerged from the morning room in a panicked shuffle. Duster in hand, she gave Ileana a silent dip of her chin.

"Didn't I tell you to unpack these trunks?" Ileana screamed. "How are we supposed to feel settled in this enormous city if we don't do some of the work ourselves?"

Nodding in triple time and scissoring her fingers, Giselle hastened away to find something with which to cut the ropes of the trunks.

Ileana sighed with annoyance, but in reality she shouldn't be irritated. When she had stripped Giselle of her youthful beauty by way of a cruel spell, Ileana had been left with a gnarled servant woman.

Ah, but it was worth it. Giselle's beauty had been too comparable to her own.

Sounds of people passing in front of the house drew Ileana's attention. Her lips set in a thin line, she glided to the bay window and pulled aside the lace curtains. On this crisp evening, the patrons that littered Green Park were dressed in their finest clothing. As they rushed to the theater or to a swank restaurant for supper, they reminded Ileana of blind ants. Scurrying to and fro, nearly colliding with one another, they were completely unaware of the secret of life—a secret she knew well. And it involved tapping into the Dark Arts.

Using black magic led to unprecedented advantages. It also supplied one with the power to alter things whether one's intentions were malicious or good. And Ileana's intentions were always malicious. After all, she had been raised by coldhearted, unloving parents. She'd been left alone often as a child, no one caring for her ugly, plump, and slovenly persona. Yet everything changed the night she saw an actress perform at the theater. The actress was a beautiful woman who glided across the stage like a ballerina. After the performance, she was hardly regaled for her talent, but more for her extraordinary beauty. Ileana was astounded at the attention the actress received. Because the lovely woman seemed to mesmerize all those around her, Ileana thought, *Beauty is the ultimate power.* That's when she transformed herself by dyeing her hair, losing weight, and studying her appearance from every angle in the mirror.

As her looks evolved, she began to gain the upper hand in every situation. Once she delved into black magic, it hadn't meant sacrificing her soul, since she never had a soul to begin with. And over time, jealousy was Ileana's foremost motivation for continuing the Dark Arts—especially when she met her impertinent stepdaughter. Alba's astonishing beauty began to upstage her own. Porcelain-skinned and warm of heart, Alba shone like a beacon in every situation . . . eclipsing Ileana . . . pushing her back into the shadows.

That, like the unkempt state of Atwood Hall, simply wouldn't do. Her gaze swept the expensive furnishings in the drawing room. It pained Ileana to think that impudent Alba had inherited a portion of Mihail's wealth. That's why the insolent girl's disappearance from Stelian Hall had made Ileana so happy. When Alba fled, she cut herself off from every Zăpădă. Believing that her stepdaughter was dead had been satisfaction enough for Ileana—until her magic mirror informed her that Alba was very much alive and living in London.

The vision of Dimitri Grigorescu becoming a vampire had prompted Ileana to move to the smoky city. After all, Simona's attempt to kill Alba with the snake had failed, and Ileana wasn't going to let Dimitri consume Alba. Not before she made Alba suffer, anyway.

Now that Ileana had her stepdaughter in her sights, she didn't intend to let her slip away again.

With a twirl of her black dressing gown, she left the window and hurried to an empty room upstairs. Her magic mirror, blackened at the moment, sat draped in a corner. Ileana had practically throttled the incompetent men who'd almost dropped it as they tried to remove it from the train.

Heart racing, she moved toward the fixture and pulled the sheet aside. The mirror glowed and waved with an unearthly blur, then sparkled with tiny glimmers.

"Good evening, my lady."

"I hope it is, my friend."

"What do you mean?"

"I am here to see to Alba's demise—and I want to know how close I shall come."

"I showed you that the serpent did not kill your stepdaughter, my lady."

"Yes, but—"

"Do not despair." The mirror cackled. "The attempt on your stepdaughter's life was primitive, at best."

"You dare criticize me," Ileana raged.

"Calm yourself... and watch carefully." The mirror rippled, then burst forth an image of Simona curled against Dimitri. He flung her away as he claimed that he might destroy Alba in the throes of passion as a *mulo*.

"Ah!" Ileana let out a chilling laugh. "I wanted to kill my stepdaughter myself, but if Dimitri destroys her while he is trying to show her love, it will cause her much more pain!"

The mirror waved and cackled. "And the best part is, if Dimitri does not destroy Alba in the throes of passion, both of them will die at the hands of the Egyptian prophecy."

"Yes," Ileana replied greedily. "It's perfect!"

"But you must remember one thing, my lady. There is a remedy for the Egyptian curse."

Her expression darkened. "What remedy?"

"The bracelet of Amenhotep. It sits inside a locked case at the British Museum."

"What is so special about this bracelet?"

"It was blessed by Amenhotep's fellow priests as soon as they learned of Princess Tousret's prophecy. Although Tousret murdered the doomed priest before he could don the bracelet, it possesses the holy powers of good."

"The holy powers of good?" Ileana scoffed. "Nonsense. They are no match for the Dark Arts."

"I agree," said a voice behind her.

Ileana wheeled around to see Simona seated in an armchair nestled in a darkened corner.

"How did you get in here?" Ileana asked sharply.

"I don't need to be invited into a place of evil." Simona gestured to the mullion-paned window.

The enchantress's nostrils flared. "Never disturb me without warning again!"

"I'm sorry. I wanted to inform you that the snake I left for Alba failed to kill her—thanks to that stupid Tuttlebaum woman."

"I know. And I should drive a stake through your heart for your ineptness."

Simona covered her chest protectively.

"Don't worry. Lucky for you, I still require your help with Dimitri Grigorescu." Ileana paused.

"I just paid him a visit."

"I already know," Ileana said cynically, swiveling to face the mirror. She eyed her smooth, fair skin and shining blond hair with approval.

"You saw me tell Dimitri that he is a *mulo*?" Simona asked.

"Yes."

"This means that Alba will eventually destroy Dimitri," Simona said as she slid closer. "But why not help them along by doubling their chances of dying?"

Ileana shot her a sideways glance. "I like the hint of evil in your voice. Go on."

"Dimitri and I are vampires. I've told you as much."

"Yes," Ileana said impatiently.

"I've also told you that I would have destroyed Alba long ago if it didn't mean losing Dimitri because of his anger."

"Yes."

"Considering those things," Simona said, "I've come up with the perfect plan. According to Romanian legend, if a male Szgamy Gypsy becomes a vampire, he turns into a sex-starved vampire that will consume his victim with his physical lust before he drains them of their blood."

"I told you, I already I witnessed your explanation to Dimitri."

"So why not place a temporary spell on Alba? If you increase her sexual aggressiveness, she will decrease Dimitri's willpower faster than usual."

Ileana threw her head back in icy, bloodcurdling laughter.

"So you like my plan?" Simona asked proudly.

"Brilliant!" Ileana arched a thin eyebrow.

"How will you do it?" Simona asked.

"I'll find a way. Still, to prevent anything from interfering with our clever scheme, you must do me two favors."

"What favors?"

"First, you must get rid of Alba's beau, Teddy Rollingsworth. He is nothing but a hindrance."

"Done," replied Simona as she reached over and stroked Otterbourne. "What is your second request?"

Ileana's lips curled into a sardonic smile. "I want you to steal the bracelet of Amenhotep and make it disappear."

Chapter Seventeen

The tang of brine and the bellow of tugboats drifted off the Embankment as Alba turned onto Fleet Street. She hastened against the crisp breeze toward the Inns of Court, a bundle of nerves. She was late for work today—and she'd been chiding herself about it ever since she'd left the dormitory.

Touching her hand to the dark shadows beneath her eyes, she scurried up the steps that led to Gray's Inn. The four Inns of Court were situated in the legal district of London which, as attested to by its noise and by its smells, wasn't far from the River Thames. Whenever the sound of water lapping against the Embankment reached Alba at her desk, it sent her back to her native Romania. The Thames reminded her of the Olt River—and of the pleasant life she used to know before her mother died . . . before her father married Ileana.

Unfortunately, daydreaming at work—and being tardy—were two things Mr. Rollingsworth frowned upon, so Alba suppressed a yawn and hurried into the great hall. She passed a set of chambers belonging to another barrister and finally entered the dark, richly paneled chambers of Mr. Rollingsworth. Settling herself at her desk, she put her head down on its surface and closed her eyes. Silence enveloped her, but only for a moment. Teddy burst through the door, bright-eyed and cleanly shaven.

Alba snapped her head up and shot him a curdling look. Surprisingly, he wasn't put off by her scowl. Rather, he smiled as he swung his arm forward and presented her with a stunning bouquet of white roses.

"Happy birthday, darling."

"Oh, Teddy," she gushed. The drama of the past weeks had pushed her birthday from her mind. As she gazed at the spectacular flowers, she felt like a sour stick.

"Beauty for a beauty," he said gallantly.

"Thank you." She reached for the bouquet, then cradled it against her chest.

"You're welcome."

"You shouldn't have."

Teddy sat on the edge of the desk. Looking his usual, polished self in a well-cut houndstooth suit and mohair greatcoat, he removed his hat without flourish. Everything Teddy did he did without bravado. Alba supposed she should find his lack of ego admirable, but she didn't. To her, it made him seem dull.

Still grinning, he looked down at her. "The flowers were a must. I had to do something to regain your confidence." He paused. "What's more, you deserve to be fawned over—after what that monster Grigorescu put you through."

Dimitri didn't do anything to me that I didn't want him to do.

Alba put her nose to the roses while her encounter with Dimitri came flooding back to her. She could feel his hand skating up her thigh. And she could envision his lengthy manhood pressed into her palm as they'd rolled about the bench of the hansom.

She chased away the erotic images under a stirred heartbeat. "You know I love being fawned over," she quipped, "but I must get some work done."

"Of course." Teddy rose. "Since Tabitha Crowe confessed to killing her son, she'll be sentenced later today."

The elderly woman's guilty verdict still gripped Alba with remorse.

Teddy straightened his tie. When he offered to put the roses in some water, Alba handed them over distractedly. "Not to worry," he said. "I'll be by your side."

She gave him a tiny smile. "Thank you. You always know how to comfort me, Teddy."

"And I always will, darling."

As Alba watched him leave the office, she wished he would stop calling her that.

In the afternoon, she and Teddy were reunited within the quiet reverence of the Old Bailey. Alba had already donned her wig and barrister gown in preparation for the sentencing. Teddy, who was dressed in his horsehair wig and gown as well, brushed his shoulder to hers.

"All rise for the Honorable Oliver Wentwood," the bailiff instructed.

Wearing the most intricate of curled wigs, Wentwood bustled in. He was a portly, sagacious man of middle age. Though he looked as if he'd eaten one too many candied sponge cakes, his reputation as a highly respected member of London's judicial system preceded him.

Wentwood gave a grave nod to the courtroom populace and took his seat in the middle of the eleven judges.

"Bailiff Murdock," he called out. "Bring in the accused."

Tabitha Crowe was escorted into the courtroom. Alba stiffened beside Teddy. Tabitha looked years older than she had during her daughter-in-law's trial. Her clear blue eyes had turned bloodshot and her complexion had grown alarmingly pale.

Alba could only imagine the conditions the woman was enduring inside Newgate Prison. Very few prisoners had the luxury of securing a private cell—and murderers were among the most hated inmates.

She watched Tabitha move to the sentencing dock, her arm clasped by the stern-faced Murdock. The accused woman shuffled forward, her ankles and wrists hindered by the shackles that bound them.

Heavens! Alba thought. *Are those chains really necessary? Tabitha Crowe is ninety years old. Who on earth is she going to hurt?*

Tabitha passed Alba and locked eyes with her. Alba's heart leapt to her throat. She never thought her first conviction would feel like this. Inspired by the mistreatment she received from Ileana at Stelian Hall, she'd dreamt of practicing law—of bringing criminals to justice. Alba knew Tabitha was responsible for the murder of her only son. Why then was it so heart-wrenching to see the elderly woman live out her just deserts?

Tabitha transferred her glance to the jury box. Today, the stacked rows were empty. Without a jury present, it was left to the panel of judges nestled behind their podiums to decide Tabitha's fate. Fear quickened Alba's pulse at the thought.

"I hope she is found guilty but insane," Teddy said in a whisper.

Alba did too, but she doubted it. She had proved that Tabitha understood right from wrong during the crime she committed. Furthermore, the accused woman showed no signs of dementia during the trial—and the fact that she'd poisoned her son over a long period of time didn't help either.

Tabitha finally reached the dock. She entered it and faced the judges who sat on the other side of the room. Murmuring from the gallery began again. The elderly woman met the legion of eyes with a calm sense of dignity. When her stare shifted to the window, the sun did not stream into the courtroom as it had on the final day of the trial. Instead the autumn sky had turned as gray as a mid-December day. Tension hung in the air—tension that felt bitter and remorseful.

Wentwood's voice broke the silence. "Under Her Majesty's Dominion," he said, "this collection of High Court judges has reached a verdict." He paused while Tabitha stood rigidly in the dock, showing no emotion save for the single tear that lined her cheek.

"Tabitha Loretta Crowe of Chelmsford," Wentwood continued, "for the heinous crime of first degree murder committed on August 10, 1888, against your son, Seymour Darby Crowe, we hereby sentence you to hang from the neck until dead. Your public execution will take place on Monday, the twelfth of November in this year, 1888."

Tabitha's knees buckled. She slumped forward with her eyes closed.

"Somebody help her!" Alba cried.

Three officers of the court came to the elderly woman's aid. They helped Tabitha to her feet while she began to sob. "I had to do it!" she hollered as she was being led away. "I feared for my safety!"

The words stopped Alba cold. Tabitha was right. She'd been left with no choice. And that was precisely how Alba had felt under Ileana's control. Ileana would have destroyed her if she hadn't run away to London. In that moment, Alba knew that life wasn't about being right or wrong, just or unjust. It was about listening to one's heart.

Strangely, her guilt over her faking her death and abandoning the Zăpădă name vanished. All she was left with was her doubt that she could continue being a barrister. After all, her sense of justice had become permanently skewed.

Teddy grasped Alba as she sagged against him. "Are you all right?" he asked.

She fought to regain her composure, but it was difficult since the wind in her lungs had been jolted out of her.

"If I didn't know better," he said, "I'd think you were a family member reacting to Tabitha's fate."

A massive headache was beginning to form in the back of Alba's neck. She said nothing as she rubbed the tense muscles.

"Tough luck, the sentencing was," Teddy remarked while the observers filtered out of the courtroom. "She seemed like a nice old woman."

"Luck has nothing to do with Tabitha Crowe's demise," Alba fired back. "It's all about the choices we make in life—and what we do with those choices."

Teddy cocked an eyebrow at her odd tone. "I think you need to rest before this evening's events."

Curse my birthday plans.

Weeks ago, Teddy had arranged an extravagant night out, complete with a fine dinner in Grosvenor Square and highly sought-after opera tickets to celebrate Alba's birthday. Considering her foul mood, she was inclined to cancel, but Teddy had invited his father and grandmother to join them.

"I'll have a carriage pick you up at eight o'clock." Teddy's eyes still twinkled despite the way she'd spoken to him. "And I don't think a chaperone will be necessary, my darling. You are like family to us Rollingsworths."

Alba arrived back at the dormitory to find an enormous dress box sitting on her bed. Stunned, she lifted its lid. A luxurious Prussian-blue gown was folded neatly between layers of tissue paper. Alba removed the dress, placed it in front of her, and moved to the mirror. With its snug-fitting bodice, extravagantly puffed sleeves, and ornaments made from lace, the dress followed the latest trend. Even its full skirt lent the dress the right touch.

Smiling, Alba returned to the box and opened the envelope that accompanied it.

You'll look stunning in blue.
T.

She sighed. Teddy was a romantic at heart, yet Dimitri was standing in the way of him gaining her affections. Alba wondered if Teddy realized that. She also wondered if his suspicions of Dimitri being a vampire would ever be confirmed.

Alba secretly wished she were dining with Dimitri tonight instead of Teddy. There were so many things she wanted to say to him. Foremost, she wanted to tell Dimitri that she was sure Ileana's presence was closing in on her—and that she needed him to protect her more than ever.

As she slipped into the dress and stole a look at her reflection, a thrill raced through her. For once she felt beautiful. The rare burst of confidence convinced her that she should seek out Dimitri this evening. *Maybe I'll get what I really want for my birthday.*

Dabbing lip stain on her bottom lip and brushing her hair to a high shine, she wondered if the forces of ancient Egypt were pushing her toward Dimitri with breathless energy. Or was it her own curiosity?

Chapter Eighteen

A string quartet strummed a Vivaldi melody as Alba arrived at Chez François.

Located in the heart of Grosvenor Square, the chic French restaurant bustled with excitement. Dimly lit and garishly decorated, the establishment boasted a slew of aristocratic types—as well as those who wished to be seen in the company of its aristocratic patrons.

Alba inhaled against her tight corset and smiled at the tiny, mustached maître d'.

"Bonsoir, mademoiselle."

"Bonsoir, monsieur."

"Vous êtes ravissante ce soir, mademoiselle."

Alba blushed. *"Merci bien."*

"De rien." The tiny man inclined his head politely, then gestured for Alba to follow him.

She felt a dozen eyes on her as she sashayed through the restaurant. Teddy had guessed her dress size accurately enough, except her full bustline had nowhere to go except up and over the dress's plunging neckline. When a distinguished-looking gentleman gave a full-body turn her way, his wife swatted him on the shoulder, knocking his pince-nez loose.

Suppressing a smile, Alba looked straight over the maître d's head. Soon they arrived at a private room in the rear of the restaurant. Her host stopped and drew back a set of amethyst curtains edged in heavy gold fringe. Inside the small room sat Teddy; his father; Harold's mother, Constance Rollingsworth; and Constance's nurse, around a circular table. After Alba thanked the maître d', Teddy helped her into her seat while his father gave her a partial rise.

"Good evening, everyone," she said.

"Happy birthday, my dear," Constance Rollingsworth greeted through pursed lips. She was a small but difficult woman who was eighty years old if she was a day. She wore her soft, silver hair spun upward into a stylish chignon while her sharp green eyes studied Alba without the aid of spectacles. *Ironically*, Alba thought, *the old woman's eyesight is probably better than mine.*

"Thank you." Alba gave Teddy's grandmother a nod as she unfolded her napkin.

"You look stunning." Teddy beamed.

"Thank you for the dress, Teddy." She touched his hand. "It was very kind of you."

In formal wear cut precisely to his lean but muscular frame, he was more dashing than Alba had ever seen him. Teddy's face brightened against his white bow tie and winged-tip collar, and his gray eyes gleamed in perusal of the gift he'd given her.

"Yes, my dear. You look beautiful," Constance agreed. "Gorgeous diamonds, I must say."

Alba put a hand to the curved necklace that encircled her neck. "This choker was my mother's." Besides the ambrotype that sat on her night table, the diamond necklace was the only possession Alba had to remember her mother by—and she cherished it greatly.

"You remember Bedford, my nurse?" Constance boomed. The volume of her voice made it apparent that it was her hearing, not her eyesight, that suffered.

"Yes." Alba gave Mavis Bedford a glance. "It is nice to see you again."

The large woman dipped her double chin in Alba's direction before she began to fuss over Constance. Mavis was built quite like a man. Her intense strength helped her lift her employer in and out of bed and the bathtub.

"For God's sake, Bedford!" Constance snapped. "I can place my own napkin in my lap. And if you think I need help eating, you'd better think again!"

Alba's cheeks flamed, as did Mavis's. Thank heavens they had secured a private table.

"Teddy, however did you get tickets to *Othello*?" Constance's expression softened as she addressed her grandson.

"Yes, my boy. However did you manage it?" Harold Rollingsworth took a sip of the scarlet wine.

"I have a box at the theater," Teddy said.

"That's my son. Quite the distinguished man about town." Harold gloated. "With a lovely woman on his arm to boot."

Alba blushed.

"You like the opera, don't you, Alba?" Teddy asked as he plunged a spoon into his lobster bisque.

How on earth could she say she preferred the ballet? "Yes, I love the opera."

"Splendid!" He seemed genuinely pleased.

And that is how the two-hour meal progressed. Between endless courses of deviled whitefish, creamed asparagus, sweetbreads, boiled fowl, salmon, pink champagne, and an impressive three-tiered birthday cake, the conversation sailed around Alba, but never involved her directly. The babble of voices and the clink of china droned through the air while Alba thought of Dimitri. Had he remembered that today was her birthday? How could he have?

She had told him the date only once, eleven years ago . . .

". . . most unpleasant business," Constance Rollingsworth was saying as she sipped her coffee.

Alba's ears perked up.

"What's unpleasant, Mother?" Harold asked patiently.

"A conversation I heard between two gentlemen at the physician's office today. Couldn't count on females at the hair salon to speak of it."

"What conversation?" he asked.

Constance scowled. "The gentlemen referred to the fact that people believe the Whitechapel Murderer is merely taking a respite—to throw the police off track."

"It has been quite a while since this so-called Jack the Ripper killed anyone," Teddy chimed in. "Over five weeks, to be exact."

Alba nodded. "The murderer may have done several things to throw the authorities off track. For instance, he might have feigned illiteracy in the letters he sent."

"Perhaps," Harold said. "The author was educated enough to observe the silent 'k' in 'knif' and 'w' in 'whil' in the From Hell note he mailed to the head of the Vigilante Committee."

"Are you speaking of the letter that was accompanied by half a human kidney?" Constance asked loudly.

"Yes, Mother. That one," Harold said. "But I don't think it's a prudent subject to discuss on Alba's birthday."

"Nonsense!" Constance clucked. "She's studying to be a barrister and this is the most interesting conversation we've had all night."

He took in a breath.

"Because the box this lunatic sent contained half a human kidney preserved in ethanol," Constance went on, "maybe he's an alcoholic himself."

"We can only speculate, Grandmamma," Teddy said as he laced his fingers together.

Constance sat up straighter. "Of course, there is another possibility. Considering how inept the police have been in the matter, maybe we are all being fooled."

"What do you mean, Mrs. Rollingsworth?" Alba asked.

"I mean, what if the kidney in the box was a hoax concocted by some juvenile medical students? And what if the letters allegedly written by Jack the Ripper weren't written by him at all?"

"I wouldn't be so sure, Mother," Harold said grimly. "I think the killer is taunting the police because he wants to get caught."

Constance gathered the ends of her fur wrap together. "One thing is for certain. His victims have received no justice. No justice at all."

"Maybe not," Mavis replied quietly, "but you must admit that the killer is a genius."

Silence filled the sequestered room.

Flustered, the nurse seemed to regret opening her mouth. "What I mean is, he brazenly murdered four women and the police can't catch him." She paused. "It's as you said, Mrs. Rollingsworth. The victims of this diabolical killer have yet to receive justice."

Alba felt as though her dinner would come back up. *Justice.* Supposedly justice had been served in the case of Tabitha Crowe.

128 • *Marina Myles*

Saving Greta was an achievement Alba could live with. But the fact that she'd had a hand in Tabitha's demise didn't rest well with her at all.

She twisted her napkin. *Who am I to determine people's destinies?* Being a barrister gave Alba a power she wasn't comfortable with. What's more, she could only imagine Monday's headlines. *Alba Spencer: heartless barrister sends ninety-year-old woman to the gallows . . .*

She decided to speak to Mr. Rollingsworth. "About Tabitha Crowe's sentencing . . ."

Teddy placed a hand on her arm. "Not now, darling. Let's not spoil your birthday celebration. Discuss it with my father in the office on Monday morning, I implore you."

Mr. Rollingsworth hadn't heard Alba speak up, so she agreed not to bring up her professional insecurities any further.

Harold Rollingsworth lit a cigar and sat back in his seat. His expression bore concern. "With all this talk of a killer running wild, Alba, I want you to promise me something."

"Of course, Mr. Rollingsworth."

"Whether or not it was Jack the Ripper who wrote these letters cannot be proved. But this madman's actions are bringing out the worst in people . . . copycats that may be getting ideas and such."

She nodded.

"The city is gripped with fear. Promise me you will go nowhere by yourself." He looked directly at her.

But how am I to see Dimitri tonight?

Seeing her old love was becoming a need that burned at her soul like the hottest fire. Swallowing her last morsel of honesty, Alba replied, "You have my word."

Dimitri grasped a single red rose as he climbed the steps to Alba's dormitory. After he adjusted his white bow tie, he knocked on the door. A heavyset woman wearing too much cheek rouge opened it. Drawing the lapels of her dressing gown around her fleshy neck, she eyed him with caution.

"May I help you, sir?"

"Pardon the intrusion, madame. I am looking for Alba Spencer. I'm an old friend and I'd like to escort her to supper for her birthday."

"You must be Dimitri Grit-gross-goo," Mrs. T. said.

He smiled cordially instead of correcting her pronunciation.

"You're as handsome as my daughters claim!"

He looked embarrassed. "Is Alba here, Mrs. . . . ?"

"Tuttlebaum. But you may use the 'Mrs.' in the loosest sense. I am a widow. Lost my poor Henry years ago. On the twenty-sixth of June . . ."

"Ah, yes. Mrs. T. Isn't that what Alba likes to call you?" He was desperate to get the loquacious woman back on track.

"Yes," she crowed. "Charming girl, Alba is. But I'm afraid she's not here. Went out for the evening with her beau, Teddy Rollingsworth."

Blast it to hell! Of course Alba had accompanied Teddy. *I made no solid plans with her.* In his own defense, he'd been searching for Ileana like a madman . . . "I would be indebted if you could tell me where they went, Mrs. Tuttlebaum. I have something very important to tell Alba."

"My stars! I don't know if I should." As she stared into his topaz eyes, it didn't take her long to change her mind. "Very well." She blushed again. "They went to Chez François in Grosvenor Square. If you don't catch them there, they are continuing on to the opera. *Othello*, I believe."

"Thank you very much. I am forever grateful." Dimitri took her hand and pressed his lips to its surface. Mrs. T. gave him a twittering "you're welcome" before he went trotting down the steps of the dorm building.

Twenty minutes later, Dimitri's hansom pulled up to Chez François. He was about to emerge from it when he caught a glimpse of Teddy helping Alba into a carriage across the street.

"Drummond, follow that carriage!" he commanded, banging his walking stick on the hansom's ceiling. The vehicle took off with a jolt and Dimitri bumped along on its rear bench. He had to catch up with them. After all, he had a sneaking suspicion that Teddy would propose to Alba tonight. What better time than on her birthday?

Teddy tossed his cigarette to the ground, but its scent followed Alba and him inside the theater. The plush lobby abounded with men in black formal wear and jewel-clad women with cascading curls, wearing elbow-length gloves. There was a buzz of excitement in the air since the opera was about to begin. Teddy and Alba had barely arrived in time for the overture because Teddy's grandmother had suffered an acute bout of indigestion at the restaurant. Harold and her nurse had offered to skip the opera in order to attend to her at home.

The house lights dimmed, prompting the crowd to disperse in all directions. Alba slipped a hand through Teddy's bent elbow as they made their way to a side staircase. Behind them, a loud banging began at the glass entrance doors.

"What the devil?" Teddy turned his head sharply. Unfortunately there were too many people barring the way for him to see what was going on.

"Some fellow is insisting upon entry to the theater," a man behind them explained. "The sod doesn't have a ticket. Why on earth would they let him in without one?"

Teddy murmured his agreement while he and Alba continued up the staircase. Once they reached Teddy's velvet-padded box, Alba settled into a Chippendale chair and leaned over the balcony's partition. Her eyes surveyed the beautiful décor of the theater—from its richly patterned walls to its scalloped private boxes and glittering chandeliers.

The gaslights lowered to a flicker and a spotlight materialized in the center of the curtains. While the orchestra dove into an exciting overture, Alba accepted a pair of opera glasses from Teddy, as she had forgotten her spectacles. The drapes parted to reveal a set depicting a seaport in Cyprus. When five singers appeared onstage, Alba watched them intently.

Throughout the opera, she felt herself carried away by the tragic love story of Desdemona and Othello. Seeing that she was touched, Teddy drew her close and feathered his fingers up her arm. He held her hand tenderly throughout the duration of the performance. In the end, Alba found herself moved to tears as Othello lamented over Desdemona's passing—before he killed himself with a dagger. The eternal bond the lovers strove for had been tragically cut short. Had it offered her a glimpse of her and Dimitri's fate?

Sorrowful chords closed the curtains and Alba melted into an emotional mess.

The gaslights sparked again. "That was lovely," Teddy whispered. Reaching up, he swept a tear from her face. Ever so lightly, his touch lingered on her face. He parted his lips and pulled her into a long kiss. The kiss didn't succeed in comforting her, though she suspected that had been his intention.

He drew away wearing a self-conscious expression. "I'm sorry, Alba. I don't know what came over me. Your reputation . . . I . . . I hope no one saw us."

"It's fine," she reassured him softly. Inside, however, she continued to feel unnerved.

"That wasn't a very uplifting opera to see on your birthday," Teddy said as he helped her stand.

"No," she admitted. She wanted to rip off her too-tight shoes and confining stockings and run all the way home. She was exhausted from fear and sentiment, and all she wanted to do was sleep.

Trying to disguise a yawn, she slid a glance in Teddy's direction. He looked hurt. "Am I as boring as all that?"

"Of course not. It's just that the Crowe sentencing took everything out of me today."

Teddy gripped her elbow. "Are you sure that's it? You must tell me the truth, Alba." Anger tinged his words. "Do you have feelings for me or not? I must know."

She was shocked by his antagonism, but she stopped herself from reacting to it. After all, Teddy had gone to great lengths to ensure a pleasant birthday celebration. "I do have feelings for you, Teddy. You are a wonderful man."

Relief brought his shoulders forward. "I'm so glad to hear that," he stammered. "I'm sorry, Alba. I just wanted tonight to be special. Please, indulge me. Say you'll have a drink with me at the Hotel Metropole before I take you home."

"Very well." She tried to smile. "If it means that much to you."

The couple left the theater. It had begun to rain, but luckily the hotel was located just across the street. As the theater patrons disappeared quickly from the streets, Teddy opened the door for Alba. He encircled her waist with his hand and drew her close.

"I want to wish you an official happy birthday," he whispered against the collar of her frock coat. He lowered his chin and closed his eyes, but the kiss he leaned in for was interrupted by a horrendous flapping sound. They turned to see a bat as dark as night swoop upon them in a violent frenzy. Hissing, the creature dodged for the vein in Teddy's neck.

"What the devil?" he yelled out. He tried to swat at the bat with his hands, but the animal's claws scraped the skin of his palms and wrists. Blood began to drip on the pavement.

Fear exploded within Alba. "Run!" she cried as the bat persisted in its attack. She grabbed Teddy's arm and pushed him toward a hansom meant for someone else.

"I'll give you fifty pounds if you go!" Teddy screeched to the driver as they tumbled inside the carriage.

"What the hell was that all about?" Teddy turned to Alba, clutching his wounded hand.

Alba tried to slow the feral pumping of her heart. Her plan to seek Dimitri out would have to wait because the time to tell Teddy everything had come.

Chapter Nineteen

Dimitri paced outside the theater like an alert panther. Giuseppe Verdi's muffled love strains seeped through the building's bricks, deepening his anger. He'd made a scene in his attempt to gain entry— and the way the staff aggressively rejected him had added to the drama.

Was Teddy proposing to Alba during the opera? The possibility flushed red-hot rage through him.

Panic clogged Dimitri's throat as he continued to pace. The end of the performance was nearing and his mouth was growing dryer than week-old bread. Completely parched, he was forced to leave the theater. As he cut through a winding alley, he tossed the rose he'd planned on giving Alba to the ground. Once he was hidden from sight, he morphed into a bat and soared to a less-than-desirable neighborhood.

Entering the blackened mouth of a side street, he spotted a young prostitute posed against a wall. He glanced around to ensure that they were alone and then Dimitri approached the girl. Her garishly painted lips spread into a smile.

"Yer an elegant one," she said. "'Andsome at that!"

She pushed herself off the brick wall and unbuttoned her coat. Her creamy cleavage rose in half-circles over her whalebone corset and shone under the moonbeams. Dimitri slipped forward, his mesmerizing eyes leading the way. The girl's eyelids grew heavy as she stroked the rise of her breasts alluringly. While Dimitri's body built with thirst, he hunched toward her and cradled her small face in his hands. Sliding his thumb over her cheek, he wet his lips in a slow, seductive motion.

"That feels nice," she purred.

She reached inside his cape and tried to fondle his shaft.

"No," he commanded. "Let me do everything to you."

Any number of men would have reacted to the young girl's advances, but not Dimitri. He wanted no woman but Alba.

He continued to caress the prosser's chin and mouth until she was like putty in his hands. Shifting her head to the side, he stared at the smooth column of her neck, and in no time, his fangs descended. Lowering his lips to her skin, he bit down. The girl moaned—first in pain and then in pleasure as a narrow trickle of blood angled to her nape.

Dimitri fed until the girl slipped to the ground, without memory of their encounter but still very much alive. As he pulled his pocket watch from his vest, he studied the time. With a whirl of his cape, he retraced his steps to the theater and arrived in time to see its patrons exiting.

Where were Alba and her ever-persistent beau?

Dimitri hastened across the street and looked inside the window of the Hotel Metropole. There was no sign of them. Transforming into a mist once he rounded a corner for privacy, he peered inside every hansom that passed in the vicinity. He even traveled to Alba's dormitory.

Where on earth can they be?

A sickening thought rose to Dimitri's mind and his gut wrenched. Perhaps Teddy had taken Alba to his house so that he could seduce her.

Anger twisted his thoughts like a debilitating disease. The image of Teddy caressing Alba's glossy hair, stroking her velvet thighs, was more than he could bear. Insane with jealousy, his fangs descended again—which caused him to morph back into human form. He gripped his silver-knotted walking cane until his knuckles turned white. As he left the wealthy London district, he planned to go to Teddy's home so that he could find Alba and rescue her. But first he needed to have something with him when he did.

The bracelet of Amenhotep.

Tonight he would steal it and then convince Alba to run away with him. If he presented her with the enchanted bracelet, she would feel safe from the cruel prophecy associated with the Egyptian amulet. *At the very least,* Dimitri thought ruefully, *she won't kill herself if she destroys me.*

There was a second half to his plan. Dimitri had made a vow to destroy Ileana before he left London. And that was exactly what he intended to do after he lured Alba to the safety of his home.

The gigantic doors that marked the entryway to the British Museum stood locked.

"I don't know what I was thinking," Alba said, reevaluating her idea to bring Teddy here.

"You wanted to show me something inside, and I'll not disappoint you," he said.

Teddy banged loudly on the doors. When no one came to open them, he took Alba around back to the employees' entrance. "My father used to bring me here when I was a child," he explained as he beat on the steel portal. "I knew everyone here. It's been two years since I visited last, but I assume Wickley is still a night guard."

"Wickley?" Alba said faintly. Her feet were killing her and all she wanted to do was sit and relay everything to Teddy. She'd tried to do so inside the carriage, but he had been in too much pain. While she had laced her handkerchief around his bloody scrapes, he'd sagged against her with his eyes closed.

"I have no idea what Wickley's first name is, but he's always been a helpful fellow." Teddy pounded on the massive door again with his uninjured hand. "Wickley! It's Teddy Rollingsworth. Let me in!"

The shrouded moon cast ominous shadows in the back alley—exaggerating the fact that they were here in the middle of the night. Alba visualized rows of eerie sarcophaguses and towering Anubis statues and her neck hair stood on end.

She moved closer to Teddy. Perhaps she was not as strong and brave as she thought . . .

"What I was going to show you inside the museum can wait until daylight," she insisted.

Teddy paid her no mind. "Wickley!" he repeated. "For God's sake!"

The door flung open and a uniformed guard with a pair of overgrown white sideburns greeted them. "Teddy! How good to see you, my lad. What are you doing here in the middle of the night?"

"My lovely companion, Miss Alba Spencer, shall tell you. But first, may we come in?"

"Certainly," Wickley said. "Your father has always been more than generous to this place. Please . . ."

The guard gave Alba a genial nod as she followed Teddy inside. He closed the door and motioned them toward a central hallway.

"What can I do for you, Miss Spencer?"

"I was here at the museum several months ago," she said. "There was a bracelet from ancient Egypt on display. Is it still here?"

"The bracelet of Amenhotep?" Wickley asked, wide-eyed. "Why, yes. It's tucked safely inside a locked case."

Alba's shoulders rolled forward with relief. She'd feared it was gone.

"I won't ask why you want to see it," Wickley said cautiously. "But promise me you won't tamper with it, Miss Spencer."

"You have my word," Alba replied.

With shaking hands, Wickley held up a lantern at shoulder height. He managed to point it in the direction of the main lobby. "Mr. Rollingsworth, you know where the Egyptian Room is, don't you?"

Teddy patted the guard on the back. "I certainly do. Thank you, Wickley. We shan't be long."

Wickley grunted as he passed Teddy the lantern and wobbled out of sight.

As Alba and Teddy made their way through the enormous repository, Alba was struck anew by all the treasures the museum held. From the famous Rosetta Stone to the Elgin Marbles and the revered Magna Carta, the British Museum was a source of pride for the United Kingdom. And rightly so.

She and Teddy climbed two flights of stairs until they reached the floor containing the bracelet. Onyx drapes trimmed in geometric Egyptian designs framed the doorway and made for a dramatic entrance to the exhibit. Drawing from her memory, Alba moved to the main display case centered by a brightly painted stone column. Teddy was right behind her. His hands encircled her waist as she leaned over the glass to look for the bracelet. She nearly complained about the intimate contact, but she had more important things to think about.

"There it is," she said.

Teddy walked around her. After he set the lantern on the display case, he peered at the spot she'd indicated with her finger.

The stunning gold bracelet sat atop a purple velvet pillow. Its coral inlays and burnished gold caught the lantern's light.

"Read the inscription," Alba instructed Teddy.

He cleared his throat and struggled to make out the words in the dim light.

The bracelet of Amenhotep

Fabricated in the year 1017 B.C., this bracelet was discovered by famed archeologist Sir Harris Farrington beneath the Temple of Luxor in the Nile Valley. It belonged to Amenhotep, a priest who served Princess Tousret, ruler of Egypt in the Twenty-First Dynasty. It is the counterpart of the amulet of Tousret, a cursed stone that dooms any female who wears it to kill her lover, then kill herself.

The curse mimics Tousret's murder of Amenhotep and her suicide following the Temple's discovery that the two were secret lovers. Amenhotep commissioned the creation of the bracelet to protect himself from the forces of darkness.

Unfortunately he did not don it in time.

The location of the amulet of Tousret is presently unknown.

Teddy locked eyes with Alba and shrugged. "Fascinating story, but I don't see how it pertains to us."

"Teddy." Alba stepped closer to him. "*I* have the amulet of Tousret."

"You? I . . . I don't understand."

"Dimitri gave it to me."

Teddy's eyes grew dark and heavy. "It's like him to give you something so foul. But I have no interest in speaking about Dimitri

Grigorescu." He slipped his hands around her waist and lowered his voice. "I want to talk about us, Alba. There is something I didn't have the courage to ask you during the opera."

He smiled and plunged to one knee. "Alba," he said, withdrawing a small box from the pocket of his dinner jacket. "I love everything about you. From your intelligence to your extraordinary beauty. Will you do me the honor of being my wife?"

He pulled back the lid of the tiny box and revealed a breathtaking engagement ring. The emerald-cut diamond, cushioned by a pair of large oval rubies, glittered in the shadows. Alba put a hand to her stammering heart. *What should I say?*

Just then the lantern clattered off the display case and landed on the floor. With the only light in the room extinguished, darkness descended on the place with an ominous hush.

Silence ensued, raising the hair on Alba's arm.

"What the hell?" Teddy asked.

A blast of cold air rushed at them unexpectedly. Teddy gasped as Simona materialized on the other side of the room, her ghostly white face set in a snarl and her knife-sharp fangs gleaming in a beam of moonlight.

"Christ!" Teddy stood immobile.

"Not Christ," Simona hissed. "I am more a product of the devil."

Fangs bared, Simona lifted herself off the ground and streamed toward him. Teddy turned to protect Alba, but Simona assailed him too quickly. He dropped the ring box in sheer horror and it went skidding across the tiled floor.

"Leave him alone!" Alba screeched. She tried to pry Simona off Teddy, but the female vampire had him captured in a choke hold. Terror convulsed through Alba, yet she wouldn't give up. She continued to pull at Simona's shoulders to prevent her from piercing Teddy's neck, but Simona flung her backward with a violent thrust. Alba went reeling into a stone sarcophagus, cracking her head upon impact.

As she lay slumped in the corner of the exhibition room, the scene before her blurred. She could focus just enough to see that Teddy was wrestling Simona with all his might. His arms were rigid against her chest while Simona's open mouth loomed inches from his jugular. Suddenly, a figure swathed in a black cape swooped down. Alba struggled to make out the man's face, but it wasn't until the figure spoke that she knew it was Dimitri.

"Get away from him, Simona!" He exposed his fangs in a seething challenge.

Simona jerked her head in his direction.

With an easy swipe of his arm, Dimitri sent her flying across the room, and she let out a bloodcurdling scream. She crashed into a display case, shards of glass shattering and crumbling beneath her weight. A single glass spear protruded from her heart. Simona stared at Dimitri with a mixture of sorrow, accusation, and anger before she closed her dark eyes forever.

Dimitri rushed to Alba and helped her to her feet.

"Are you all right?" he asked gently.

She nodded groggily and leaned against him. He felt strong and warm and she yearned for him to gather her in his arms. But there was Teddy to attend to.

"What the devil just happened?" Teddy thundered, pulling himself to a standing position.

Dimitri and Alba looked at one another. "He mustn't know I am a vampire," Dimitri whispered.

Still disoriented, Alba didn't answer him.

"Do you trust me?" Dimitri asked quietly.

"Y-yes," she said as she rubbed the back of her neck. Blood coated her hand.

Dimitri strode slowly toward Teddy without saying a word.

"What is the meaning of this, Grigorescu?" Teddy demanded. "Have you been following us?"

The closer Dimitri came to Teddy, the more entranced Teddy became. His eyes drooped as if he were under a spell—and by the time Dimitri reached him, he'd slumped into Dimitri's bent arms. Alba had never seen anything like it.

Dimitri laid him on the ground while Alba eyed the ring box that sat nearby. "I'm sure the crash summoned the night guard," he said. "I have only seconds . . ."

Alba watched Dimitri retract his lips and bare his vicious-looking fangs. His eyes, which glowed an unearthly crimson, stirred something deep inside her. As she saw an extraordinary bloodlust take over Dimitri's face, waves of lust exploded through her. Any decent woman would have averted her eyes from the sight of a demonic creature, yet she couldn't tear her gaze from his features.

Dimitri pushed Teddy's head to the side and then put his mouth to the exposed skin.

Piercing the largest vein that bulged from Teddy's neck, he drank for five or six seconds.

When he stood, Alba took a step back. She finally looked away as he yanked a handkerchief from his dinner jacket and wiped the blood stains away.

"He will remember nothing," Dimitri said.

"But he'll become a vampire!" Alba replied in a panic.

"No," he said. "I did not take enough blood."

Footfalls sounded on the stairs beyond the black curtains.

"The guard!" Dimitri whispered. "I'll take Simona's body and disappear. You must get Teddy home."

"Thank you for saving his life," Alba whispered back. She stared into Dimitri's bewitching eyes—eyes that smoldered an intense gold even in the shadows of the room. Her heart surged.

"I shall come for you at ten o'clock tomorrow night, my sweet," he said.

She nodded numbly. Before he left, Dimitri spun the handkerchief around his hand and pummeled it straight through the display case that housed the bracelet of Amenhotep. After he seized the artifact, he lifted Simona's bloody corpse into his arms and disappeared in a cloud of bluish mist.

Alba snatched up the ring box bearing the name "Cartier," then bent over Teddy's body. She managed to stuff the box into her reticule before Wickley shuffled into the exhibition room.

The elderly guard eyed Teddy on the floor.

"What in the name of sweet Christmas happened here?" he asked.

"A vampire." Alba tried to swallow the dryness that lined her throat. She inched in front of the display case so that Wickley wouldn't see that the bracelet was missing. "It attacked Teddy," she said. "They fought . . ."

"Good God!" Wickley said. "Are you all right, Miss Spencer?"

She tried to ignore her throbbing head. "I'm fine."

"Where is the vampire?" The guard's eyes darted around the room.

"She disappeared."

"She?"

"Please, Wickley. Can you help me get Mr. Rollingsworth into a carriage?" Alba asked. "I shall attend to him at his house."

Despite his confused state, Wickley agreed. He knelt beside Teddy and put a trembling finger to the puncture wounds that marred his neck. "Are you sure you don't want to take Mr. Rollingsworth to the hospital?"

"No." She shook her head. "We must be very discreet."

"Oh, yes." Wickley seemed to catch on. "Mr. Rollingsworth wouldn't want anyone to find out about this."

"Thank you for understanding, Wickley. Now, can you help me lift him?"

As she and the guard managed to carry Teddy down the main staircase, the horror of the night replayed in Alba's head. Only one good thing had come of it: she'd have more time to think about Teddy's marriage proposal.

Chapter Twenty

The night was cold and steeped with dampness as Dimitri moved in and out of the city shadows. While he cradled Simona's limp body, mixed emotions about her death swelled inside him. She had always been a vicious thorn in his side—a devil woman who'd brought him nothing but trouble. Yet, long ago, they had been friends. It was an innocent time in Dimitri's life—when adolescent infatuation reigned over everything else.

Now Simona was dead because of him. Or maybe in spite of him. He couldn't be sure. What he did know was that he had never loved the temperamental girl. And that very obstacle led to her downfall.

At least she can't hurt Alba now, Dimitri considered as he reached the edge of the River Thames.

Big Ben chimed the two o'clock hour, and amid the shoddy surroundings, his heart grew heavier. Simona would go to a watery grave here in the middle of this smoky, impersonal city—with no relatives or friends to mourn her.

Dimitri had chosen the industrial district of London for the disposal of the body because the docks were empty this time of night. However, the stench was overwhelming.

He laid Simona on the ground for a moment, then moved to the frigid waters of the embankment. As he resisted the urge to cover his nose, a barge sounded its horn in the distance. Dimitri watched the boat meander through the muddy waters until it disappeared from sight. The image of the empty river and the shift of Big Ben's hands jolted him back to the urgency of the moment.

He grappled in the dark for something with which to weight Simona's body. Although he regretted the fact that she would not have a proper burial, he couldn't risk being involved with her dramatic demise. He'd come too far in his quest to save Alba—and he would stop at nothing to see it through.

Urgency shot up his spine as he spotted a large rock nestled along the rubbish-ridden shore. He hoisted it into his arms, moved back to Simona's body, and laid the rock next to her. Looking at her face, his stomach roiled. It had taken on a strange, greenish hue. She resembled the vampire they had unearthed in Castle Bran's graveyard—and the memory surged bile to Dimitri's throat.

He gladly looked away in search of something he could secure the rock with. There, in the overflowing rubbish bin, lay a knot of rope discarded from a parcel. He quickly tied the rope to the rock and the rock to Simona's waist, then waded into the icy water. Murmuring something respectful, he dropped her body into the soft waves and watched her uncanny face disappear into the water's depth.

Exhaling, Dimitri trudged out of the river. When he reached a broken piece of cement, he sat upon it and drew his knee up. His thoughts turned to Alba. *Will she come with me tomorrow evening?* Something told him she would. Alba knew Dimitri was a vampire now, but she didn't seem afraid of him. Perhaps it was the Egyptian amulet at work, but he preferred to think that she would come of her own accord. Of course, if she had been enchanted by the amulet's curse, it was no matter. Dimitri had the bracelet of Amenhotep.

He hadn't gotten a proper look at the trinket inside the museum, so he delved a hand beneath his greatcoat. His hand fumbled inside the empty pocket, and he froze.

Where the hell is the bracelet?

Standing, he ripped at the lining of each pocket. The bracelet must have fallen out of his coat while he was in the water! Could it have sunk to the bottom of the black river—never to be found again?

Panic gripped him. He splashed back into the water. He was about to thrust his head beneath it when he heard voices. A group of vagrants was nearing. Dimitri peered over his shoulder and saw the degenerates teetering about in their drunken state, laughing loudly at one another's jokes.

He scowled. If Simona's body happened to wash ashore—and witnesses attested to his presence here—he was doomed.

Forced to abandon his search for the bracelet, Dimitri emerged silently from the water and slipped away into the night.

Alba rapped on the Rollingsworths' front door. "Please, Reeves. Let us in!"

She feared that making a commotion would wake Harold Rollingsworth, but she couldn't support Teddy's weight much longer. He was propped against her at a sharp angle, one arm slung around her neck as she grasped his waist. Teddy had managed to regain partial consciousness in the carriage that transported them here, but now he was murmuring delusional words with his head flung back.

Alba knocked again. Thankfully Reeves opened the door. The sleep-rumpled butler bore a horrified expression but said nothing as he lunged for Teddy. A moment later, Mavis Bedford appeared behind Reeves—both of them in their dressing gowns.

"What happened to Mr. Rollingsworth?" she asked.

Alba and the butler brought him across the threshold. "He's been attacked," said Alba.

"My God," Mavis gasped, eyeing Teddy's badly bruised neck and bite marks.

"Let's get him to his bedchamber before Master Rollingsworth wakes up," Reeves suggested.

The two women helped the servant move Teddy toward the staircase. After they'd managed to get Teddy settled in bed, Reeves went to fetch a glass of whiskey. Teddy was still muttering a string of inaudible words while Alba and the nurse removed his shoes and jacket.

"Unbutton Mr. Rollingsworth's shirt," Mavis instructed. "I need to take his pulse and listen to his heart."

With shaking hands, Alba removed Teddy's silk cravat and dinner jacket and unbuttoned his starched shirt. She propped his torso away from the headboard so that she could slip the shirt from his body. She couldn't avoid the brush of her fingertips against Teddy's bare chest. It was as muscular as Dimitri's, yet Teddy's skin was much paler and tufted with copper hair.

Alba's cheeks burned. She drew her eyes away and stared at the floor. She'd gone from never seeing a man naked from the waist up to snatching two glimpses in a matter of days.

Reeves reappeared with a snifter of whiskey and the medical bag Mavis asked for.

Mavis leaned over the bed and put a stethoscope to Teddy's heart. Meanwhile Alba pulled a chair close to the bed and clasped Teddy's hand tightly.

"I'm so sorry this happened," she whispered to him in a soothing voice. "But please don't worry. You will recover."

At least Dimitri said you would.

"Mr. Rollingsworth seems to have experienced a traumatic shock. Do you want to tell me what happened?" Mavis asked.

Alba swallowed hard. "Teddy was attacked."

"By whom?"

"I think the more accurate question is, *what* attacked Teddy?"

"I don't understand."

"Teddy was bitten by a bat."

The masculine-looking woman retracted. "How odd. I thought bats could only be found in the countryside."

Alba hated to lie, but it seemed an easier alternative than telling the outlandish truth. "I saw the creature with my own eyes."

"I have no experience treating a *bat* bite." Mavis spoke the word as if it were something poisonous she wanted to extract from her mouth.

"Nor can I give you any advice on how to do so." Alba paused. "I suppose the best thing to do is keep an eye on Teddy."

"Keep an eye on him? Miss Spencer, I don't think you understand the gravity of the situation."

Perhaps not. In fact, Alba wasn't sure of anything at the moment. Her head ached and she felt completely disoriented.

"Mr. Rollingsworth lost a great deal of blood," Mavis stated firmly. "He is cold as ice and he needs a blood transfusion."

"We cannot take him to the hospital," she cried. "People wouldn't understand . . ."

The nurse raised a thin eyebrow. "Understand what, Miss Spencer?"

Alba looked at her imploringly. "I'm in no position to explain everything, but I'm sure Mr. Rollingsworth would like for this episode to remain confidential."

"What exactly are you asking, Miss Spencer?"

"I'm asking for your discretion, Miss Bedford." She paused. "Can you perform the blood transfusion here?"

The nurse hesitated. "I . . . I suppose so." She hesitated again. "Oh, very well. Expose your arm."

Alba removed her elbow-length glove while Teddy moaned. She hovered over him and he pulled her closer. "Couldn't protect Alba . . . I'm sorry . . ."

"I'm fine, Teddy," she said. "I'm right here with . . ." Her vision clouded, and thanks to the tremendous pain at the back of her head, she slumped weakly across Teddy's knees.

"Gracious!" Mavis circled the bed.

The nurse put a hand to the bloody gash at the base of Alba's skull. Alba could barely make out the words "administer a painkiller" and "stitch up the wound." Then she plunged into a deep sleep.

Throughout the night, Mavis attended to Teddy and Alba alternately, offering Teddy rounds of lemon-barley water and taking Alba's vital signs until morning broke.

Dawn's light slipped through the lace curtains and Alba woke with a start. The sound of her rousing woke Mavis as well. "How is Teddy?" Alba asked.

"I gave him my blood last night." The nurse, who looked alarmingly pale, touched the sizeable bandage that encircled her arm.

"Thank you, Miss Bedford." Alba offered her a grateful look. "The Rollingsworth family is very lucky to have you."

Mavis nodded and appeared satisfied—as if she'd received the compliment she had been waiting for.

Alba moved to Teddy's side. As she studied his face, she saw that he'd regained some color in his cheeks. However, he was clenching and unclenching his jaw violently. When his head rolled from side to side, Alba squeezed his hand for comfort. Then she thought of the ring box. *Is it still in my reticule?*

She reached into her handbag to make sure it was still there. She was tempted to pull it out and return it to Teddy, but then she realized he had slipped into a peaceful sleep.

Alba stood, her skirts rustling. Mavis bolted out of her chair. "You're going home?" the nurse asked.

"Yes," Alba replied. "Teddy is in good hands and I'm sure Mrs. T. is worried out of her mind about me."

"Before you go, Miss Spencer, let me say something." The nurse stopped Alba by placing her hand on her arm. "I suspect you haven't told me the truth about what happened to Mr. Rollingsworth. And you have never explained the startling gash on your head."

Alba thought it best to keep her encounter with vampires to herself. "Rest assured Teddy did get bitten by a bat. And I fell against a lamppost trying to swat it away."

"It seems an extraordinary story," Mavis said.

"You'd be wise to remember your place, Miss Bedford," Alba replied curtly.

Grunting with doubt, the nurse turned to check Teddy's pulse.

Alba seized the chance to leave the Rollingsworth home unseen. She returned to the dormitory with the weight of the world on her shoulders. It was as if her entire existence had changed in a matter of days—and that change began the moment Dimitri reappeared in her life. She'd started to lie as if it were the most natural thing in the world. Teddy's behavior was also growing bizarre, and the way Alba viewed her position as a barrister had become completely skewed.

Not only were these changes driving her to the edge of a dangerous precipice, they had unlocked things she'd forbidden to a remote recess of her mind. Her plan to go with Dimitri tonight, however hazardous it might prove, was a perfect example of her gravitation toward danger. He was dominating her life—and she had little control over the transition.

Was the Egyptian amulet to blame?

Refusing to think about it anymore that morning, she came through the door of the dormitory.

"Alba!" Mrs. T. gathered her in her arms as if she were a lost child. "You had us worried sick! I was on the verge of notifying Scotland Yard. Where in St. Peter's have you been?"

Alba felt the woman's heart beat to an insane rhythm—a rhythm only a mother's concern could fuel—and she erupted into tears in the middle of the embrace. "It was horrible," she choked out. "I didn't know what to do . . ."

"There, there." Mrs. T. gave her a squeeze. "As long as you're alive and well."

The Tuttlebaum girls bounced out of the bedroom, one nearly tripping over the other. They gathered around Alba and their mother, each asking different questions in the same high-pitched voice.

"Calm yourselves, girls," Mrs. T. urged. "Alba has returned safely. If we all sit and listen, I'm sure she will tell us the entire story."

Like the dutiful daughters they were, the girls complied. Evelyn made a pot of tea while Elaine and Eugenia set a pile of raspberry scones on the kitchen table—around which the eight females gathered.

"Sorry we ate all of your favorite apple ones from the Captain," Eugenia apologized.

"It's no matter," Alba said. She wasn't hungry, but she was exhausted. Still, she stared into the girls' patient faces and decided she owed them an explanation.

"You dears are the only people who know what I ran away from in Romania," she began.

"Yes," cried Mrs. T. "That witch of a woman! If I had my way, Ileana Zăpăda would plummet off the London Bridge, straight to her doom." Mrs. T. crossed her arms and sat back in her chair. "Wouldn't mind giving her a push myself."

"Please let Alba talk, Mother," Elaine said.

The rotund woman fell silent and rolled her eyes.

"I ran away from my stepmother because I had to protect myself," Alba said. "She planned to kill me—and now she's here in London."

Gasps circled the table.

"She's here?" Edith spoke through a mouthful of pastry.

Alba's fingers trembled around the fluted teacup. "Ileana is a malicious person, I agree. But it's time I confessed something myself."

"Confess?" Ella echoed. "That can't be good."

"Shh," urged Evelyn. "She'll tell us everything if you're quiet."

Alba's audience settled in and listened intently as she relayed the story of how she, Simona, and Dimitri had desecrated the grave of Vlad Dracul's lover in the shadows of Castle Bran. She admitted that the sacrilege still haunted her deeply. She also told them that Ileana had been using Simona to taunt her—from prodding Simona to steal the amulet in the first place to convincing Dimitri to pass it on to Alba to curse her. Alba also relayed the night's events inside the British Museum, ending with a show of her head injury.

"There is no doubt that Ileana wants to destroy Teddy," Alba asserted. "It's another way she can hurt me."

"'From ancient grudge break to new mutiny,'" Ellen said softly. "That's from *Romeo and Juliet.*"

Her sisters groaned with annoyance.

"You mustn't feel bad for any of this." Mrs. T. patted Alba's hand. "Besides, I don't believe in vampires or black magic. Just a lot of hocus-pocus phooey, if you ask me."

"You're wrong, Mrs. T." Alba's bottom lip quivered. "Teddy lies in bed at this very moment with two bite marks in his neck—and I am responsible."

"Teddy's been bitten by a vampire?" Edwina fretted. "Alba, you must go back to him."

"I intend to. I need to wash up first and change my clothes. Meanwhile, Constance Rollingsworth's nurse is watching over him. She is the one who stitched my injury."

"Will Teddy become a vampire?" Edwina flushed profusely. "Oh, please, Alba. Tell him I'm very worried."

"I don't think he'll become a creature of the night," Alba replied.

"How can you be so sure?" Edwina asked.

"It's a hunch."

"There you have it, Edwina." Ella scowled. "Now, can't you see that Teddy is completely infatuated with Alba, not you?"

"You're horrible, Ella!" Edwina said. "'Art thou so bare and full of wretchedness?' That's from—"

"Who cares what blasted play it's from!" Ella countered.

Edwina scowled. "Just because you're the eldest girl and you have no suitor doesn't mean—"

"Girls!" Mrs. T. threw up her hands. "That's quite enough. It's time for your ballet class. Gather your things while I tend to Alba."

Falling into silence, the sisters scattered around the parlor, grabbing pairs of tights from the mantel and plucking up pointe shoes.

"Come with me, my dear," Mrs. T. instructed Alba. The large woman helped her into a nightgown, then into bed. "God knows if that nurse treated your wound competently."

"I do have a splitting headache."

"You see? That means you must lie down before you go back to the Rollingsworth house. I'm going to give you one of my special headache pills."

Mrs. T. disappeared. A moment later she entered the bedroom carrying a large white pill and a glass of water. "Take this."

Alba propped herself against the pillow and did as Mrs. T. advised.

"Now. I want you to listen to what I have to say." Mrs. T. gave her a stern look.

Alba's eyes widened because she'd never seen the woman's pleasant expression drop before.

"I swore to your lovely mother that I would take care of you if anything—God forbid—happened to you. She was sick for a long while before she died, you know."

Alba nodded. Mrs. T. rarely spoke of her mother, so she was paying careful attention.

"As sure as the sun will rise tomorrow, I know this Dimitri Grigorescu is trouble. I can feel it in my bones, Alba. He came looking for you last night. I was going to tell him to mind his own business—that you are practically betrothed to Teddy Rollingsworth—but he *bewitched* me with those brimstone eyes of his."

"Bewitched you?" Alba would have laughed if Mrs. T.'s expression hadn't been so grave.

"As sure as I'm standing here, he cast a spell over me. It's the same thing that happened to those girls."

"What girls?"

"The prostitutes that lunatic cut up." Mrs. T. did the sign of the cross. "Whoever killed those poor women lured them straight to it. The Whitechapel Murderer *enchanted* them into doing what he wanted."

"Those women were paid companions," Alba reminded her.

Mrs. T. sat on the bed and the mattress sagged. "You're a smart girl, Alba, but you aren't comprehending what I'm trying to tell you. The victims of this Jack the Ripper began dropping off around the time Dimitri Grigorescu came to town."

Alba drew back. "Are you implying that Dimitri is Jack the Ripper?"

Mrs. T. crossed her arms. "I may not look very intelligent, but I can put two and two together."

The insinuation ripped the air from Alba's lungs—as it had when Teddy suggested the very same thing. "You don't know Dimitri. He has tremendous integrity—and he holds women in the highest regard."

"People change, Alba. Especially people you haven't seen for eleven years."

As the headache pill Mrs. T. gave her began to take effect, Alba closed her eyes to the disturbing notion.

Chapter Twenty-One

Alba slept all day and into the night, thanks to Mrs. T.'s special medicine. As ten o'clock neared, her eyes popped open. The Tuttle-baum girls were snug in their beds and the moon shone on their serene faces. They were dear girls, and their mother was even dearer, but if they knew Dimitri was a vampire they would surely take action against him.

When Mrs. T. had suggested that Dimitri was the maniacal killer stalking the bowels of London, Alba had defended him out of instinct. But did she really know him anymore? If he was capable of ending someone's life as a bloodsucker, maybe he wouldn't stop at mutilating innocent women.

Alba flipped over and stared up at the ceiling. Where was Dimitri? Fear mingled with excitement as she glanced at the bedside clock again and tried to will its hands to move faster.

A thump rang out. She bolted to an upright position and her eyes swept the long room. Thankfully, none of the girls stirred. Heart hammering, her stare darted to the window. There, the silhouette of a dark figure materialized in the moonlight. The figure leapt from the balcony to the small landing beneath the window in a graceful bound, his black cape rippling behind him. The man's face was shadowed, but from the cut of his wide shoulders and narrow hips Alba could tell it was Dimitri. Her heart continued to stutter as she pushed the window open for him.

"Dimitri." She inhaled sharply. His stare grazed the curves of her body beneath her sheer lace nightgown. Sliding closer, he wrapped his arm around her waist and she was astounded at the hunger in his almond-shaped eyes. As they shimmered like polished gold in the moonlight, they captured her with temptation and commanded her without words. Before she knew it, he lifted her off the ground and they dissolved into a cloud of blue mist. In her entranced state Alba's fears fell away to a womanly desire. Dimitri could have asked her to leap off the uppermost point of Parliament and she would have done it.

"My sweet Alba." She heard Dimitri's low voice in the mist. "Let me protect you from Ileana. I want to watch over you tonight."

They touched down in the courtyard of his mansion and soon they were back in their human forms before the parlor fire. Dimitri hadn't let her go yet and she melted into the fold of his cape. She gripped his waist desperately, suppressing a fountain of tears. He smelled familiar and manly and wonderful. And she never wanted to let go.

He took her hand and led her to the sofa. "How is your head?"

"It still throbs," she said.

He edged her close with an arm wrapped around her waist, and a thrill shot through her.

"You slammed into that sarcophagus with full force. Damn Simona . . ."

Alba shook her head. "We needn't worry about her anymore. We should concentrate on Ileana and poor Teddy. He needed a blood transfusion after you . . ."

"Bit him?"

"Yes," she replied softly.

"Did you give him your blood?" He looked alarmed.

"No. The Rollingsworths' nurse did." She paused. "Dimitri, she saw the bite marks on Teddy's neck."

He got up and paced before her. "It's no matter. A vampire is a very abstract thing. Most people don't believe in the undead—even when they see the evidence we leave behind."

"I know who believes in vampires," Alba said as she wrung her hands in her lap.

"Who?"

"Mrs. T. It seems you have entranced her."

Dimitri joined her on the sofa again and smiled. "I suppose I'm getting good at that."

"You must be careful whom you hypnotize." Alba frowned.

"You're right. Not all vampires are alike." His tone changed. "When I was a child in the Gypsy camp, there was talk of *mulo* vampires. *Mulos* are strong, unstoppable creatures who were Szgamys before they crossed over. When I grew up, I realized these creatures got their power from consuming their victims sexually."

"I still don't understand."

He took her hand. "After *mulos* seduce their victims into bed, they exhaust and destroy their partners sexually before drinking their blood."

Alba put a hand to her neck and gulped. She met Dimitri's stare. "Would you do that to me?"

He raked a hand through his hair and scowled. "You have no idea how much you fuel my lust."

"You showed great restraint at the hospital," Alba argued. "I'm trying not to be afraid of you, Dimitri."

"Then come away with me," he said. "I shall take you to a place your insane stepmother will never think to look for you. It's the only way you can be safe from her—and from this killer who lurks in the alleyways."

Would being alone with Dimitri mean being alone with Jack the Ripper? Alarm seized her. Yet as she gazed into his vivid eyes, she was able to sweep the worry under the rug, if only for the moment.

"We cannot run away from this vampire's curse." She paused and looked at his hand as it lay over hers. "But I'm glad we have the bracelet of Amenhotep. It will help us beat the Egyptian prophecy."

He said nothing.

"Dimitri. You do have the bracelet, don't you?"

"I had it," he said with pain in his eyes, "but it dropped into the Thames when I sank Simona's corpse."

Fright pulsed through her. "You have to find it!"

"I already looked for it. But I'll go back again—and I won't give up until I locate it."

"Having the bracelet is the only way to ensure that we'll remain together. I don't want Ileana to defeat us."

"Don't worry," he said. "We won't be separated again." He knelt before her, his handsome features waving in the shadows of the firelight.

Despondency bombarded her and a single tear rolled down her cheek. "I hope you're right. At the very least, we must stop Teddy from standing in our way."

"I had a vision last night." Dimitri leaned closer. "Did Teddy . . . propose to you?"

"Yes," Alba replied without hesitation. There was no sense in lying.

His straight nose flared with impertinence. "And what was your answer?"

"Simona appeared and I didn't have time to give him one."

"What *is* your answer?" He inserted his hand into her billowing sleeve and trailed his fingers up her arm.

"I cannot marry Teddy," she said softly. "Not when I feel the way I do about you."

She watched desire rise in his golden eyes. She sucked in a breath as he gathered her to him eagerly. And when he slanted his mouth over hers and captured her lips with a scintillating kiss, she sighed against them. Their tongues collided, eliciting the very passion that had exploded between them on the bench of the hansom.

Enthralled, Alba clutched the lapels of Dimitri's greatcoat. She silently cursed all of the clothing between them. She wanted to feel his smooth, bare chest against her breasts and his hand between her legs. Oh, those skilled hands that had sent her to heaven the other night . . .

Dimitri kissed her over and over and she became breathless. "Where is Jochen?" she asked without tearing her lips away.

"He's out for the night," Dimitri rasped. "We'll be alone all evening."

He smoothed his other hand along her back and up to her neck. Her hair was partially caught in a chignon and Dimitri fingered one of the curls that dangled from it. He drew back to look at her. "You have no idea how long I've wanted to make love to you," he whispered.

"Show me how long," she murmured in return. "I don't care if you hurt me."

* * *

Alba's daring words shot a thrill to every corner of Dimitri's body. *Alba wants me as much as I want her.*

Anticipation thrummed through him. He quickly pulled her to her feet. There was no chance of thinking rationally at the moment, for he was useless against the commands of his desire. He kissed Alba again, and as she pushed his coat off his shoulders then to the floor, he held the gaze of her blue eyes. She fumbled with the buttons of his vest as embarrassment reddened her cheeks. Dimitri urged her to carry on with a string of kind words—and when his vest joined his coat on the floor, his shaft reacted. The feel of her hot breath feathering across his face engorged it to a stiff rise.

Alba proceeded to open Dimitri's shirt while he focused on her beauty. Her fair skin glimmered against her hair and the fan of her lashes thickened in the firelight. In that moment, she looked like a princess—and he was determined to be her prince.

Bending at the knees, he scooped her into his arms and whisked her to the bedchamber. As he sat on the edge of the bed, he perched her on his lap like a treasured artifact meant to be admired. With a flaming desire, his stare traveled from her indigo eyes down farther, to her ripe breasts that strained against him, heavy and aching for his touch. His cock hardened even more as he took her exquisite face in both hands. As he pulled Alba's lips to his, her sounds of delight came in tiny gasps. Her mouth tasted like sweet, sun-drenched honey, but this time Dimitri kissed her to explore her eagerness—and prompt her willingness. Her response to the kiss was completely uninhibited, even visceral in nature, and it was precisely how he wanted it.

She clapped both hands over his cheeks and yanked him closer. Dimitri assumed she was a virgin, but he could be wrong. She seemed like an open book at the moment, ready for anything. *Has Teddy already corrupted her?*

Pushing the thought from his mind, Dimitri felt the blood surge wildly through his veins. She squirmed against his erection. *Holy Christ.*

His cock strained painfully against his trousers. *Can I hold out much longer?*

Alba yanked his shirt away and pressed the tips of her breasts against his flat nipples. The sensation nearly sent him over the edge. Her heart was thudding as well; he could tell that much. And as she sat against the rise of his cock, her eyes fluttered shut. She shifted her bottom toward it in tiny circles, moaning as she moved.

Dimitri grabbed her left leg and swung it over his hips so that she was facing him—straddling him. She opened her eyes and released her mane from its chignon. In a slow, erotic motion, her black locks tumbled past her slim shoulders and cascaded over her arms like ribbons of taffy.

"Dear God," he murmured as he put his tongue to her nightgown and traced the outline of her nipples. After all, she had thrust her breasts forward at mouth level.

"Taste me," Alba whispered. "I want you to taste my breasts."

He obliged in no time. Tugging on the upper half of her nightgown, he exposed her full, teardrop-shaped mounds. As he bunched the perfect spheres together in his fist, he ran the tip of his tongue over the hard buds. Side to side. Back and forth. He enjoyed nipping at the pearls—sucking, teasing, and licking them to a high charge.

"You're like an angel," he murmured gruffly.

She lowered her chin to look him in the eye. "And you are my dark angel."

He released her breasts and swept his thumb over her rosy lips.

"I'm here with my hair down and my breasts bare," she said. "Do you think I am a whore?"

"Never, Alba. I love and cherish you with my entire soul."

"Then God help me," she murmured as she bent to kiss him. "Because I love you too. And I shall offer myself to you tonight."

Her words snaked sin around him more persuasively than Adam and Eve's serpent. He had to have her. Could he resist killing her?

So far his fangs hadn't descended, yet Alba's scent was beyond alluring. He longed to bite her and release her blood to flow into his mouth.

Gripping the bottom of her nightgown, he fought the urge with all of his might. Then he guided her hand to his hard shaft. "Fondle me," he whispered into her lush hair.

Leaning forward, the tawny tips of her breasts brushed against his mouth. She unfastened his trousers with her eyes ablaze and reached deep inside his pants. When she found his penis, tall and erect, she ran her fingertips around its rigid rim. He arched his head back.

"Am I touching you the right way?" she asked.

"Oh, yes," he replied. "Now stroke it."

She squeezed his cock. And when she caressed its slick surface in an up-and-down motion, Dimitri's mouth began to water. The lust he felt was overwhelming. Catching Alba's mouth with another fiery kiss, he lifted her off his lap. They stood for a moment while she raised her nightgown over her head and he pulled off his trousers and underclothes. Once they were naked, he laid her on the bed. And as he spread his weight over her, he kissed her hotly, receiving a whiff of her perfume. She smelled delectable—like something fresh and undeniably sweet. Breaking the kiss, he ran his tongue down her milky-white neck. And beneath her layer of perfume, he could smell her impassioned blood flow. The scent fueled fervor in him like he'd never known before. Breathing in the unique woman that was Alba, he flicked his eyes to hers.

"I shall be gentle," he said.

Her eyes twinkled in response.

Realizing that the moment he'd dreamt of had finally arrived, he glided a hand up her leg and edged her thighs apart. Her knees fell to the mattress, an open invitation to which he responded with enthusiasm. He had anticipated seeing her sweet center and he didn't have to wait another minute. His stare traveled over her stomach until it landed on the curls that framed her pink cunny. She was like a goddess, almost too perfect to touch. Gingerly, he combed the nether hair with his fingers and then pressed his hand against her damp mound. She seized his wrist and lowered his hand so that his fingers were stroking the slit of her petals. He parted her core and her womanhood responded with a release of ambrosia that astounded him.

"Do what you did to me in your hansom," Alba whispered, her voice thick with lust.

He gave her a devilish smile as he thrust two fingers deep inside her. This time she placed her hand over his to intensify the sensation. She shifted closer to him while his mouth found her breast. He moved his hand in and out of her while he sucked her nipple and she clasped the bedsheets.

"Lord above." She pulled in a breath. "How do you know how to do that?"

He wasn't about to tell her that he'd learned it from Simona.

Smiling, he felt her cleft swell around his fingers, and when it started to beat, his cock rose even more.

He withdrew his hand and she pulled him closer—until she spotted the scar that marred his right shoulder.

"Is this from that night in the graveyard?" she asked, tracing the puckered skin with her fingertips.

"Yes."

"I'm so sorry," she whispered.

He gathered her in a firm embrace, his rod wedged between her damp thighs.

"Now make love to me, Dimitri." She panted.

As he buried his head into the pillow next to her hair, her hot breath tickled his earlobe.

Reaching down, he guided the tip of his shaft to her readied core. She sprayed kisses along his neck, then, nuzzling close, she dug her fingers into his back.

The scent of her blood pounded Dimitri's brain.

Self-restraint. He could ignore the fragrance of blood in the hospital, but this was a different matter. This was Alba's blood. It was a scent he was becoming addicted to.

He tensed and his balls tightened. Then he froze.

"Damn it to hell!" he snarled as he rolled off her. "I can't do this!"

Chapter Twenty-Two

Alba wasn't acting like herself. Blinded by red-hot desire, she could only assume there were other forces at work at the moment. She had nearly yanked Dimitri back between her legs and begged him to finish, but as her senses cleared, she realized he was right. If he made love to her, he might destroy her.

Still panting, she eased into his chest and held his hand. "You did the right thing," she whispered.

He grasped her hand fiercely. "I'm sorry—but I can't risk harming you. You mean too much to me."

"Just hold me tight." She kept her voice steady, but frustration lay beneath it. As Dimitri embraced her, she tried to hide her spilling tears. *My God*, Alba thought. *What must he think of me?* Had she spawned distaste in him?

A moment ago, it was as if she'd slipped into another person's body—the body of a brazen woman. By throwing her inhibitions out the window and thrusting aside inexperience, it was she who had become the seducer.

Was this how finely mannered women in the reign of Queen Victoria acted behind closed doors? Alba could only wonder. Self-degradation raced through her, until another explanation rose to mind. Had Dimitri "bewitched" her, as Mrs. T. put it?

If so, she didn't care. Intimacy with Dimitri was like being on a heavenly cloud. And as she lay listening to his frantic heartbeat, she suspected very few women would complain about being hypnotized that way.

Dimitri tilted her face up to meet his. When she stared into his astonishing gold-flecked pupils, he stole her breath away. Lying still, she studied his perfectly set features—until her gaze reached his blood-encrusted mouth. With a wrench of her stomach, she reminded herself that Dimitri was a vampire. No doubt his fangs had dropped during their intense lovemaking, slicing his lip. And while he hadn't hurt her, she'd been lucky. *This time.*

She sat up. As she retrieved Dimitri's shirt from the edge of the bed and pulled it on, Dimitri looked up at her. Flat on his back, he had his muscular arms spread wide while his flaccid penis curled to the side above a bent knee.

"Do you feel like talking?" she asked.

He nodded.

Tonight Dimitri had captured her heart inside a special box no one else would ever unlock. But she was desperate to know everything about him—including what it felt like to be a vampire. Sliding alongside him, Alba propped her head on one elbow. "In those years we were separated," she began, "what was your life like?"

"To answer your question, Barrister Spencer," he said, grinning charmingly, "my life was rather boring, actually. After the ever-generous Dr. Rhessa helped initiate my education as a doctor, I put my nose to the grindstone. I studied day and night, working my way through university to pay for my books, clothing, et cetera."

"So you were extremely focused."

"Yes. But as I plowed through my internship in Edinburgh, I never erased your image from my mind. Even when I accepted my first post at the hospital in Wales, I did it for you."

She smiled. "And that's when you became a fabulously wealthy surgeon."

"I wouldn't say 'fabulously' wealthy. It is the beginning of my career—and I'm afraid I extended myself quite a bit when I bought this house." He rolled to face her.

"Why did you do that?" she asked. "You didn't have to impress anyone here in London."

"I felt the need to impress you," he said softly.

She reached for his hand. It felt cold yet strong inside hers. "All that impresses me is your spirit, Dimitri. You've always been the bravest, most determined person I know. I was devastated when you left me."

"I didn't leave you. I told you, the message I entrusted to Dr. Rhessa never made it past Ileana. You ran away soon after that and I began to search for you."

"Thank you for not giving up on me. But it seems I haven't escaped Ileana's reach completely." She cast her eyes away as a pit of terror swelled in her stomach. "Will she stop at nothing to destroy my happiness?"

"Some people revel in others' misery," he said. "I'm afraid Ileana is one of those evil people."

She hesitated. "You suggested that we go somewhere together. I'm ready to leave London."

He traced the outline of her face, and adoration sparkled in his citrine eyes. "I'll take you back to Romania. I keep a leased flat there. It's small and a bit seedy, but we can drink wine and stay up all night long. It shall be the perfect place to hide."

"How long will we have to hide?" Alba asked.

"Until I can destroy Ileana," Dimitri said grimly. "She's a witch who doesn't deserve to live."

"I suppose she is no match for you—your being a vampire, I mean." She knew she hadn't broached the subject very gracefully.

He snaked a hand around her waist and caressed her skin through the shirt. "I'm no fool. It upsets you that I've become a creature of the night."

"'Upset' is hardly the word." She frowned. "Part of me is terrified that you'll bite me."

"You tempt me beyond description, but I shall resist the urge to drink from you with my entire being."

"Then . . . you cannot guarantee you won't make me a victim?"

"You have my word that I'll use all of my powers to keep you out of danger."

She squeezed his hand and nuzzled closer. "I want to know what being a vampire is like."

He looked uncomfortable. He removed his hand from her waist and stared at her with haunted eyes. "It is hardly fun and games. But I'm responsible for only one man's death here in London."

"Who?" Alba asked pointedly.

"A vagabond. I killed him before I learned to completely control my thirst."

She gasped. "Are you speaking of the degenerate they found behind McGroder's Pub?"

He nodded.

"I thought Simona killed him." The confirmation that Dimitri had murdered someone stabbed her with alarm. Meanwhile, Mrs. T.'s suggestion that Jack the Ripper began his killing spree when Dimitri arrived in London sprang to mind.

"Although Simona has more willpower to stop drinking than I, I'm sure she has purposefully killed people since she arrived here. It's best that she's dead," Dimitri said as he flung back the bedsheet. Securing a dressing gown, he padded to the hearth.

While Dimitri busied himself with making a fire, Alba drew her knees to her chest and rocked back and forth on the bed. *Am I really willing to leave everything behind and go back to Romania?*

It would change her life as she knew it. Then again, she would have no life if Ileana succeeded in her evil calculations.

Flames began to crackle and Alba joined Dimitri on the plush carpet. She fastened a few of the shirt's buttons while he stirred the fire. A moment later he turned to face her.

"Alba," he said, "as you've guessed, I cannot guarantee your happiness or well-being. Ours would be an unconventional love affair. You will have to live the life of the night if we're to be together. When I sell this house, I won't have to work for a while. That way I can take care of you . . . protect you."

She broke eye contact with him and stared into the dancing fire. "I don't need you to protect me from anything but Ileana."

"I'm also here to prevent you from becoming a vampire," he reminded her.

"I have a feeling neither of us has control over that," she said despondently.

Cupping her chin, Dimitri directed her gaze back to his face. "You may be right. But you're a strong woman—it's one of the things I love about you. I hope you can summon that strength when you glimpse into the dark side. I'm afraid it's a mortifying place."

"I've seen Ileana use black magic firsthand. I agree. It was beyond frightening."

He paused, stroking her loose tresses. "Before you're to be safe with me, you must do something first."

"What?" she asked.

"You must let go of the past."

"I'll try," she whispered.

His fingers trailed along the line of Alba's jaw and her pulse leapt. She didn't know what had come over her, but her passion for Dimitri was insatiable. Without thinking, she slid her hands against his silk dressing robe trimmed with diamond stitching and let her hands drop farther. When she untied its sash and pushed it open, she glimpsed his rock-hard arousal.

"You drive me to insanity," he murmured in his velvety Romanian accent. "But we cannot make love."

"I'll take my chances." Unable to stop herself, she arched against Dimitri's chest, pressing her mouth to his with a blazing kiss. Desire waved through Alba with the force of a hundred galloping horses. Dimitri's hands drifted to her chest, where they formed half-circles beneath her breasts. While she whimpered with pleasure, he fondled and squeezed the spheres though the shirt.

As his thumbs whispered across Alba's erect nipples, she gripped his arms and urged him to slide his touch lower. Her center was already damp and as the scents of their arousal mixed, she licked her lips. Dimitri purred. He stroked her clitoris, and as he probed her creases patiently, expertly, the sensation built Alba's desire. She stole a look at Dimitri. While he pleasured her, the shadows thrown off by the lit hearth accentuated his lean cheeks and carved jawline. Smiling like a mischievous cat, he delved his fingers deeper inside her core. Alba sucked in a breath. As he caressed her center, he claimed her mouth with a hot kiss and she climaxed against his hand. When he pulled her swiftly to a standing position, his dressing robe fell away and she stared at his glorious body gleaming in the firelight. His wide shoulders complimented the narrowness of his hips and his pectoral muscles moved like molten metal as he urged her against the wall. With her back to him, Alba wondered how attractive her bare bottom looked from this angle. But as he began to knead it with moans of pleasure, it seemed that Dimitri didn't mind the image at all.

"You have an ass fit for a queen," he whispered gruffly into her ear. Pressing his arousal against her buttocks, he covered her with his solid body, crushing her flat against the wall. He skimmed his hands over her derrière and her eyes widened as he touched her in a place she thought women were never touched. Hardly breathing, she closed her eyes and enjoyed the sensation of his skilled hands roaming her body. He slithered a hand under her shirt and cradled her breasts again. Then with his other hand, he guided his penis into her folds, stroking her dampness with its tip. Dimitri nudged her hair over her shoulder and ran his tongue along the column of her neck.

"You are so beautiful—" His voice was raw with desire.

Alba could feel his energy radiating behind her. *Can he smell my blood? Will it lead him to violence?*

Her eyes flitted to a silver sconce that lined the wall over the hearth. Her distorted reflection shone back, but Dimitri's did not. To see if his fangs were bared, Alba whipped her head around. Dimitri had a firm grasp on her hips, while his neck and head were bent back in ecstasy. He raised his head to meet her gaze and she saw the sharp points of his incisors glimmer in the firelight.

Terrified, Alba broke away. Her heart pounding incessantly, she thrust him a look tainted with fear. Still, he encircled her waist and tugged her closer. And while he embraced her, all she could envision were his fangs. Suddenly, she regretted playing with fire.

"I . . . I should be getting back to the dormitory," she stammered.

"I'm sorry, Alba," Dimitri said breathlessly. "It seems that I cannot control myself around you."

"No, it's my fault." She paused as she squirmed farther away from him. "I kept pressing you."

Lust still lit his eyes. She watched his chest heave up and down with the heaviness of arousal and his fists curl into tight balls. He spun away from her while he tried to compose himself. "I will get you home," he said, frowning. "Then you must gather your things. When the sun rises, you should make arrangements to leave for Romania tomorrow night."

Alba said nothing. How could they go away together and endure the torture of never being intimate? A wave of angst spilled over her as they dressed. Although she held on to Dimitri tightly during their flight back to Bloomsbury, she was grateful when they touched down on the dormitory ledge. As he leaned in for a heated kiss, he reminded her that he would come for her the following evening. She gave him a nervous smile and slipped silently back into her bedroom. All she could think of was that tonight had been an over-whelming paradox. She'd experienced extraordinary fulfillment— yet she was more frightened than she had ever been.

Damn you, Dimitri.

Chapter Twenty-Three

Dimitri felt drugged. Alba had intoxicated him with her sensuality and he could barely think straight. As he made his way back home, her luscious image became fixated in his mind. Even the crisp night air did nothing to clear his head.

No doubt she'd seen his monstrous fangs. The truth was, Alba had fueled his thirst to an extraordinary degree—and he'd come within inches of biting her neck. Luckily, he had restrained himself, but it'd been hell.

Was going away with her really a good idea? Because he was a *mulo*, his thirst was building more than he thought possible, and he was starting to second-guess the decision.

He'd almost reached his house after escorting Alba home when he decided he would have time to feed and make a medical round in Whitechapel. After securing his Gladstone bag, he traveled to the sooty East End. The quiet streets attested to the fact that most of the city was terrified by Jack the Ripper's murders. *Will I be able to find a victim from whom I can drink?*

As luck would have it, he spotted two flamboyant prossers in the distance. The women were busy parading their bodies shamelessly beneath a gaslight. Obviously, they didn't have the luxury of fearing the Ripper.

Dimitri approached the younger prostitute. Wearing a mini-bowler hat and a choker with a flower on it, the fair-haired girl sauntered toward him. While they exchanged mutual smiles, they walked arm in arm to the rear of a tailor shop. Dimitri pinned her gently against the wall, and when he slid in closer, he mesmerized her with his stare. Feeding with no resistance, he listened to the girl's pleasurable moans. Afterward, he took off unnoticed as she melted to the ground in a trance.

Alba would despise me if she had seen the attack. In fact, he hated himself for it as well. But drinking was a necessity. Without his daily dose of blood, he would perish. What good would he be to Alba then?

Dimitri reached Miller's Court, where he proceeded to make his rounds. In a series of house calls, he checked on ailing prossers and aged tenants inside their tiny doss-house rooms. Glad to leave the depressing rookeries behind, he stopped inside the East End clinic next. There he treated a downtrodden man who was suffering from the flu, delivered a baby, and treated an elderly woman's painful arthritis.

At three-thirty A.M., he returned to his house on Park Lane. Too tired to bathe, he removed his waistcoat and donned his dressing robe over his bloody clothes. Entering the drawing room in a relaxed state, he drank two glasses of wine and got even sleepier. Too fatigued to go to the basement, he settled on the sofa, where he drifted off.

A banging at the door split the dark, dead silence of Dimitri's sleep.

"It's the police, Dr. Griffin. Open the door!"

Dimitri tried to sit up, but daylight was upon him. His eyes darted to Jochen, who appeared in the parlor's archway. His servant cum friend was fully dressed—and didn't look as though he'd been awakened by the banging.

There was another series of furious knocks.

"Shall I open the door?" Jochen asked as he helped Dimitri to an upright position.

Sunlight bored through the window, and though it hadn't landed on Dimitri directly, he felt disoriented and weighted by its haze.

"Did they say they were the police?" Dimitri slurred his words as he nearly fell back to sleep.

"Yes," Jochen said. "I think we should let them in."

"Of course," Dimitri murmured.

Jochen moved to the ornate entryway with Dimitri slumped against him. A police chief had his grim face pressed to the glass door panes and his fist raised to knock again.

"Dr. Griffin," the gentleman said breathlessly once he and two additional police officers entered in a rush. "My name is Chief Constable Ethan Prindle . . . of the Commercial Street Police Station. I'm here to inform you that there's been another grisly murder in Whitechapel."

Dimitri's gut surged. He'd been in Whitechapel last night. Had the fair-haired prosser died? Had someone seen him drink her blood? No, he'd been very careful . . .

His stare shifted to Jochen. Perhaps the police were here to collect him. Or better yet, maybe this was all a dream.

"A prostitute named Mary Kelly was killed in her house in Dorset last night," Prindle informed him. "Her mutilated body was found at ten-thirty this morning."

Christ! What time is it? "That is most unfortunate," Dimitri said. "But what does it have to do with me?"

"A man fitting your description was seen entering Mary Kelly's house." The constable inhaled. "Dr. Drake Griffin, we are taking you in for questioning in the murder of Mary Kelly, also known as Marie Jeanette Kelly. Take him away, boys."

The brawny officers began to escort Dimitri out of the house.

"How dare you!" Dimitri cried as he wriggled in their grasp. The sash of his robe unfurled and his robe fell open. "You have the wrong man!"

"Jesus, Mary, and Joseph!" the taller of the two officers said in an Irish lilt. "Just look at his bloody clothes!"

"Wot for," the other officer cried. "Listen to 'is speech as well. And I can smell his breath. This man is drunk!"

Prindle surged forward. "I hereby arrest you for the cold-blooded murder of Mary Kelly."

Dimitri resisted, but in his weakened condition, he was no match for the policemen. "My cloak!" he bellowed to Jochen. "Get it and throw it over my head!"

Jochen moved as if he had wings and did as Dimitri instructed. As Dimitri was led outdoors, his legs gave way. The officers maneuvered him toward the police wagon with difficulty. One of the officers drew his club and struck Dimitri in the knee full force. Jerking forward in pain, Dimitri sank lower to the ground. Despite the agony that radiated through his body, he continued to resist the burly men. Then he felt the crack of a club at the base of his skull.

Before he lost conscious, he murmured to Jochen, "Get Alba."

A pot of chamomile tea sent forth a calming aroma as Alba sat at the kitchen table. It was early morning and the dormitory was quiet—as the girls and Mrs. T. were at the ballet studio and Justina had slinked away to a quiet nook.

Alba poured herself some of the tea and then took a sip. Thank God she'd stolen back here unseen and unheard last night. It had been twelve-thirty in the morning; she'd noticed the time on her night-table clock.

She was about to drink more of the hot tea when she heard a knock on the door. Puzzled, she opened it and saw Jochen Rhessa standing before her. A troubled look waved over his blotchy face.

"Jochen?" Alba became even more puzzled when her gaze drifted to the bundle of fabric he had clasped in his hands.

"Miss Zăpăda." He spoke in rapid Romanian. "I'm sorry to disturb you . . ."

"It's all right, Jochen. What is it?"

"It's Dimitri. I mean Dr. Griffin," he stammered as his cheeks flushed. "He's been arrested."

"My God!" Panic squeezed Alba's heart. "Why?" was all she could ask.

"There was another East End murder last night. It seems the police have mistaken him for Jack the Ripper!"

She hadn't yet read this morning's newspaper. "Please. Come in." She motioned Jochen toward the kitchen.

They sat at the round table where Alba urged her fellow Romanian to tell her everything. Jochen recounted the events of the arrest in a fast flow of words—after which Alba leaned back in her chair, completely astounded.

"And you say the police claimed this Mary Kelly was mutilated—like the four other victims Jack the Ripper destroyed?"

Jochen gulped and nodded his response.

"What time did Dimitri get home last night?"

"I don't know. It was my night off and I'd just gotten home myself when I found him asleep on the sofa." He paused. "He asked me to come to you for help, Miss Zăpăda."

Dimitri will need a barrister. The thought gripped Alba like a tight vise. She cleared her throat. "You may call me Alba," she said kindly, though she didn't smile. How could she under the circumstances? She hated to think what Dimitri had done after he'd dropped her off at the dormitory. When they had parted ways, he still seemed fully charged and on the verge of losing control. Then she chastised herself. *Don't rush to conclusions. As difficult as it may be, I must believe the best scenario, not the worst.*

"The police are mistaken," she said hurriedly. "I'm sure of it."

"I think you're right," Jochen responded. "But how do you explain the witness who saw Dimitri enter Mary Kelly's house?"

Her stomach clenched and she looked away to hide her alarm.

"Will you come to the police station?" Jochen asked.

"Of course." She rose and pulled on her overcoat. "What are you holding?"

"Dimitri's clothes. He was taken away in his dressing gown."

Alba's stomach fluttered. *His forest-green dressing gown trimmed in diamond stitching.* She knew it well—and the image of him in it sped her heart. The vision of him baring his fangs had terrified her, but he still held a sacred place in her heart. And now he was alone in a dank prison cell.

Did he feed last night?

"Very well." Her voice cracked with emotion. "Let's go."

Chapter Twenty-Four

Snip. Snip. Snip.

Ileana Zăpăda watched another rose tip drift to the ground. In the glass-lined conservatory of the Kensington house, she'd been cutting up flowers for hours.

Beauty in its purest form must be destroyed. Whispering the motto she lived by, she eyed the basket of roses Giselle had provided for her amusement. Now, in the afternoon haze, she plucked another flower from it. With an insistent chop of a pruner, she severed the head off the cherry rose and reveled in its wilted state.

This type of botanical demolition helped Ileana think. And following the images she'd seen in her magic mirror this morning, she had a great deal of thinking to do.

Ileana had watched it all in the mirror: Alba swallowing the headache pill she'd managed to slip in and taint moments before that twittering Mrs. T. gave it to her. Dimitri whisking Alba to his Park Lane home like a valiant knight and his vow to protect Alba. She had even seen their enflamed lovemaking—which had been fueled by the sexual confidence the pill provoked in Alba.

Still, Alba hadn't coaxed Dimitri to destroy her—and Ileana threw her head back in laughter at the realization. *Perhaps she's not as beautiful as everyone says she is.*

No doubt Alba thought Dimitri had cast a spell over her, but she was wrong. Ileana's lust spell had worn off the same way a conventional pill stops working. But Alba was none the wiser.

Damn Dimitri. He has too much willpower for his own good. No doubt he'd learned to resist much and do without more as a filthy Gypsy.

Refusing to rely on his *mulo* powers any longer, Ileana had fixed him. She'd gone to the police, claiming that she saw Dimitri solicit a prosser in Whitechapel last night. What's more, she had stated that she saw him enter Mary Kelly's house. When Ileana gave the police chief a detailed description of him, the chief had believed her.

Now the fact that Alba failed to prompt Dimitri to destroy her in bed didn't matter. It was all too delicious for words.

Giselle appeared just then to scoop the roses off the floor.

"Leave them!" Ileana thundered. "I like to watch them shrivel and die."

The hunched servant fled the conservatory, wide-eyed, while Ileana's thoughts turned back to her stepdaughter. "I had the chance to kill Alba many times since I arrived in London," she murmured to herself. "But I want the girl to suffer before she dies. And watching her true love deteriorate in prison before he faces the gallows will do the trick nicely."

Ileana butchered another rose as her cheeks heated. *If Alba doesn't kill herself from grief after Dimitri hangs, then she shall die at my hand.*

But I must be smart about it.

Abandoning the dead roses, she swept upstairs and stepped in front of the enchanted mirror she'd had mounted on the wall. As she raised one eyebrow at her pristine reflection, she noticed the tiniest of wrinkles across her forehead. Her eyes flashed in anger and her expression became shadowed as the mirror rippled and waved.

My beauty must never fade.

"Mirror, mirror, on the wall, who is the fairest of them all?" she asked.

"Today you are the fairest, my lady," came the imperious voice.

"Today?" Ileana growled. "What do you mean *today*? What does the future hold?"

"Your appearance will wane with time. It has begun to do so already. But your stepdaughter's beauty will never change."

Outraged, Ileana picked up a poker. She smashed the mirror into bits and shouted, "I will never be outshone by Alba. *Never!*"

The dimly lit corridor inside Newgate Prison glowed a depressing shade of green. Shuddering against the draft that ran along the hallway, Alba drew the collar of her half cloak together. The institution smelled of violence and tragedy. But worst of all, it smelled of stolen freedom.

Dimitri.

How was he faring without his casket—or whatever he was accustomed to sleeping in? Was he getting his much-needed blood supply?

Alba envisioned him wasting away in his cell, shriveling from the sunlight that streamed into it, and the mental image sent bile to her throat.

Pushing away the vision, she tried to focus on why she was here. She was desperate to know if Dimitri was guilty—if he was capable of butchering this woman known as Mary Kelly. Of course she'd learned in law school that she must not ask a client anything point-blank, so she needed to coax the information out of him.

Nerves racing, Alba was shown into a windowless room that contained nothing but a table and two chairs. The guard who had escorted her from the registration gate said nothing as he pointed to one of the chairs. Alba sat as instructed and fiddled with her gloves once she'd removed them. Staring at the empty chair across from her, she grew frightened at the idea of seeing Dimitri. No matter how much she tried to erase the vision of him as a vampire from her mind, she was fixated on how violent he could become.

A gate clicked open and he was thrown into the room with her. They locked eyes. In his stare, Alba saw a startling humility.

"Alba," he said softly. He sat and started to reach across the table for her hand, but then he retracted it. *No physical contact allowed.*

When Dimitri finally spoke again, his eyes were shadowed from either pain or hunger. It was impossible for Alba to tell which.

"Thank you for coming," he said. "As Jochen no doubt told you, I've been arrested for the murder of a prostitute in Whitechapel," he said. "The murder took place last night."

"Were you in the East End?"

"Yes."

Her throat constricted.

"But I didn't pay a visit to Mary Kelly."

Alba drew back, her heart pounding. "Are you certain you didn't go inside her house?"

"Yes, I'm certain. She wasn't listed on my scheduled rounds. Alba, I didn't kill her. You have to believe me!"

"Let's not get ahead of ourselves, Dimitri," Alba said as calmly as she could. "We need to summon Mr. Rollingsworth and Teddy. They will take you on as a client."

"No!" Dimitri's tone was sharp. "I want you to defend me. Teddy and his father may assist you, but you know me better than anybody. That means that you have the best chance of freeing me. And I need to get out of here—to protect you from Ileana."

Ileana. Alba didn't know what she was more afraid of, her conniving stepmother, Dimitri's sharp fangs, or defending him and failing.

"Dimitri," she said carefully. "I've only acted as a barrister once and, unfortunately, that experience left a bad taste in my mouth. Tabitha Crowe will hang because of me. I don't think I can be responsible for someone's fate again." She paused. "Especially if that someone is *you.*"

Alba had the sudden urge to leap out of the chair and flee the room. It was painful to see Dimitri suffer, but more than that, she couldn't bear to see him face the gallows. *Why did you come to London, Dimitri? You should have stayed in Romania.*

"You can't be blamed for that woman's death," he insisted. "She brought the verdict upon herself. But you feel for her because you're a good person, Alba. That is why I believe in you. Now it's time you believed in me."

She broke her gaze from his. "Tabitha Crowe followed her heart and did what she thought was right. But I don't know if you are telling me everything, Dimitri. Did you go to Whitechapel to feed last night?"

"Yes."

"There, you see? We couldn't possibly use that sort of testimony in your defense." Her voice faltered. "I hate to say it, but I don't know if a jury will side with you."

He looked agonized. "You're giving up on me that easily? After all these years, I never gave up on you."

Alba's heart felt as if was breaking. "But a witness is able to put you at the scene of the crime."

"Blast it to hell!" Dimitri said as he pounded his fists on the table. Even the officer in the corner jumped at the noise. "I don't know who attested to that—or why that person is lying through their teeth."

Alba pulled in a breath. "You may be charged with all the crimes of this infamous Jack the Ripper, Dimitri. What's more, I can't help but think of the Egyptian amulet's curse. If I don't defend you effectively and you hang, I may kill myself afterward from grief."

"That's another reason I need to get out of here and find the bracelet!"

She remained quiet. He shot her a pained look. "So that is your answer?" he asked. "You refuse to defend me?"

She nodded as tears pooled in her eyes. "I know Mr. Rollingsworth will get you exonerated."

"If that's the case," Dimitri said grimly, "this may be the last time we ever speak. Listen to me carefully. I know you are at odds with many things, but let your mind take you back to our child-hood—to when we loved each other unconditionally. Like a fool, I put you in harm's way during that night in the graveyard. I swore I would never do that again. Now your stepmother wishes you dead, and I am the only one who can defeat her powers of black magic. You know that. But more than that, you know that I love you and that I adore you. And that my heart would never lead me to savagely kill any woman for the sake of violence."

Hot tears stained her face. Dimitri was right. Somehow she knew he would never murder for the sake of vehemence. What's more, they were in this together. If Alba wanted their precious bond to remain intact, she mustn't be afraid of defending Dimitri. She was a capable woman, and while she didn't know what the future held, she knew Dimitri wouldn't survive in prison much longer if he wasn't freed soon.

She had no choice but to defend him. Reaching across the table, she squeezed his hand despite the strict instructions she'd been given. "I love you, Dimitri," she said. "And by God, I will get you cleared of this heinous crime."

Chapter Twenty-Five

Alba grabbed her reticule and left Newgate in a rush. She hailed a hansom and instructed its driver to take her to the Rollingsworth house.

As the carriage rolled forward, her heartbeat quickened. She hadn't seen Teddy since Simona had attacked him, nor had they discussed his marriage proposal. *How is his present physical and mental state?* She could only hope Teddy would agree to see her.

Reaching over, she patted the handbag perched against her leg. She could feel the outline of the ring box Teddy had given her beneath its lining. It was about time she returned it to him—and though she was going to break his heart with her answer, she couldn't possibly ask Teddy to help her in court without clearing the air between them first.

The marble façade of the Rollingsworth home glittered like a frosted white wedding cake in the two o'clock sun. Hands shaking, Alba knocked on the door and waited. Reeves answered her knocking in full livery and eyed Alba with relief.

"Good afternoon, Miss Spencer."

"Good afternoon." She forced a smile.

"Please come in."

"Thank you."

She stepped into the foyer and handed Reeves her coat. He did a little bow before he hung the garment on a coatrack.

"Young Mr. Rollingsworth has been asking for you, Miss

Spencer," he said in a low whisper. "He is still very weak, but he's insistent that he pay you a visit."

"Where is he? In his rooms?"

"No. He's settled on the sofa in the back parlor. I shall announce you first, then I will come and fetch you."

She nodded and Reeves disappeared. Her gaze wandered to the drawing room—where Dimitri's birthday celebration had taken place. What a tangled mess their lives had become since then.

A moment later the aging butler came shuffling down the corridor. "Mr. Rollingsworth will see you now, Miss Spencer."

Alba followed Reeves through the portrait-lined hallway to a room she'd never been in before. Teddy was on a horsehair sofa, just as Reeves had described. Sitting upright, he was clutching a plaid blanket that covered his legs. Because he was wrapped in his bedclothes minus his usual neck tie, Alba could see the red, swollen bite marks Dimitri had left on his neck.

"Alba!" Teddy's pale face lit up while she crossed the room.

"Teddy," she said softly. She knelt before him, and when she stared into his bloodshot eyes, she felt sick with the knowledge that she was about to cause him more pain. "How are you feeling?"

"I'm much better. Miss Bedford has been attending to me quite diligently."

Mavis Bedford. Despite her position as a nurse, the woman was judgmental and unfriendly. Those qualities made her someone Alba didn't wish to see.

"I'm glad you're receiving fine care." She gave Teddy a small smile—which she dropped a moment later.

"I'd hoped to see you when I awoke from my stupor," he said. "Miss Bedford told me I was murmuring odd things . . ."

"You didn't say anything startling, I assure you." She paused. "Do you remember what happened inside the British Museum?"

His face turned red. "I bloody well remember that cryptic exhibition room—and proposing to you on one knee. After that, my mind is a blank."

Alba gave an inward sigh of relief. "I feel terrible for suggesting we go there. But I still have the ring you presented me with, Teddy. We shall get to that in a minute, but first I want to talk about your neck. Do you know what happened to your neck?"

"Miss Bedford said that after you brought me home you claimed I'd been attacked by a bat."

She nodded and reached for his hand. He looked different this afternoon. With his mussed hair and unshaven jaw, he appeared ruggedly handsome—a style she didn't recognize. "I have no idea how, but a bat streamed into the exhibition room."

"The same bat that attacked me outside the Hotel Metropole?"

"I think so." She paused. "You tried to fight it off, but it dove in and bit you. You were very weak, so Miss Bedford performed a blood transfusion."

"You gave me your blood?" Teddy asked.

"No," Alba replied. "Miss Bedford did. I was too weak because I fell and hit my head while we were trying to shoo the bat away."

"My darling. Are you all right?"

"I suffered a nasty cut, but I'm fine."

Teddy rearranged his position, but he still looked uncomfortable. When he snatched a glance at her left hand, she could tell that he wanted to broach the subject of their engagement.

"You say you have the ring I presented you with?" he asked in a hoarse voice.

"Yes." She removed the small box from her handbag and set it in his lap.

"The fact that you're not wearing it gives me my answer."

"Teddy." She could barely get the words out. "I'm so sorry. I want to love you that way, but my heart belongs to another."

"Let me guess." Fury shook his body and his eyes housed a dark storm. "You're in love with Dimitri. That bastard! He stole you from me!"

"It's no one's fault. Dimitri and I have a history together." She looked away, unable to bear the pain in Teddy's face. "Sometimes ties from the past are too strong to be broken."

"That's hogwash, Alba. Just say it. Even if you take Dimitri out of the equation, you will never feel for me what I feel for you."

Harold Rollingsworth entered the room. "What's all the fuss about?"

"Mr. Rollingsworth." Alba stood awkwardly.

"Thank you for paying Teddy a visit, Alba. He's been most distressed in your absence."

"I'm fine, Father," Teddy said coldly. "Remember, I am a big boy."

"Indeed you are." Harold put his hands on his hips and gave his son a small smile. "Although I miss tossing you up in the air as a wee toddler."

"Father . . ." Teddy's voice was a mixture of embarrassment and sternness.

"I don't mean to interrupt your conversation, but I have some grave news." Harold clasped his hands together. "Alba, your friend Drake Griffin has been arrested for murder."

Teddy shot Alba an alarmed look. "What the devil?"

She wound the strap of her handbag around her fingers nervously. "Yes, I know. I came to tell Teddy, but I haven't gotten to that part yet."

"Please, Alba. Be seated." Harold gestured to a winged-back chair situated near the sofa. He remained standing while she sat and turned her attention to Teddy.

"Dimitri has been arrested for the murder of a prostitute in Whitechapel," she said. "His valet contacted me, and when I went to the prison, he asked me to represent him."

"And you said?" Teddy's tone rang with sarcasm.

"I accepted. But I cannot do it alone. I think Dimitri is innocent, but I need the assistance of you and your father."

"Of course we shall help you, my dear," Harold chimed in. "I have met this Drake Griffin on a number of occasions, and I say he could not have butchered that woman."

"Don't expect me to be a part of your team," Teddy said. "I'm still very weak."

"You'll be fine, young man." His father's timbre was solemn. "Buck up. This is your friend we are talking about—and I wouldn't expect any less than your finest work in court."

As Alba observed the exchange between Harold Rollingsworth and his son, she knew how much Teddy didn't want to disappoint his father.

"Very well," Teddy said. "Count me in."

Alba nearly cried out with relief, until she remembered that the Rollingsworths had no idea that Dimitri was a vampire. How was she going to proceed without making them privy to the fact?

Chapter Twenty-Six

The newspaper headlines the next day were horrific.

St. Bart Surgeon Jack the Ripper
Leather Apron Has Been Caught!
Local Surgeon Drake Griffin Arrested in
Whitechapel Murders

Alba tried her best not to listen to the newsboys on the corner as they shouted the slanderous lies. She dodged the media circus outside the Inns of Court as she raced into her office and shut the door behind her. She had stayed awake all night, mulling over the time line associated with each of the Ripper's crimes. She had also constructed the angle she would use in Dimitri's defense. She would play up the notion that Dimitri was a surgeon, a man who had devoted his life to helping people. Yes, he possessed medical knowledge—a prerequisite that lent the Ripper the ability to kill in the fashion he had—but Dimitri didn't have the moral fiber of a murderer. He wasn't inherently bad, but something told her Jochen Rhessa was.

She spun her chair around and looked out the window. As lazy waves lapped against the Thames's embankment, the wheels in her head started to spin. Jochen was an outsider, a man who hadn't the grades or the bedside manner to become a doctor. He'd always been odd, and as Alba remembered, Jochen had turned to stone when his mother abandoned him. He had retreated into a deep depression, much like a turtle seeks solace inside his shell. Jochen's father was kind, but it hadn't been enough. Perhaps Jochen's temperamental personality and the abandonment he suffered had caused him to resent women altogether.

Jack the Ripper certainly resented women.

Hope began to build in Alba's chest. If she could *prove* that someone else was the killer, Dimitri would have to be acquitted.

The door burst open and in walked Teddy. Still unshaven, he swayed toward Alba. The nearer he came, the more she could tell he'd been drinking.

"Good morning, my beautiful Alba. Alas, I have no roses to give you today."

She flung him a disapproving look.

"I'm glad you're here and not running off to see your true love." He slurred his syllables.

"Stop it, Teddy."

"You're right. I really should end my infatuation with you. There is no time to indulge ourselves in petty fantasies. After all, it's time to save the life of the man who ruined my life!"

Alba bit back a harsh string of words. "Maybe you should go home and sober up."

He leaned his powerful form over her desk. His breath reeked of whiskey. She jerked her head away.

"I've been hitting the bottle, it's true," he said. "Who wouldn't? I just lost the love of my life to my friend. A friend who may or may not be a fiend."

"Dimitri isn't a fiend!"

"No?" Teddy asked mockingly. "Remember, people say he's a vampire. A bloodsucking monster."

"What are you talking about?" Alba said as nonchalantly as she could.

"Come now." Teddy frowned. "You saw the teeth marks on my neck."

She leapt to her feet, knocking all the papers from her desk. "Teddy Rollingsworth. You know I don't believe in vampires. If you go home at once, I won't tell your father about your appalling behavior."

He slid closer to her, his eyes glazed over with desire. The scent of liquor wafted across her face and her stomach constricted.

"Scold me like a schoolboy again," he whispered.

She slapped his face. "You're disgusting."

He stepped away in surprise, but the action seemed to sober him up. "My God, Alba. I'm sorry. I'm acting like a pathetic, broken-hearted fool."

She looked down, her cheeks hot with anger. "I forgive you, Teddy." If she was going to get Dimitri out of prison, she needed his assistance.

"No. I truly want you to accept my apology," he stammered.

"Accepted."

"I cannot believe I behaved that way. I'm so sorry."

Tears rimmed her eyes. "I'm sorry too. For hurting you."

She hesitated at first, then allowed him to pull her into an embrace. "We've known each other much too long for this to affect our friendship," she said into his jacket.

He nodded. After clearing his throat, he pulled away and sank into the desk chair.

"Right then. How can I help?"

"I'm going to track Dimitri's whereabouts on the night of the murder," she answered as she tried to compose herself. "Can you find out where Dimitri's butler was on the same night?"

Teddy rubbed his temples. "Dimitri's butler?"

"Yes. He's an odd man by the name of Jochen Rhessa. Dimitri and I knew him in Romania, and he came to London around the time of the first Whitechapel murder."

"Do you think he could be the real killer?"

She gave him a steady glance. "I have a sneaking suspicion that he is."

For three weeks, Alba, Teddy, and Harold Rollingsworth worked on Dimitri's case, gathering information—or ammunition, as Harold liked to call it—from dawn to dusk. Meanwhile, Jochen brought packages to Dimitri upon Alba's instruction. The packages contained fruit and pastries and cheese—all secretly injected with animal blood. It was an odious task, but Jochen had agreed to do it. And when he delivered the food to Dimitri, it had passed inspection by way of Alba's idea: he was to offer one bloodless pastry to the guard upon each visit.

As the defense team learned that the court date had been set for December seventh, Alba grew anxious. Dimitri had begun to deteriorate in prison, and during one of her visits he claimed that the animal blood was barely sustaining his existence. His comment that it tasted nothing like human blood set her stomach roiling. She tried to banish the vision of him sliding close to a tawdry prostitute . . . bending her head to the side . . . piercing her jugular vein with his sharp fangs.

"All right, Dimitri," she said during her final visit to him before the trial started. They were sitting across from each other in a holding room. "It's time to go over your testimony."

"Why must I testify?" His eyes had receded into dark spheres. "I look like hell, and I'm turning into a madman in this infernal place. My appearance in the witness box can't possibly help matters."

"The jury wants to hear you say that you are innocent."

"I am innocent." He gathered her hand across the table. Luckily, the guard in the corner had fallen asleep in his chair. "I'm starved for you, Alba. I miss the scent of your hair—and the softness of your skin. I want to feel you touching me."

After he tugged open a few of his shirt buttons, he pressed her hand to his chest. He was thinner, but Alba could still feel the hard ridge of his muscles.

"Dimitri," she whispered in protest.

The guard's head came crashing forward and the action knocked him from his sleep. Alba snatched away her hand while the guard eyed them and crossed his arms.

Alba met Dimitri's gaze. "Tomorrow I want you to stay close to me in court and be responsive to what I tell you. The most significant thing you can portray is your sensitivity to women."

Dimitri nodded. "Who will be your opponent?"

"A barrister named George Hargraves."

"Is he any good?"

"Unfortunately, he is a piranha."

The possibility that Dimitri Grigorescu was the gruesome Whitechapel murderer initiated talk of the trial of the century. In turn, the frenzy disseminated into an astounding event. On the first day of the trial, cameras flashed, scribblers pushed and shoved each other furiously, and a full-blown audience of news seekers circled the building like vultures homing in on their last meal.

Inside there wasn't a seat to be had in the gallery. Heart thrumming, Alba glanced at the curtains drawn over the windows. Luckily her request that the courtroom be darkened in light of "Dimitri's allergy to sunlight" had been accommodated. She didn't know if the shadows would cure the lethargy Dimitri suffered in the daytime, but she hoped for the best.

George Hargraves stood and the room quieted. He moved toward the twelve-member jury panel with a solemn expression. A large, arrogant man, he possessed a long chin disproportionate to his short forehead.

Alba sucked in a breath.

"Violence. Crime. Filth," he began. His dark brown eyes roved over Alba as if she were a first-year law student. "These are common sights in London's impoverished East End. Whitechapel is home to a maze of dank, dirty streets. It's a grim neighborhood, and perhaps that is why a sadistic killer chose it as his stomping ground. Eighty-thousand people, most of them unemployed, live in Whitechapel's rotten, reeking tenements. The residents of these slums are people with smallpox and hungry children who have nothing to eat but scraps. What's more, Whitechapel is home to countless single mothers ill with the knowledge that they'd do anything to break free of their pathetic social station."

Dimitri scowled as he sat beside Alba. It was obvious that he disliked Hargraves intensely. While his eyes followed the blustering barrister, she took a glance at his handcuffs. Not only did the shackles connect his hands, its chain bound him to the table. It made Alba wonder: If Dimitri were free of the cuffs, would he have the strength to evaporate into a blue mist and float out the window?

"We, as a society, must protect these unfortunate residents of our city," Hargraves continued. "Dr. Drake Griffin has been on the streets of Whitechapel often. He knows them well because the East End clinics are part of his rounds. In addition, the streets are elements of his duty as a surgeon at St. Bartholomew's Hospital."

All eyes turned to Dimitri. In response, he straightened his posture.

Hargraves paced in front of the jury. "But don't let Dr. Griffin's handsome, debonair appearance fool you. He has expert anatomical knowledge, just as the killer of Polly Nichols, Annie Chapman, Elizabeth Stride, Catherine Eddowes, and Mary Kelly displayed. This heartless murderer slit these women's throats before he tore out their organs and disemboweled them."

Gasps sounded from the gallery at the shocking description.

"Drake Griffin arrived in London from Wales just before the first Whitechapel murder was committed. And most importantly, gentlemen"—Hargraves looked directly into the jurors' eyes—"he was seen going into Mary Kelly's house on the night her body was ripped to shreds."

He paused for dramatic effect. "Thank you."

Alba felt like fleeing the courtroom. It was always her first instinct when a crisis arose. But Dimitri needed her. He was depending on her talent as a barrister, and she was going to prove his innocence in her own way.

"Gentlemen," she said, standing. "Everything my colleague, Mr. Hargraves, said was true."

Murmurs and gasps raced around the courtroom. Even Dimitri shot her a dubious look.

"It's true that the Whitechapel District is a horrific place—and that its unfortunate residents must be protected. It's also true that Dr. Griffin has a connection to the East End. But I say his connection to the murders is purely coincidental. It is sheer happenstance that he arrived in London when the Whitechapel killings began. And it's pure coincidence that he made his medical rounds in the East End on the night Mary Kelly lost her life."

She paused to verify that her statements had seized everyone's attention. They had.

"What's more, there is another explanation for the report someone made about my client going into Mary Kelly's house. I present to you the possibility that Mr. Griffin is being framed."

With that, she sat down and raised an eyebrow at Hargraves. After thrusting her a look that said, "I may have underestimated you," he swiveled away defiantly.

Chapter Twenty-Seven

The trial, which seemed to go on forever, was a terrible strain on everyone.

Alba had assumed she was well prepared, but everywhere she turned George Hargraves was there to counteract her theories. When she tried to convince the jury that the murders of Polly Nichols, Annie Chapman, Elizabeth Stride, Catherine Eddowes, and Mary Kelly weren't linked, Hargraves brought attention to the fact that all of them were perpetrated at night—and that they'd taken place on or close to a weekend.

Alba had countered with the fact that the murders must have been committed by someone with a steady weekday job that left them free on the weekends. In return, Hargraves fired back that the killer probably planned things that way to throw suspicion away from himself. To Alba's chagrin, the arrogant barrister also pointed out that Dimitri had been at work on the evening of the first two murders, but that he'd left the hospital early on those nights. And when the other murders had taken place, he wasn't at the hospital at all.

When Alba had brought up the three letters allegedly sent to the media from Jack the Ripper, Hargraves juxtaposed her notion that Dimitri couldn't have written them because they were inarticulate. He proposed that Dimitri was smart enough to try and confuse the authorities by an apparent lack of academics.

The witnesses didn't aid Alba's endeavors either. During her questioning of the police surgeon, she raised the detail that not all the murder victims were brutalized the same way. Some of the women's faces were mutilated, some were not. Some of them had certain organs removed, while some had not. The surgeon agreed, but then disintegrated her supposition by suggesting that the killer had been interrupted. He went on to say that he believed the murders were committed by one person because the victims' throats were cut from the left to the right—at precisely the same angle.

Exasperated, Alba watched as Hargraves pushed the defense's case to the edge. He proved that Dimitri was right-handed, that he possessed the kind of surgical knife used in the murders, and that the cessation of the Whitechapel murders coincided with his incarceration.

Finally, the day arrived for Dimitri to take the witness stand. On a positive note, the rumors that he was a vampire had been dispelled. (How could he have sustained the lengthy trial without drinking human blood?) What's more, the witness who'd seen him enter Mary Kelly's house had disappeared. Still, Alba and Harold Rollingsworth huddled anxiously together in the Old Bailey as a haggard Dimitri entered the courtroom. Moving as slowly as someone who'd been drugged, he took his place beside Alba. She had never seen him look so fatigued. He could barely keep his eyes open, and despite the fashionable clothes he was wearing, it appeared that he'd been stripped of all his resolve.

"Stay with me, Dimitri," she whispered. "This shall be over soon."

Just then, Teddy burst through the courtroom door and hastened to his father and Alba.

"I have something on Jochen Rhessa," he whispered to them. "We must ask for a delay and bring him in to testify."

Alba bolted out of her seat and addressed the Honorable Oliver Wentwood. "My lord, I must ask for a delay."

Wentwood, who had grown even more portly since Tabitha Crowe's trial, braided his hands over his huge belly. "May I ask your reason, Miss Spencer?"

"New information has come to light that shall aid in my client's defense, my lord. If you grant us time this morning, we will present you with solid evidence this afternoon."

Wentwood conversed with the other judges in a low tone. Then he nodded in concurrence. "You have piqued our interest, Miss Spencer. You shall have a four-hour continuance. But I daresay you've set high expectations for yourself."

"Understood, Your Honor." She watched the bailiff take Dimitri away and she couldn't help but wonder if he would survive the rest of the trial. She wondered the same for herself. Her nerves were shot and her lack of sleep was catching up with her, yet she knew her troubles paled in comparison to Dimitri's.

Stay strong.

Teddy helped her pack her papers inside her case. "Jochen is being held at Scotland Yard. I obtained a warrant for his arrest last night."

"On what charge?" she asked.

"He was seen in the East End on the night of Mary Kelly's murder." Teddy took in a breath. "In fact, he stepped out with Kelly's neighbor and friend, Dotty Malone. This Malone woman just came forward. She claims that Rhessa beat her—and she thinks he is capable of more than that."

Alba could taste victory on her tongue. She and Teddy made their way to the brick compound and asked to see Jochen. When Jochen was thrust into an interrogation room with them, Alba wrinkled her nose. She could smell liquor on his breath from across the table.

"Miss Zăpăda," Jochen began. He looked desperate and confused. "Why are you here? Can you help me?"

Alba glanced at Teddy, who gave her an encouraging nod. "As you know," she said, "I've been defending Dimitri. If the truth does not come out, he will hang for a murder he didn't commit."

It seemed to dawn on Jochen that they were there to interrogate him, and he became edgy. "Did that bitch talk?"

"Bitch?" Teddy repeated.

"Dotty Malone."

"Jochen." Alba scowled. "Miss Malone told the police that you were with her in Whitechapel on the night Mary Kelly was murdered."

"That whore doesn't know what she's talking about."

"Dotty Malone was a friend and neighbor of Mary Kelly, Jochen." She paused. "What aren't you telling us?"

His fleshy eyelids drooped and he slumped forward. He didn't say anything for a very long time.

Teddy leaned forward. His hulking shoulders formed an intimidating silhouette. "Rhessa. A man you've known for many years is about to face the gallows. If you tell us the truth now and testify in court, you might be granted some leniency."

Jochen's bloodshot eyes darted from Teddy to Alba. "I didn't kill Mary Kelly. You have to believe me. Putting me on the witness stand will do Dr. Griffin no good."

"Damn it!" Teddy pounded on the table. "You'll face the jury right now and you will tell them exactly what happened on the night of November ninth whether you like it or not!"

Jochen's forehead formed deep ridges. "Who are you exactly?" he asked.

Teddy sat back and glared at Jochen from beneath the rim of his beaver hat. Suddenly, he looked uncomfortable. "I am part of Dimitri's counsel. And I'm his former friend."

Alba pulled in a breath. "We shall see you in court shortly, Jochen."

"I will have nothing to say!" Jochen's voice echoed behind Alba and Teddy as they exited the tiny room. Feeling more lighthearted than they'd been in days, they traveled back to the Old Bailey.

"I daresay that sod will make a persuasive witness on the stand," Teddy said. "He's ugly and disheveled and looks as though he's suffered a ghoulish past. The jurors will believe he's capable of extreme violence."

Alba had studied Jochen's appearance as well, but she'd come to a different conclusion about it. "There is only one problem with the way Jochen looks. His description doesn't match the majority of witness testimonies. Most say the Ripper was tall and elegantly dressed."

"But," Teddy said as they elbowed their way through the swarms of reporters, "there is one witness who places a stranger with Rhessa's stocky build and hair color in the vicinity of Elizabeth Stride's murder."

"I don't know if that sole description will be enough."

Twenty minutes later, they rejoined Harold Rollingsworth at the semicircular defense table. "Thank God you've come back," the elder Rollingsworth said in a low tone. "The natives are getting restless."

Alba shot a look at the judges—and at the twelve jury members who sat below them on tiered benches. From this distance she couldn't tell if they were agitated or not.

Where are my spectacles?

Teddy handed her a paper containing relevant facts about Jochen. Alba murmured a thank-you as she quickly scoured them. Then she handed the paper back to him. The side door opened and Dimitri was brought in. Saying a silent prayer, she watched Jochen enter the courtroom directly behind Dimitri. Anxiety climbed up her throat. It was a good thing Teddy was questioning Jochen since she might be too emotional.

Will he do an effective job?

"Jochen?" Dimitri whispered harshly to Alba. "*He* is your new development? What has he done?"

"Miss Spencer." Lord Wentwood's sharp tone prevented her from answering him. "You may question your emergency witness."

Jochen had made himself slightly more presentable, but his appearance still bordered on the rough and slovenly. He climbed into the witness box and removed his deerstalker cap. As he was being sworn in, he raised one beefy hand and scowled at the sea of people before him.

Alba stood. "My colleague, Barrister Rollingsworth, will be questioning Mr. Rhessa, your lordship."

"Very well."

"Mr. Rhessa." Teddy greeted Jochen as he approached the witness box.

To Alba, Jochen's face looked fuzzy from this distance, but she strained her eyes to make out the details of his expression.

"Please state your present post of employment," Teddy instructed.

"I have been hired as a butler for Dimitri Gri—I mean, Dr. Drake Griffin."

"Gentlemen of the jury." Teddy raised an eyebrow. "I must backtrack for a moment. Drake Griffin was born in Romania. His given name is Dimitri Grigorescu. He legally changed it when he began to study medicine in the United Kingdom."

Murmurs of surprise filtered through the courtroom.

Jochen grasped the railing in front of him with disdain. "I've been nothing but a loyal servant to Dr. Griffin."

"The jury will decide that, Mr. Rhessa. Now, when did you first come to London?" Teddy asked.

He concentrated. "It was the end of August, it was."

Teddy held up the sheet of paper he'd shown Alba. "Mr. Rhessa, according to your landlord at the Shires, a tenement in Whitechapel, you arrived in London on Wednesday, August 29, 1888." He paused. "Do you know when the first gruesome East End murder took place?"

"N-no."

"On Friday, August thirty-first."

"That doesn't prove anything!" Jochen fired back.

Alba stole a glance at Dimitri. He looked completely torn up.

"I propose to you, Mr. Rhessa, that during your brief stay in Whitechapel, you got to know many of the unfortunates there. Is that a fair statement?"

"Yes, I suppose."

"I may not know much about prostitutes," Teddy said, "but I know that many of them try to have normal romantic relationships outside of their work."

"I don't understand what you're getting at."

"Did you try and court these prostitutes, Mr. Rhessa?"

Jochen's face turned scarlet. "There's no crime in that."

"I'm suggesting that you tried to have a romantic relationship with these prostitutes, but that they refused you," Teddy said.

"You're wrong," Jochen growled.

Teddy strode to the front of the witness box and held Jochen's gaze. "Would you consider being refused by a prostitute humiliating, Mr. Rhessa?"

Alba bit her lip and rubbed her weary eyes. *I hope we aren't wrong about Jochen.* She couldn't bear to send an innocent person to the gallows. She stuffed her hands into the pockets of her billowing black robe. *My spectacles!* She hastily donned them and inhaled a breath to steady herself.

"I knew Mary Kelly," Jochen replied, "but that doesn't make me a murderer!"

"I believe you are lying." Teddy leaned on the railing. "You knew the area of Whitechapel, Mr. Rhessa. You were familiar with the prostitutes and their schedules. And you have a medical background. After all, you were studying to be a surgeon alongside Mr. Griffin, were you not?"

More startled murmurs shot around the room.

Jochen flashed angry eyes at the crowd.

"Please answer the question," Teddy prodded.

"Yes. I was studying to be a surgeon," he said reluctantly.

"Mr. Rhessa," Teddy continued, "I put to you that you were uncontrollably jealous of Mr. Griffin for two reasons. He succeeded in becoming a doctor when you failed. And he was admired by your father when you weren't. I have a feeling that if you didn't kill Polly Nichols, Annie Chapman, Elizabeth Stride, Catherine Eddowes, and Mary Kelly out of vengeance for the way they rebuked you, you killed those women to frame Dr. Drake Griffin."

"I did no such thing!" Jochen cried. "People claim Jack the Ripper is tall and dressed like a gentleman. I don't fit that description!"

"I'm afraid jealousy makes you capable of anything, Mr. Rhessa. Perhaps you hired someone who looks like Griffin. Maybe you killed Mary Kelly then paid someone to testify that they saw Dr. Griffin enter Mary Kelly's house on November ninth. Did you do any of these things?"

"No!" As his body shook with rage, Jochen lunged forward and took a swipe at Teddy.

The attack sent Teddy's horsehair wig to the ground. The sight of him without it struck Jochen with horror.

"You!" Jochen burst out. "I knew I'd seen you somewhere before! You were in Whitechapel the night I escorted Dotty Malone home. You were dressed in a top hat and cloak, but you removed your hat when you approached a prosser. You were there!"

"You're mistaken." Teddy scowled as he put his wig back on.

"I know it was you," Jochen raged.

The pounding of Wentworth's gavel did nothing to restore order in the courtroom.

Jochen pointed a finger at Teddy, his face crimson. "I also saw you in Whitechapel two nights after I arrived in London. *On the night Polly Nichols was killed.*"

Alba felt her gut wrench. *Teddy?* Could he be all the things he was accusing Jochen of? Was he jealous enough to try and frame Dimitri? Or had he killed the prostitutes as a result of a twisted mind?

Alba's mind spun. She looked away and caught a glimpse of Teddy's legal case, which sat on the floor. With the aid of her spectacles, she could see that the case was trimmed with Teddy's initials, JTR. John Theodore Rollingsworth. Or just maybe, *Jack the Ripper.*

Chapter Twenty-Eight

Alba must have passed out from the strain, for when she opened her eyes, she was seated at a table with her head upon it. Harold Rollingsworth was sitting beside her patting her hand. He looked devastated.

"Where am I?" she asked groggily.

"You fainted, my dear, and I brought you here, to a private chamber of the courtroom."

While she studied the cozy, wainscoted chamber, the events she'd witnessed in the courtroom came streaming back to her. "Teddy," she murmured. "He might be a killer."

Rollingsworth ran a hand over his white curls. "My son didn't kill anyone."

"Has he been detained?"

"Yes. But he hasn't been charged with anything yet."

"And Dimitri—"

"I'm afraid he won't be released anytime soon. I plan to talk to the lead judge since Teddy and Jochen have become new suspects," Harold replied quickly, "but you know as well as I that filing for a mistrial can be a lengthy process."

She made a move to get up. Her knees buckled.

"Have patience, Alba. I've ordered you some tea to revive you."

She desperately needed her strength at the moment, so she sat back down.

A kindly-faced, elderly woman bustled in. She held a tray filled with a clattering teacup and an apple scone. "Here you go, my dear," she said, placing the tray in front of Alba. "I'm Mrs. Grayson. I see to the judges' needs here at the Old Bailey."

"Thank you," Alba replied.

The woman offered her a gentle smile before she left the room.

Alba began to fix her tea when the court bailiff stuck his head through the crack in the door. "Mr. Rollingsworth, your son is asking for you."

"Am I allowed to see him?"

"Yes, sir."

Harold bolted out of his seat. After telling Alba he would return shortly, he disappeared.

Reaching for the scone, she could hardly believe what had just taken place. She hated to admit it, but Teddy as the sadistic killer made sense on one level. The same level, in fact, on which he'd proclaimed Jochen had a motive. *Jealousy*. Just maybe Teddy had committed the first two Whitechapel murders before Dimitri came to London of his own accord, but after seeing Alba's connection to Dimitri, Teddy became inspired to incriminate him. And because Dimitri's medical rounds took him to the East End, he had fallen into that plan far too easily.

Although Alba's glimpses at Teddy's dark side had been few and far between, she'd certainly seen them. Perhaps he held a deep resentment of women that stemmed from his being given up for adoption at birth. If Teddy was the Whitechapel killer, Alba thought, he also harbored a raw propensity for violence—a propensity he'd managed to keep hidden beneath his pleasant demeanor.

The possibility that she didn't know him at all pierced her heart like a sharp arrow.

Alba took several bites of the scone. Suddenly she felt queer. Her upper lip began to perspire and her mouth went dry. She thrust down the pastry. A burning sensation spread through her entire body and she sagged against the table in front of her.

What on earth is happening to me? Then she knew. *I've been poisoned.*

Spots clouded her eyes, but she could still make out a female figure hovering over her as she crashed to the floor.

"Alba." It was Mrs. Grayson's face—but it wasn't Mrs.

Grayson's voice. "I finally found you, my not-so-innocent step-daughter. You are in my hands now."

Ileana.

Eyes closed, Dimitri huddled on a filthy cot in the corner of his cell. Suddenly, a vision of an incapacitated Alba jolted his world of imprisonment. He sat upright, feeling her silent pain as she slipped into a catatonic sleep. In the black shadows, he realized that his precious Alba had just surrendered to one of Ileana's spells.

Holy hell! The stone-hearted witch finally got to her!

Knowing that his visions were always correct, Dimitri's senses turned topsy-turvy and his heart struggled to pound against a devastating vise. While panic, sorrow, and an uncontrollable rage twined together, Dimitri drove his fist into the wall. He'd been wasting away inside the prison like a pathetic weakling—and he hadn't protected the woman he loved.

Yanking on the bars, he cried, "Guard! I need you!"

I must have human blood. It was the only thing that could supply him with enough energy to escape. And he had to get to his beloved Alba.

Maybe he could feign illness. Once the warden entered the cell to check on him, Dimitri would attack. The plan was a long shot since the wardsman never got within four feet of him.

"Guard!" he called out again.

The reed-thin officer didn't come, but to his surprise Edith Tuttlebaum appeared.

"Miss Tuttlebaum! How did you get back here?"

"For once my red hair does me justice." Her voice contained only a fraction of her usual good humor. Edith placed her face between the bars and clasped them with trembling hands. "Dr. Griffin," she whispered. "Alba is gone!"

When Dimitri stepped close to her, he could smell her blood. The metallic but sweet scent prompted his fangs to drop. He tried to speak without widening his mouth.

"I sensed that something happened," he said.

Edith looked alarmed. "How did you know?"

"I had a vision . . . her stepmother cast a spell on her."

"My God!" Edith pressed her face closer to his. "This can't be."

Dimitri scowled. "You hardly know me, but you must believe me."

"You and I are not well acquainted, Mr. Griffin, but Alba has faith in you. She wouldn't have defended you otherwise." Edith took a glance up and down the narrow corridor. "Now she needs you, so we must get you out of here."

"How?" Despite the urgency of the moment, weakness pulled at Dimitri. The small amounts of animal blood he had received barely allowed him to function.

"I know you're a vampire," Edith said. "I saw you materialize outside the dormitory window—on the night you swept Alba away. I never told anyone."

He studied the torment in the girl's green eyes. *Would she allow me to bite her?* "Now that you know I'm a vampire, you know I require human blood. Will you let me take some of yours?"

"Yes," she said cautiously. "Will it leave me alive?"

He nodded. "You will feel only momentary pain. Then you'll remember nothing."

"Very well," she said courageously.

"Are you certain?" Dimitri asked.

She nodded. "Alba is like a sister to me. And I owe her a favor. On the night I accompanied her to the hospital, I shouldn't have told Teddy that she went home with you. To think that Teddy Rollingsworth might be Jack the Ripper . . ."

Dimitri gave a shudder. It was true that he, Jochen, and Teddy were all in the East End the night of Mary Kelly's murder. But Dimitri was willing to bet Teddy was the brutal killer. "Where would Alba's stepmother have taken her?" he asked.

"Alba suggested that Ileana might be living in her family's house in Kensington Gardens. She wouldn't be able to perform her dark magic in private at a hotel."

"Did Alba tell you what this house looks like?" he asked.

"She described it as a Georgian-style home with a brick edifice and stained-glass windows. It belonged to her father."

A plan started to form in Dimitri's mind. *It's essential that I get out of here.* To do that, he needed to start hypnotizing Edith.

"It's time, Edith. Brace yourself," he said.

She nodded.

Breathing deeply, he sent a commanding energy from his topaz eyes to her viridian ones.

"Call for the guard," he instructed.

Enveloped in the trance, she turned slowly around. "Guard!" she said. "I feel ill."

Dimitri reached a hand through the bars and pulled Edith to him. She stretched her head to the side and he bit down on her neck. Her blood filled his mouth and soothed his parched throat. And as the red liquid streamed into his veins, a tremendous force rushed through him. Like a phoenix rising from the ashes, he'd been re-born.

He held Edith's tiny body upright while the wardsman rounded the corner.

"What's wrong, miss?" the guard asked.

"She blacked out," Dimitri replied, careful to keep his bloodied mouth hidden in the shadows.

The guard took hold of Edith, and Dimitri saw his chance. He yanked the round key chain off the guard's belt, then punched the guard on the jaw. The guard and Edith fell to the ground in unison.

Dimitri's heart pounded as he fitted key after key into the lock. Finally one was a match. *There! I'm free!* He streamed down the hall, leaving the clamor of the other prisoners behind him. If he thought for an instant that any of the inmates were innocent, he would have opened their cells too.

Reaching the first window along the corridor, he stopped in his tracks. After he morphed into a mist without being seen, he seeped past the open window and into the miasma of twilight. It didn't take Dimitri long to reach Kensington Gardens and find the home that fit Edith's description. When he circled the quiet structure, it ap-peared dark from every angle.

Are Ileana and Alba inside?

He decided to chance it. Fanning out his cape like a pair of black wings, he leapt in preternatural flight to the second story. As he peered into a curtain-framed window, he realized that the purple haze of dusk had settled over the neighborhood. Dimitri saw no one beyond the rooftop, so he drew a handkerchief from his jacket and busted the glass pane. Pulling his frame into the house, he found that the room was empty—save for a chair in the corner and the shards of a broken mirror on the carpet.

He was about to make his way to the corridor when the glass pieces glowed and rippled. Astounded, Dimitri took a step back. No doubt this was one of Ileana's magical tactics. The mirror had been broken into only eight or nine large chunks, so he fitted them back together like a jigsaw puzzle. Gazing down at the reassembled mirror, his eyes widened as it spoke.

"All the king's horses and all the king's men couldn't put Humpty Dumpty together again," it said. "But you have, Dimitri Grigorescu."

"Where is Alba? Where has Ileana taken her?" he thundered.

"My mistress has thought ahead. She sent her housekeeper back to Romania and has taken your beautiful Alba somewhere no one will find her."

"Tell me where, damn it!" Dimitri raged.

The mirror cackled ominously. "Where else do you take a prisoner you want the world to forget?"

Dimitri thought for a moment. "The Tower of London?"

"Indeed," it answered. "But I'm afraid you're too late, brave Grigorescu. She has been poisoned by a pastry dipped in special cyanide."

"No! Ileana shall pay!"

"What a battle." The mirror's voice echoed as Dimitri vanished into the starry night. "An enchantress of black magic duels a scorned, bloodthirsty vampire. Who, I wonder, shall win?"

Chapter Twenty-Nine

The River Thames shimmered calmly in the moonlight, but Dimitri soared over it as angry as a provoked tiger. Christmas had come and gone two days ago—but seasonal cheer still glowed from London's windows and sparkled in the tinseled garland that wrapped the lampposts. However, he was in no mood to admire the holiday ambience.

Speeding past Big Ben as it loomed over the snow-blanketed city, Dimitri knew that the Tower of London wasn't far now. While his body quivered with wrath, all he wanted to do was put an end to Ileana and steal back to Romania with Alba. He supposed he'd have to settle for one out of the two—unless he was willing to do the unimaginable to save Alba.

The infamous Tower, with its rag-stone construction and pointed spires, sat adjacent to the riverbank inside an eerie cloud of fog. Over the years, the medieval castle had housed hundreds of prisoners, perhaps the most famous of those being Anne Boleyn. Now the intimidating structure seemed to beckon anyone willing to glimpse her beheaded ghost.

Dimitri, nauseated with the knowledge that he'd left one prison to break into another, scowled as he touched down on the bridgeway between two of the landmark's towers.

If I were Ileana, where would I have taken Alba?

Then he knew. *The Bloody Tower.* The place where most of the compound's atrocities had taken place. It was far from where the Crown Jewels were kept and no doubt it would be free of guards at this hour.

He hoisted himself to the windows of the turret and peered inside its topmost room. There, illuminated by the light of a torch, stood Ileana looking down on Alba. Alba lay sprawled over what appeared to be some sort of torture device, her hands captured in ropes above her head. *The rack.*

Even in her torturous state, Alba looked like an angel, and Dimitri's heart surged. Free of her horsehair wig and black barrister robe, she was clothed in a simple blue dress. As she reposed in eternal slumber, her milky skin paled against the ruby red of her lips and the gloss of her ebony hair. *She is more beautiful than life itself—thank God she doesn't seem to be in pain.*

In the hollow of a turret directly above Dimitri, the sound of ravens' wings beat loudly. Ileana snapped her head to the window and caught sight of him. The look she gave him oozed a calculated evil.

Unfurling his fists, Dimitri evaporated through a crack in the ancient bricks and imported himself into the room. Once he morphed back into human form, he moved forward determinedly. Meanwhile, Ileana floated around the rack table, her hands clasped behind her back.

"Dearest Dimitri," she said. "We finally meet face-to-face."

As Dimitri's glance shifted to Alba, he sucked back tears of grief. "How dare you take Alba from me! She never did anything to you."

"Oh, my lovesick vampire. Don't you know anything?" Ileana eyed him with pity. "Alba's beauty threatened everything I live for."

"You are jealous of someone half your age?" Dimitri roared. "Only a creature of the devil could be so heartless."

Ileana tsked. "Speaking of evil creatures, you shouldn't be so critical. I've seen you do it. You slip close to young, unknowing women while the scent of their blood fuels your excitement. I bet you drank someone's blood recently—or you wouldn't have escaped from prison."

While Ileana spoke, Dimitri fired off options in his mind. *Should I bind her to the rack and stretch her to death? Should I slam her against the wall and break every bone in her body? Or should I simply toss her out the window to her death?*

He stiffened, his eyes burning into hers. "Becoming a blood-sucker wasn't something I chose."

"Alas." Ileana pouted dramatically. "The minute you gave Alba the Egyptian amulet and crept into the cemetery at Bran Castle, you put her life in extraordinary danger. I witnessed all of it in my mirror."

Dimitri had never despised anyone more in his life.

Soon the titillation in Ileana's steel-colored eyes dimmed. "The good news is that I'm getting what I want in the end. *But you* ... I don't know why you're even here. I can't let you bite Alba and bring the vampire's curse to life."

We'll see about that, Dimitri thought.

Ileana continued with a diabolical smile. "I'm not surprised that Alba didn't kill you—or herself, thanks to the Egyptian prophecy. Apparently the prediction holds no power over the vampire's curse. You must have disturbed a very important vampire that night at Bran Castle."

I did.

"It's no matter. For all intents and purposes, Alba is dead," she said. "Deader than a doornail, as they say!"

Dimitri lunged for Ileana, but she jerked back and rose off the ground, her fingernails projecting into claws and her eyes growing serpent-like. She withdrew the bracelet of Amenhotep from a pocket of her dress. "You were so upset when you lost this, weren't you?" Waving the bracelet tauntingly in front of him, she threw her head back in hysterical laughter.

Then it dawned on Dimitri. The moment he became a vampire, the curse of Tousret's amulet didn't apply to him or Alba because he was already dead and Alba hadn't killed herself. He'd wondered about the curse affecting them all along, and Ileana had just supplied him with the answer. It seemed the vampire's prophecy had dueled with the forces of ancient Egypt, and this time the power of Petra Laskov's curse had trumped everything.

Smiling voraciously, Ileana came closer and stuffed the bracelet into the front pocket of his jacket. "It's a shame that this can do you no good. But it's more of a shame that Alba is gone."

Once she landed on the ground again, she retracted her hand. Dimitri grabbed hold of her wrist. Snarling at him, she whipped her free arm around and revealed a sharpened wooden stake.

"I knew you would appear, Dimitri!"

They began to struggle, but Ileana was stronger than Dimitri anticipated. While he managed to send her crashing against the stone wall, she came back seething like a savage. With blood dripping from her head wound, she flew at him with the stake. Dimitri tried to duck and move out of the way, but his foot slipped on a puddle of her blood. He landed on his back, and while his vision clouded, Ileana brought the stake slamming down at his heart. By way of a miracle, it struck the metal of the bracelet and ricocheted off.

Dimitri locked eyes with Ileana, panic seeping into her own.

He yanked her to her feet, sending the stake plunging to the ground. When he saw that it'd become wedged in a crack in the brick floor, Dimitri grabbed Ileana roughly and lifted her in the air. She wiggled in his muscled arms, but she couldn't free herself. She eyed the sharpened stake as he dangled her over it.

"You wouldn't dare." Her eyes grew round and black.

"I must—to get what I want in the end," Dimitri said as he dropped her onto the pointed stake.

Ileana's scream died in her throat. Dimitri turned away and patted the bracelet of Amenhotep inside his pocket. *It came in handy after all.* He moved quickly to Alba. Dropping to his knee, he brought her ice-cold hand to his cheek.

"Can you hear me, my love?" His tears began to flow. "Ileana is gone. I thought her death might bring you back to me, but it hasn't." He reached forward to stroke her petal-soft cheek. "We've had an odd time of it, haven't we, darling? We ran from our past, changed our names, and transformed ourselves into things we aren't. But I think I'm most guilty. I was obsessed with making myself a respectable gentleman to win your hand. Still, I think we were happier when we were young and true to ourselves. I loved you for you and you loved me for me. And as long as the earth orbits the sun, that will never change."

Smiling ruefully, he pressed her stiff hand to his lips. Then he reached inside his vest pocket and produced the rustic promise ring he'd carved for her in Romania when he was sixteen. "I've been carrying this around for a very long time."

He slipped the ring on her finger. It was a perfect fit.

"Try and find it in your heart to forgive me for what I'm about to do," he whispered. "I cannot allow you to sleep forever, so you must undergo one . . . last . . . change."

He stood and leaned over her reclining body. In her deep sleep, Alba's blood scent had dissipated, but Dimitri's fangs descended anyway. Pulling his lips back, he lowered his mouth to her neck and bit into the cold, fragile skin that covered Alba's jugular vein. He drank and drank.

And while all the memories they had created together danced through his mind, he punctured his wrist with his fangs and brought it to Alba's mouth. As the blood trickled past her lips, he offered her immortality.

Dimitri drew back. Alba remained still for a few moments. Then her eyes fluttered open—those delphinium-blue eyes that made his spirit soar. Gathering her to him, he felt the odd pump of a vampire's heart against his chest. *I've done it.*

"What happened?" Alba asked in a weak voice. "I remember being at the courthouse—and Ileana . . ."

In a swift recount, Dimitri told her how he'd bitten Edith in order to escape from prison. Then he pointed to Ileana's impaled body. Alba recoiled and buried her face in his jacket. He ended the explanation with the daunting news that she was a member of the undead.

"I . . . I'm a vampire?" The words caught in her throat. She began to tremble and shake in his arms. "I don't believe it."

"It was the only way. Please forgive me."

After a long cry, Alba pulled away and met his gaze. "I don't know what to think."

"You're like me, which is a better alternative to sleeping forever." He paused. "At least we can be together now."

She nodded, yet anguish shadowed her features.

"Perhaps this will make you feel better." Dimitri ran his thumb over the ring on her finger.

"What's this?" she asked.

"I made it for you during our summer in Romania."

She wiped her tears away and raised her hand to look at the ring. "It's beautiful." After a pause she added, "If I had to guess, you wanted to give me this instead of the Egyptian amulet the day we went to the graveyard, didn't you?"

"Yes. But Simona convinced me that the necklace would impress you more than any cheap wooden ring."

Alba brought the token to her heart. "She couldn't have been more wrong." Grimacing, she touched her bite marks with the tip of her other hand.

"Alba." Dimitri's expression grew solemn. "Do you forgive me for bringing you over?"

Her tone was sorrowful but firm. "I know you had no other choice, Dimitri. The sleep of death consumed me at the courthouse, and there was no turning back. Except your way."

"I suppose the vampire prophecy played itself out after all," he said solemnly.

She sagged against him.

He stroked her smooth locks and inhaled her scent. Her fragrance was different now, but just as sweet and enticing. He held her at arm's length so that he could look into her eyes and study her soul. "You need to know that we will be together. *Forever.*"

Her eyes softened and he knew that she would be his princess for all eternity. He would never tire of her and he would never have to watch her grow old. He dropped his mouth to her lips and claimed them with a kiss—a kiss that proved his undying devotion. She moaned against the pressure of his mouth, and he understood just how she felt. At the moment, she could swear she was a stranger inside her own body, confused but in possession of an incomparable energy. Her senses were magnified a hundredfold— and she was willing to try things she hadn't experienced before.

He broke the kiss and met her stare. "I love you, Alba."

"I love you too," she whispered breathlessly. "Do you want to know the last thought I had before I fell into that horrible sleep?"

He nodded.

"I regretted that we never made love."

"Then," he said, helping her to her feet, "making love is the first thing we shall do."

Chapter Thirty

No doubt the police were looking for them, but Dimitri wasn't going to let anything prevent him from being with Alba. He knew he couldn't take her back to his Park Lane house—nor could he take her to the Bloomsbury dormitory. Thankfully, he'd decided on the perfect location.

Following Dimitri's lesson on how to alter her physical state into a mist, Alba traveled with him to the Kensington Garden house and slipped through the window he'd broken earlier. Once they had morphed back into humans inside the house, Alba grasped Dimitri's hand and led him into the corridor. Down the carpeted hallway they treaded, until they came to a closed door at its southern end.

"This was my grandmother's house," Alba said, her expression glazing over with sentimentality. "I was twelve when I came to London with my mother." She pushed open the door. "And this was my room."

Draped in soft shades of blues and grays, the room was furnished with an ornate canopied bed, an elegant vanity, and velvet curtains trimmed with large tassels. It was thoroughly feminine—but grown-up enough to make a twelve-year-old girl feel like a young woman.

Alba stepped forward and grasped the pole of the canopied bed. Her hands shook around it.

"Is it just as you remember?" Dimitri asked. He lit a candle and set it on the bedside table, then stepped in close enough to press his chest to her back.

Alba nodded. "Thank God Ileana didn't change it."

"She will never disturb anything again," he whispered in her ear. "Alba, I want to erase the last month of our lives from your mind."

He curled her hand into his while his mouth dropped to her neck. Warm, wet kisses slid over her skin, and goose bumps sprang up on her arm.

"You mean everything to me," he said. "Now I finally have the chance to show you."

As unhurriedly as an island breeze blows over a beach, Dimitri cupped Alba's breast. He caressed the soft mound through the material of her dress, and she moaned. His body felt hotter than a raging fire against hers—and Alba closed her eyes against the energy. She tilted her head to the side so that he could nuzzle her neck as he played with her breast. The bite marks he'd left behind were incredibly sore, but she refused to dwell on the pain. Not only had Dimitri's fangs redirected their fates, they had bound one another to a parallel destiny.

"When I awoke, your face was like the brightest sun I had ever seen," she said softly.

"You weren't scared?" he asked in a whisper.

"I wasn't scared until you told me I was like you."

"Are you still scared?"

"No," she whispered back. "Because you're all I need in any lifetime."

Alba felt his erection pressing into her backside and she sucked in a breath. As his every muscle flexed against her in anticipation, she suspected that he was about to burst with the rapture he was restraining. And she desired him the same way. While she couldn't begin to understand all of what took place today, she knew that she belonged in Dimitri's arms at this very moment . . . wrapped deeply in his world . . . loving him completely and profoundly.

He spun her around and when he locked eyes with her, his passion found its way to the center of her heart. Lips swollen with lust, he bent forward and kissed her, sending a thousand white-hot flames to her every recess. Crushing her closer, he glided his fingers into her hair, loosening her hairpins. Her tresses exploded in waves around her shoulders, and as he deepened the kiss, she became as breathless as she had as a teenager. Uttering a little cry against his mouth, Alba clutched him with desperation. He responded with a fierce groan. Then he took her clothes off. Her overskirt dropped to the carpet, followed by her dress and bustle. And when he peeled away her corset and filmy fichu, her breasts spilled forward, an offering to him.

Left in nothing but her underpants and stockings, Alba clung to Dimitri again. He gathered her closer, but this time, her nakedness did not cause her to flush with embarrassment. She liked the feel of him being fully clothed against her bare skin.

Virile and strong and indestructible, he stepped back and let his gaze roll over her body. Then he kissed her again. She smiled as his unshaven cheek brushed across hers. And she smiled even wider when he reached down and tugged off her underclothes and stockings.

"I'm going to take you very slowly," he said as the garments floated to the floor. "And with more passion that you could ever imagine."

Dimitri directed her toward the bed. Once he spread Alba across the mattress, he straightened up and removed his clothes. Soon his broad chest, chiseled stomach, and ramrod cock increased her desire for him. Wearing a hungry look, he took her face in both hands—and as she whimpered with anticipation, his hot tongue slipped into her mouth and plundered the open space. Alba's heart raced. She yearned to feel his stiff manhood in the damp juncture of her thighs, but she realized that taking things at an unhurried pace meant they could savor every moment of their lovemaking. After all, they'd waited eleven years to solidify their love—and there was no rush now.

As Dimitri hovered over her, moonlight bathing his face, his pale skin shone like polished silver. While his topaz eyes came alive, they filled with excitement as he took in the sight of her—from her face and shoulders, to her erect breasts and her hollow stomach.

"Let me kiss you all over," he murmured.

As more wetness gathered in Alba's core, Dimitri pressed his lips to the tiny recess at the base of her throat. Then he ran his tongue up her neck and lowered his hand to stroke her damp curls. Her folds were ripe for his fingers to explore. As her petals contracted like violets shrinking from the sun around them, she arched off the mattress and Dimitri let out a groan. His mouth wandered to her breasts. He retracted his fingers and rubbed the aching mounds with his palms. Giving another grunt of desire, he found her darkened nipples with his mouth. For a long while, he lapped at the hard buds, teasing, pulling, and commanding them into sharp points.

"You are magnificent," he murmured in a voice raw with lust.

As he thumbed her erect nipples back and forth, a furling heat quickened Alba's pulse. And her center flooded with more cream than she thought possible.

"Now I want to kiss your stomach," Dimitri said.

His fiery lips traveled to the indent of her belly button. The sensation of his tongue thrusting in and out of it caused her body to shiver with delightful convulsions. As she raised her arms over her head in sheer surrender, Dimitri's thick prick hardened against her shin. It proved that he was enjoying giving her pleasure. That was Dimitri. Assiduous and devoted to the end—and the thought made her smile.

He urged her thighs apart. After sending her a mischievous grin, his head disappeared between them. Alba sucked in a breath. *Is Dimitri going to kiss me there?* Her nipples tightened, and as he pressed his tongue against the cushion of her thigh, anticipation swept through her. While his fingertips petted the skin that framed her core and his mouth found her drenched folds, she let out a little cry. She fisted his hair, which shimmered like sea glass, and when his tongue made contact with her cleft, she swore she saw heaven's gates.

"Good God," she murmured.

Sliding his tongue halfway inside her folds, Dimitri probed the recess. Then he gripped her thighs and pulled her core closer to his mouth.

"You taste so sweet. I want to make you come again," she heard him say in a muffled voice.

Inflamed, she bit her lip while his tongue flattened on a magical spot. The bead hidden in her petals began to pulsate and Dimitri held it in his mouth so that he could taste her climax. As hundreds of tingling daggers racked her body, she moaned and thrust her head to the side, the sensation almost more than she could bear.

"Now you're ready for me," he whispered.

He rose up on his knees and Alba ran a hand down his cut torso.

With muscles stacked so close together they looked like brickwork, his chest heaved in breathless grunts. He grabbed his rock-hard penis and directed its tip toward her center. After supporting himself on his free arm, Dimitri rubbed his engorged staff against her slickness. Completely roused, he rocked into Alba, filling her with a satisfying warmth. Her fingertips strayed along his torso as he thrust his cock fully forward and ecstasy streaked through her.

He's inside me and we are making love. There were times in their relationship that Alba had doubted it would ever happen. Against all odds, they'd created closeness without physical intimacy. *How many couples are capable of that?*

Pumping his way to bliss, Dimitri craned his neck forward and captured her mouth. Her hair became tangled against his face and his strong chest crushed her breasts, but neither of them seemed to care. She held on to him desperately, as if the thrill and the meaning of their lovemaking would end the minute she let go. She pushed her hips up to meet his thrusts and he moaned.

"Yes. Dear God—like that," he said.

Perspiration pooled on his forehead. His bangs dripped and his biceps bulged as he took Alba's raised hips and gripped with a fury. His slim hips banged against her core and she began to feel her center vibrate again.

She inhaled a sharp breath.

"Christ, Alba," he said sharply. "I can't hold out any longer."

His cock was swollen to maximum size inside her channel and she knew he was about to spill his seed. In a blind frenzy, he ejaculated his desire while she climaxed for the third time.

Slumping over, he wrapped his powerful arms around her. And as he breathed against her in heavy gasps, his embrace calmed her and filled her with hope. It also banished the vacancy she had suffered ever since they were separated. She didn't have to pour her efforts into creating a new life anymore. Now she could simply love Dimitri—without the debilitating fear that he'd put her in danger again.

She melted into the curve of his chest, envisioning the endless stretch of their future. He held the key to all that was important to her, and in his arms she belonged.

Dimitri caressed her face and smiled.

"That was incredible," she whispered.

"It was," he agreed. "It was everything I hoped it would be." He nuzzled her neck and drew her closer. "I thought I lost you, Alba. That was the worst feeling in the world."

As she lay enveloped in his arms, Alba's blood coursed through her veins like a mighty river. It was as though she possessed ten times the blood content she'd had before Dimitri bit her, and her brain began to pound with an unfamiliar urgency. She became desperately parched, thirsty beyond control. Her fangs descended— and she hardly recognized her thoughts and behavior. Wild-eyed, she gripped Dimitri's hand.

He rose up on his elbow and looked down on her. "I know what you're going through. You are thirsty—and you feel you'll die without blood."

"Yes," Alba hissed. "I don't want you to see me like this!"

"Don't worry. I went through the very same thing."

"I'm afraid, Dimitri."

"Don't be. You will hate yourself if you feed on a stranger and you're unable to stop. I will let you drink from me again."

As the flickering candlelight mingled with the glow of the moon, his fingernails grew. He reached up and sliced open the skin above his left nipple. A thick stream of blood poured forth. Alba lunged for it, but he stopped her.

"You must understand something," he said firmly. "If you consume my blood consciously, you will become the same kind of vampire as I."

"The same kind of vampire?"

"Remember I'm a *mulo*—the strongest, most sensual kind of vampire there is. Besides my lust drive, you shall inherit my visions."

"I'll have premonitions?"

"No. You will see events as they are happening at a different location. But I must warn you, Alba: if you envision something terrible, you may be powerless to stop it."

"I don't care," she said, famished. "I need blood."

Relinquishing her arm, he nodded. She leaned forward and pressed her open mouth to his muscled chest. Then she drank from the cut he'd made. The taste was tremendous. Indescribable. It reminded her of something sour and sweet, tangy yet sharply coppery—and the energy it supplied her with made her feel invincible.

As she drank Dimitri's blood, it fueled her need for sex, as he warned it would.

His lips curled as he caught a glimpse of her insatiability. Without saying a word, she rose on her haunches and straddled his narrow torso. As she looked down on him, she loved the way his glossy eyes twinkled in the candlelight like stars.

"I want to make love again," she said quietly.

She traced the jut of his hip bones before she trailed her fingers along his handsome face. Cradling his chin in her hands, she lowered her mouth to his for a red-hot kiss. He parted his lips and received her tongue, moaning against the brush of it. Sitting over his hips, Alba felt his erection bob behind her. Smiling, she pulled away and reached backward to find the bulge of his sac between his legs. She fondled it while he pressed her breasts together and brought them to his mouth. Alba slithered her hands up his towering penis as his tongue circled her tawny nipples. Once he'd gathered one of her hardened buds between his lips, she swayed her backside against his prick, causing it to grow to a new height. Then she quickly slid her hand up and down the length of his shaft.

Dimitri squeezed his eyes shut, grunting with desire. As she stimulated him, he uttered, "You drive me to insanity."

"I can tell," she said playfully.

"That feels like heaven," he murmured.

She rubbed the tip of his penis with her thumb and his eyes flashed open devilishly.

"Now I want you to sit on it."

Already ripe, Alba did as he asked. Gone was the trepidation that came with virginity. She wanted him to be pleasured and she wanted to feel him inside her again. His cock fit inside her like a thick hinge in a tight groove. Dimitri grasped her small waist and lifted her body up and down over his penis. The action lifted his sex to the brink of ejaculation.

"Make yourself peak before I do," he whispered.

"How do I do that?" she asked.

"Constrict your muscles around me while I suck on your breasts."

Leaning forward from the waist, she offered her breasts to him. He took their points in his mouth greedily, hungrily. Meanwhile, she hunkered down over his sex, pressing her center into its bulk.

Wiggling and gyrating caused her folds to flutter—and as Dimitri's tongue swirled over her buds, she climaxed for the fourth time that night.

Excited by the fact that Alba had reached her own pinnacle, Dimitri ground his pelvis in the air. Holding her hips captive over his, he created a fantastic friction. She watched his face convulse with desire just before he shot his cream into her. Smiling, Alba slumped forward and gathered his head to her chest.

"Listen," she coaxed. "Listen to the wild beat of my heart."

He nodded. "It's the rhythm of something supernatural."

Bathed in perspiration and struggling to breathe, Alba rocked off Dimitri. He pulled the coverlet over both of them before he bundled her in his arms. He kissed her temple. "We will enjoy endless nights like this . . . forever."

Alba closed her eyes but her mind sped. Although the room was dimly lit and she was physically exhausted, she wasn't sleepy.

In my other life, I would have been fast asleep by now. Since Dimitri didn't seem groggy, they talked for hours, pledging their love, planning their next move.

"What time do you think it is?" she finally asked.

"Maybe two or three o'clock in the morning." He paused. "Before the sun rises, we must prepare for our deep sleep."

Alba muttered a lazy response as she clung to Dimitri. This was bliss—and she didn't want anything to interrupt it.

"We'll have to leave this city," Dimitri said quietly.

"Yes," she replied. But she wouldn't be sorry to abandon a profession she wasn't suited for—and she certainly wasn't going to miss the horrible business of Jack the Ripper.

The candle flickered out. Alba heard Dimitri's steady breathing beside her in the dark, yet she knew he was awake. She willed her eyes to close again. That's when she had the vision. A man, tall and elegantly dressed in a dark suit and a top hat, was moving through the dense London fog. He held a Gladstone bag—and as he plowed through the shadows, his hand curled around the handle of the knife hidden beneath his coat.

Jack the Ripper!

Alba gulped against the visualization. Heart pounding, she strained to see the man's face, but she couldn't. However, she did witness the killer pass the Bloomsbury Library—a library located dangerously close to the dormitory she shared with the Tuttle-baums.

He is coming for one of the girls.

"Dimitri!" she shrieked, shooting upright.

He sat up too. "What is it?"

"I have to go. The Whitechapel Murderer is going to kill again!"

"The Whitechapel Murderer? But Teddy and Jochen are in prison . . ."

"It's not Teddy or Jochen. The Ripper is prowling the streets of Bloomsbury and he's about to kill another woman . . . I saw it!"

"Are you sure?"

"Yes! He's nearing the dormitory."

"Christ!" Dimitri's face went ashen. "Hurry and dress. I'm coming with you."

Chapter Thirty-One

As Alba soared through the frosty night, she felt like screaming. She wanted to warn Mrs. T., Edith, Ella, Elaine, Evelyn, Eugenia, Ellen, and Edwina, but she had no means of doing so.

While barges sounded in the distance, she and Dimitri streamed over the curves of Tottenham Court Road. Much to Alba's relief, there wasn't a soul in sight as they neared Bloomsbury. They touched down on the empty street of the dormitory and morphed into human form. Although Alba saw nothing amiss, the sense that something was wrong still churned her stomach.

Creeping closer to the dormitory with Dimitri by her side, she noticed that the front door stood ajar. *How unusual.*

Then Alba spotted a dark figure lying on the ground near the open door. Partially shrouded in shadow and partially illuminated by a street lamp, the figure remained still. An eerie silence filled the air while Dimitri knelt beside the body. When he nudged the figure onto its back by its shoulder, Alba's eyes grew wide. It was a young bobby, his navy blue and silver uniform awash with blood.

"His throat's been cut," murmured Dimitri.

Alarm prickled her spine and she hugged her arms around her body. "The Ripper is near," she said. "I can feel him."

Dimitri stood and reached for her hand. "This bobby was probably stationed here in hopes of catching me when I escaped from Newgate."

She nodded numbly. "We must check on the Tuttlebaums."

Dimitri gave her a brief kiss and dropped her hand. "You stay here—I bet the murderer is inside."

He vanished into the building before she could protest. Now that she was alone, her heart slammed against her ribs in a panicked rhythm. She stole a look at the dead police officer while her thoughts flew to Teddy and Jochen. If they weren't Jack the Ripper, *who was?*

Just then, Justina shot out of the front door of the dormitory. The cat passed Alba and scampered into the frigid evening air. Alba's pulse thrummed as she called its name and chased after it. Moving like lightning, she hurried along the empty, snow-patched street.

Jack the Ripper is near. He has come for me, not the Tuttlebaum girls. Alba felt it in her bones.

She considered turning around and fetching Dimitri, but whoever killed the bobby would surely kill Justina if given the chance. She must pursue the cat on her own. *Besides, I'm a vampire now. Dare the murderer go up against my newling powers?*

She ran after Justina all the way to Chancery Lane. She was far from the dormitory now, and fright gripped her as she lost sight of the feline in the rolling fog. As she leaned against a gaslight, Alba heard the sound of purring coming from an alley. Summoning all of her courage, she made her way around the corner and into the mouth of the dimly lit passage. Goose bumps prickled her arms. She wasn't cold; it was her way of bracing herself for what was to come.

Passing behind a darkened bookstore and a tiny meat shop, her eyes darted to the end of the alley. She was grateful to see clearly without her spectacles—a benefit of being a vampire, she presumed.

As she neared the fence that marked the alley's dead end, she saw the contours of a male silhouette take shape. The ominous figure was clothed in a flowing black cape, tall hat, and dark gloves. A Gladstone bag sat at his feet. Alba gasped. Jack the Ripper held Justina in one hand and a large, gleaming knife pressed to the cat's abdomen in the other.

Alba moved forward intrepidly. When the killer adjusted the brim of his hat, she realized it was Dr. Ionel Rhessa, the Zăpăda family's former physician! Horror and anguish stabbed at her. "Dr. Rhessa! You're Jack the Ripper?"

"Yes, my lovely Alba."

Gone were the doctor's thick spectacles, but Alba still recognized his round gray eyes, ruddy complexion, and mutton-chop sideburns.

"I am so glad our paths have crossed again," Rhessa said as Justina squirmed in his hand, "though I took steps to assure they would. In order to watch you all the while, I accepted the job as Dimitri Grigorescu's hansom driver."

Drummond? *My God.* Dimitri hadn't recognized Rhessa in the dark—with a scarf wrapped around his mouth and neck . . . without his spectacles.

Alba remembered the photographs of the Ripper's mutilated victims, and her throat constricted.

"I know what you're thinking, Alba. After all, you were always intelligent."

"What am I thinking?" Her voice quaked. *That you're a heinous monster? That if you don't release my cat, I'll kill you?*

"You're thinking that I look considerably different," he said. "Allow me to explain. When my wretched eyesight put an end to my medical practice, I underwent a cutting-edge operation that corrected my vision. Since then, I've been employing new methods of surgery myself."

"You mean you've been experimenting on innocent women?"

"Innocent is hardly the word," Rhessa said, pressing the knife farther into Justina's fur. The cat let out a loud meow. "Women are cruel and heartless creatures, like the wife who left me. By using their seductive ways, they steal men's hearts only to crush them into smithereens." He paused. "And do you know which kind of women are the worst?"

Alba's hands formed fists against her skirt as she shook her head.

"Prostitutes. A whore will pretend to love you—then laugh behind your back."

Alba assumed Rhessa knew this from firsthand experience. She cleared her throat and pushed her shoulders back. "So you were able to experiment on a subject you abhorred?"

"Yes. It was most satisfying."

Her gut clenched. "I suggest you put Justina and your knife down. We have much to catch up on."

"No, Alba. I cannot do that."

Justina squealed in pain and Alba's knees faltered. "You must turn yourself in to the authorities, Dr. Rhessa," she said quickly, tears pricking her eyes. "My friend, Theodore Rollingsworth, may go to prison for the murders you committed in Whitechapel!"

"You have nothing to worry about." Rhessa sauntered closer. The heels of his boots smashed the rubbish strewn over the damp cobbles. "I've been saving you for my last victim. Once you're dead, I've left a note supplying the details of the East End murders inside this Gladstone bag. The bag also contains hair samples of all my victims—as well as more evidence I took from every crime scene. After these things are found, your friend will be exonerated and I will disappear."

"Did you sign your name on the note?" Alba challenged.

Rhessa made a low tsking sound. "I already gave them my first name—on one of the letters I sent to the Central News Agency."

Of course. "Jack" is the English version of "Ionel."

"But," he went on, "if I reveal more of my given name, I won't be able to escape London in peace."

Rhessa stopped within four feet of her. Alba looked into Justina's pleading eyes as the scent of the physician's blood wafted under her nose. She felt empowered. She clenched her fists again, the urge to attack pouring over her like a relentless avalanche.

"Do you take me for a fool, little Alba?"

"I am no longer the Alba you knew."

"No?"

Alba's fangs descended, but she hid them. "No. But before I show you how I've changed, I want to know why you want to kill me."

"You are a link to my past. To the darkest time in my life—when my wife deserted me and my son disowned me."

"Jochen told Dimitri Grigorescu and me that you were dead."

"Dead to him, he meant."

Alba forced a hint of gentleness into her voice. "I implore you, put my cat down and drop your knife. We can go to where Dimitri is. He'll want to thank you for helping him."

"Dimitri brings us to the *real* reason I've been saving you for my last victim. When you left Romania, you abandoned him and broke his heart. I had high hopes for you, Alba, because you seemed different than most women. But ultimately you deserted the man you loved—just as my wife did."

Rhessa's eyes turned to flat stones. "I'm sure Dimitri will be crushed when he hears of your mutilation, but I am beyond caring."

"That, and the fact that you would have let him hang for your crimes, make you a monster," she said with derision.

His eyes blazing with anger, Rhessa tossed Justina in the air. Alba let out a cry as she caught the feline in both arms. The doctor grabbed Alba and pressed the knife to her throat. The cold of the metal made her stomach undulate. She had died once already. Would she be dead again a few hours later?

Alba struggled against the deranged killer, the cat teetering in her arms. Justina leapt to the filthy ground while Alba elbowed Rhessa in the rib cage. Then she gave him a kick so powerful it flung him against the fence.

A voice beside her made her jerk her head to the side. "I could feed again tonight, but I would never give a maniac immortality." Dimitri was by her side, and Alba's heart surged.

After she gave him a nod, Dimitri bared his gleaming fangs and streamed off the ground. As he lunged at the doctor, Rhessa's eyes filled with the same fear his victims had most likely known in their final moments. In one single crack, Dimitri snapped his neck. Relief poured over Alba and she looked away.

A police whistle rang out in the night. Dimitri grasped her hand and tugged her toward the gate in the fence. She shot a look at the Gladstone bag as it lay on the ground, but there was no time to extract the letter Rhessa spoke of. As Dimitri coaxed her out of the alley, Alba could only hope that the police would find it—because if they did, they would finally have their killer.

The whistle blew again, this time closer.

"Are you ready to leave this place?" Dimitri asked in a hushed tone.

She hesitated at first but then she nodded. Scooping Justina into her arms, she clutched his waist as he drew her to him tightly. With an impassioned kiss from Dimitri on her lips, Alba vanished into the night—leaving London, her cruel stepmother, and her extraordinary encounter with Jack the Ripper behind on the way to an infinitely better place.

Epilogue

Romania
Six months later

The peaks of the Carpathian Mountains shimmered beneath a waning moon. Dimitri and Alba strolled hand in hand to the open meadow beyond Stelian Hall, the summer wind ruffling their hair . . . carrying with it a sweet, floral scent. The meadow was alive with countless white poppies. And because of its natural beauty, it had become Alba's favorite place since Dimitri purchased Stelian Hall.

The couple settled on a patch of grass near a hollowed-out log. Alba spread out her white dress, adjusted her lace shawl, and curled against Dimitri's shoulder.

"You look beautiful tonight." He eyed her with admiration.

"This dress is nice and light," she chirped happily. "You made a good suggestion."

Dimitri drew his knees up and rested his elbows on them. He looked back at Stelian Hall, its turrets reaching the cloudless night sky with stoic patience.

"This place puts my apartment in Bucharest to shame." Dimitri laughed. "Are you glad I bought it?"

Alba smiled. "Yes. It holds good memories of my father as much as it holds bad ones of Ileana, but I'm not afraid to make a fresh start."

Dimitri reached over and stroked her cheek. Bending forward, he pressed his lips to hers, and Alba felt a familiar rush of delight pulse through her. She never grew tired of Dimitri's kisses—or of their ardent lovemaking. Seemingly, the world had stopped since they came to Stelian Hall. And she was happier than she'd ever been.

He coaxed her to lie down and rolled halfway on top of her. Their legs tangled while she ran a hand through his black hair. It glimmered in the moonlight as it always did, and his handsome face beamed with its usual elegance. All that was familiar about Dimitri made Alba grateful that she would never see him age. Being a vampire was a strange lifestyle, yet Alba had adjusted to it quickly. Her only regret was that she and Dimitri could never be legally wed. It was a complaint she'd been forced to throw to the wayside, as there was no changing their circumstances.

She moaned with pleasure as he flicked his tongue forward. She received it readily and closed her eyes as a warm breeze fluttered over them.

He pulled away to look into her eyes. "You make me so happy."

She sighed and stroked the curve of his lean chin. "I hope we never have to leave here."

"I feel the same way." He pushed a curl from her forehead. "There is nothing for us anywhere else."

"I do miss Mrs. T. and the girls," she countered with a quirk of her lips. "I got a letter from them today."

He smiled. "What did it say?"

"Mrs. T. wrote that the girls are dancing in *La Traviata* this season. Ellen has been given a solo piece."

"That's wonderful!" Dimitri shifted onto his back. Alba laid her head on his chest while he took her hand in his. "Did Mrs. T. mention Teddy—or Jochen?"

Alba nodded. "Since Teddy was released from Newgate, he has returned to the courtroom with full dignity. Mrs. T. writes that it was difficult for him to live down the fact that he visited a prostitute or two in the East End, but his disposition helped him through the scandal."

"How does Mrs. T. know all this about Teddy?" Dimitri marveled.

"He's remained close to the Tuttlebaum girls. In fact, he escorted Edwina to dinner."

"They're both romantics at heart," Dimitri said, plucking a poppy from the ground and twirling it by its stem.

"Yes. They would make a lovely pair."

"And Jochen. What did Mrs. T. say about him?"

"When he was released from police custody and found himself without a job, Mrs. T. offered to secure a post for him at the local café. She knows everyone there."

"Did Jochen take her up on the offer?"

Alba shook her head. "She wrote that Jochen came into some money. How do you think that happened?"

Dimitri cleared his throat. "Instead of giving the bracelet of Amenhotep back to the British Museum as I should have, I gave it to Jochen. Then I wrote Mrs. T. asking her to give him Tousret's amulet from your jewelry box. Upon my request, Jochen sold them to a private collector."

"And I presume that upon your further instruction, Jochen gave Mrs. T. and the girls a portion of the impressive sale." She smiled.

"You presume correctly," Dimitri said dreamily.

As the moon hung low overhead, Alba snuggled in closer. She let out another contented sigh. Dimitri sat up suddenly.

"It's time," he said.

Alba arched an eyebrow in confusion. "Time for what?"

"Do you know what today is?"

"It's June twentieth."

"Yes, but do you know the significance of this day?"

She was speechless.

"We met twelve years ago on June twentieth."

Alba was touched that he remembered such a detail. Her lips quivered with emotion and she smiled.

Dimitri opened his hand. There lay the dried white poppy he had delivered to her in London.

"How did you get this?" she gasped.

"I asked Edith to send it to me."

He pulled her to her feet, as excited as a schoolboy. "I want to make this day our anniversary of sorts. Stay here." He moved to the hollowed log and stuffed his hand inside it. "I put something in here twelve years ago. Let's hope it's still there."

He removed a tiny package wrapped in burlap, and when he opened it, he revealed a ring carved out of alderwood, slightly larger than hers. "I made one for myself that summer," he said sheepishly.

"Dimitri—" Her voice caught.

"You will be the most beautiful bride there ever was. Now, hold your flower in front of you."

She laughed gaily and did as he asked. He fastened her white shawl over her head like a veil as tears of happiness streamed down her cheeks.

Dimitri turned to face her and held out the ring he'd hidden in the log. "Before we exchange vows, I want you to read the inscription I carved."

Pressing her lips together, she held the rustic ring up in the moonlight. It read: *Pentru totdeauna şi întotdeauna.* Forever and Always.

"How perfect," she murmured. After they took turns exchanging vows, she slipped the ring on his finger and he drew her into a heart-pounding kiss.

"Have you finally learned to like surprises, Alba?"

"Yes." She choked the words out against his soft mouth. *Damn you, Dimitri.*

Eighty miles away, high up Transylvania's winding mountain roads, sat a centuries-old castle steeped in shadow. Its owner—a reclusive collector of art and antiquities—studied the amulet of Tousret and the bracelet of Amenhotep, for which he'd just paid a fortune. He had done so in hopes that the jeweled pieces would finally lead him to his soul mate.

Innocent and extremely beautiful, the woman this mysterious collector was about to seduce had no idea that her dark Prince Charming was coming for her. Nor did she know that he was an extremely powerful lord of black magic . . .

AUTHOR'S NOTE

Snow White and the Seven Dwarfs by the Brothers Grimm is the first fairy tale my mother ever read to me. Dazzled by the idea that true love's first kiss could bring someone back to life, I became an instant fan. (I was Snow White for Halloween that year. I even had Snow White bedsheets!)

As I grew and my writer's imagination came into play, I began to mull over the classic fairy tale in a different way. What if Snow White had been shrewd enough to outsmart her cruel stepmother without the help of the huntsman? And what if her prince had been more of a central character . . . a dashing and elegant hero fierce enough to stop the black-hearted Queen in her tracks?

I'm excited that these possibilities played out in *Snow White and the Vampire.* I admit that I took some fictional liberties with English Law in this novel (the first woman to defend a murder suspect in England actually did so in 1929), but it was great fun stocking the story full of what-ifs—especially my favorite one: What if Snow White could only be awakened by true love's first "bite"?

If you liked *Snow White and the Vampire*, I hope you'll look for *Sleeping Beauty and the Demon*, the next Cursed Princes romance, in August 2014.

THE CURSED PRINCES

HUNGER AND DESIRE
CAN TWINE INTO
MADNESS...

Beauty and the
WOLF

MARINA MYLES

Also available!

www.ingramcontent.com/pod-product-compliance
Lightning Source LLC
Chambersburg PA
CBHW021239260626
47155CB00004BA/1227